Sexpossessed

Ian Saul Whitcomb

Wobbly Cockatrice Productions

Also by Ian Saul Whitcomb:

I Married a Galaxy-Conquering Alien Space Monstrosity

ISBN-10: 0692324755
ISBN-13: 978-0692324752

FOR K ...

who brought a new cat into my life at a time when I already had too many cats. As a bonus, dedicating this to you allows me to make my dedication look like the word "Fork." No one ever said love was easy.

CONTENTS

CHAPTER ONE

I guess there are several reasons I should have said "no" when Bill offered to let his dead sister possess my girlfriend.

I mean, for starters, I didn't really know Bill that well. He was a fun guy, a blast to play RPGs with, and had given me some good tips on local microbreweries. But he was oddly mysterious about his job, where he lived, why he showed up ten minutes late for absolutely everything ... I can't say he had my full confidence. Plus, not only did I not know Bill that well, I certainly didn't know his sister. And considering Bill's level of irresponsibility, I'd probably think twice about letting any relative of his borrow my car – much less the love of my life's body.

And that's before we even get to the creepiness factor. Possession. Undead spirits. Things from Beyond. The possibility that those "Paranormal Seeker" assholes might show up at my house with cameras.

But those reasons would only have occurred to me if I thought he was being serious. Which, I mean, come on, how could I?

This came up when we were having a Car Theft Dark at Able Schnabel's over on Sutter. As often happens with my friends, Bill remarked what a lucky bastard I was, and because Liv's the only obviously lucky thing about my life, I knew what he was talking about, and because I'd had a couple my monitor was on the fritz and I started moping about how she was probably going to leave me sooner or later and how she was currently on a tear about me not being daring enough, not getting out there and experimenting with new things like I should.

"Which is kind of weird coming from a 26-year-old who owns a working SuperNintendo console and marathons Star Wars at least twice a year," I grumbled, complaining about two of my girlfriend's most beloved qualities in that way you can only manage when you're at least partially buzzed.

Bill didn't answer me right away, but looked into his beer like it was a crystal ball. I took the opportunity to polish off my glass and wave at our server for another. The impenetrably dark beer finally finished relaying its mystical communiqué to Bill. He looked over at me.

"Is this a sex thing, Tim?"

I balked for a second, because even though my monitor had been jacked by the beer, it hadn't been *completely* jacked. If I said yes, he might ask for details, and like I said, I didn't know Bill all that well. Would I want to tell him exactly what my girlfriend was wanting me to do? Probably not.

"If it's a sex thing," he went on, after a smooth tip of his glass and a swallow, "I've got an idea for you."

Now, except for opinions about where to get a good beer, I didn't put much stock in Bill's ideas. His characters in D&D had a knack for hare-brained schemes that ended up getting most of the adventuring party killed. Whenever a new sci-fi movie came out, if he liked it, I hated it. He had tattoos covering every inch of his forearms, and the first tattoo he ever got said, "People with tattoos are idiots."

But this thing with Liv really had me worried, and I was willing to listen to just about any idea on how to fix it, and I was boozed-up enough to forget the mantra our whole group would repeat whenever one of Bill's characters said he had an idea: *"Never listen to Bill's ideas."*

Somehow we always listened, though, and almost always went along – maybe because it was only D&D and if some characters died we might be able to Wish them back to life and if not then we could always roll up new characters. Bill's ideas were 100% guaranteed to be entertaining, even when they were fatal.

So I said, "I'm listening."

He made a conspicuously clandestine show of remaining silent while our server, a tiny but happy-looking Asian guy, brought my new pint. It was a glass full of night with a beige cloud on top.

"Okay," Bill said once the beer-hop had gone, "she's got a kink you're not keen on, and she's trying to push you into it by saying you're dull and chicken."

"Well, no, Liv's not –"

"Yeah, yeah, I know she wouldn't put it that way." He waved a hand like my reflexive defense of Liv was a fly to be shooed away. "But that's still how it's working out, right? She wants something, you don't, and that means you're not adventurous enough in her book, which bugs you. On target?"

I hunkered down over my beer and nodded. My jaw felt tight.

"Then what you need is to prove you can be as kinked up as she can. Tell her you want to do something freaky, but suggest something that's in your comfort zone instead of hers."

"You mean a swap? But then I'd still have to ... uh ..."

"No, no, no," he said, looking up at the ceiling. "She wants to do X, so you suggest Y. Whether she takes you up on it or not, offering to do Y means that the problem isn't you being too chicken, it's her wanting you to do something you don't want to do. Then she's the bad guy trying to pressure you instead of you being the wimp who won't do this thing to make her happy."

I wiped off a beer-head moustache while I thought about that. I've known a lot of girls that Bill's strategy would never work on, but with Liv, I thought it would.

"So I just have to think up something kinky she doesn't want to do."

"Or even better, something she *does* want to do that proves you can perv with the best of them. If she's busy enjoying your new freakiness, it'll be easier to put her own pet twist on the back burner."

I opened my mouth, but Bill went on before I could say anything.

"And I've got just the thing."

* * *

Let's establish here that Liv is like some kind of nerd goddess out of a nerd's pantheon of mythological nerd beings. She's tall and lean and built like an African super-model, by which I mean African-African as opposed to African-American: exotic and super-dark with amazing teeth and a giant open-mouthed laugh that makes you want to tell her every joke in the world just to see and hear it. Her parents adopted her from Ethiopia or Kenya or something, a couple of dreamy-eyed white American liberals who had every intention of exposing her to as much of her native culture as they could, except that they got killed in a car crash when she was four and left her in the hands of their one halfway-suitable relative, Liv's Uncle Nate.

Now, Uncle Nate's main goal in life was *not* raising a culturally aware adoptive daughter from Africa. He was, however, a cool guy who didn't mind having someone to play video games with, talk comic books with, listen to Led Zeppelin and the Who with, and, when she got old enough, teach to play Dungeons and Dragons. They lived in San Diego and went to ComicCon every year until she was ten or twelve, by which point Nate thought it was getting too big and commercial, which Liv agreed with because Liv was smart and Nate was right.

Let's also establish that I am a full fifteen years older than Liv, and admit that yes, that's weird. If being raised by Uncle Nate hadn't gotten her into pretty much every single hobby I loved, I could never have imagined asking her out, much less asking her to move in with me, which I'd done the second month after we met. She's a young and beautiful and flawless creature of the 21st Century on the outside and a total geek throwback to

1982 on the inside. It's so preposterous for me to have a woman who looks like her as my girlfriend that every once in a while I wonder if I'm really dating Uncle Nate's psychic residue and not the real Liv at all.

Next: I'm kind of OCD about certain things. Like I don't like to eat with my fingers. Yeah, I know where they've been and I know how many times I've washed them – I just don't like it. I eat pizza with a fork and knife. I skip fried chicken completely. Mostly Liv is okay with this. She even thinks it's funny sometimes. But when it gets in the way, she can be impatient. A couple of times she has suggested going to this Ethiopian restaurant one of her friends likes. I'm not completely opposed to trying new ethnic foods, but I always need to know what kind of utensils they use. In Ethiopia, they apparently have this spongy flatbread they scoop everything up in, so even stew is finger food. I didn't want to go, and we both knew why. But Liv still had to ask.

"Why not?"

The fact that she asked irritated me. She knew perfectly well why not. So I said, "I don't know. It just doesn't sound appealing."

"But you think I'm appealing, and I might be from Ethiopia."

"Or you might be from Kenya, in which case things from Ethiopia could still suck." I mentally thanked Uncle Nate for never being able to remember what country Liv's parents adopted her from.

My intimidatingly beautiful girlfriend rolled her eyes and then narrowed them at me. "This is the finger thing, isn't it? The place has forks. I made sure to ask Shawna when she was telling me about it."

"I can't go into a place where they eat with their fingers and use a fork. It would be rude, like I thought their culture was stupid."

"You eat pizza with a fork."

"I look finicky eating pizza with a fork. I'd look racist eating Ethiopian food with a fork."

This made her growl. "Good God, no one's going to think you're racist when you're eating dinner with *me.*"

But she dropped the subject and we went for Chinese food instead. (At a fancy Chinese restaurant with washable chopsticks. I can't deal with those bamboo ones in the open paper sleeves where you have to break them apart and there are splinters coming off.) Eventually she was going to ask a third time and then I'd have to go, because I had a rule for myself that refusing to do something three times made you an asshole. Liv sensed this rule as if by magic at some point – I never told her – and she wouldn't ask a third time about anything that was really a big deal to me.

She had asked my OCD self two times now to fuck her in the ass.

* * *

"Okay, Tim, what's Liv playing in the game right now?"

"A necromancer with a vampire fetish." Bill knew this. He played with us every week. (Although he always showed up ten minutes late.)

"And what did she play in the campaign before that? The one with the snake cult, where the subterranean temple accidentally caved in on us?" Yeah, accidentally.

"A necromancer with a zombie fetish."

"And what's that face you're making right now?"

"I didn't know I was making a face."

"You are. It's a creeped-out-but-turned-on face. You make it every time one of Liv's characters detours the game so she can dominate something undead and boink it."

"I didn't know I made that face."

"Well Liv knows. And she grins and scoots her chair closer to yours every time she sees you make it."

Thinking back, I realized Bill was right.

"So ... what, you want me to dress up like a vampire and fuck her?"

"No," he said, as if talking to a simpleton. "She doesn't scoot her chair over because necrophilia turns her on. She does it because necrophilia turns *you* on and gives you the heebie-jeebies at the same time."

"Dude, that's disgusting. I do not have a dead-body fetish." I took a big pull on my beer. Then I took another one. Why the hell was my throat so dry all of a sudden? Fuck. "And anyway, even if I did, I can't surprise Liv with a zombie costume or a vampire costume and ask her to hump me in it. Every time I try to buy her clothes for a present it's a disaster. Either she can't squeeze into them or they're like a tent on her."

Bill raised his glass up almost to his lips. "You don't need to buy her a costume."

"Then what?" I asked while he downed what was left.

He set the glass on the table with a *clunk*. Leaned over at me on his elbows and spoke very quietly.

"My sister was way heavy into all kinds of occult shit before she died –"

"Jesus, I didn't even know you had a sister. I'm sorry."

A wave like it was nothing. "She's been dead a couple years and she was kind of a bitch anyway. The point is, I still have some of her stuff, and there's this necklace she said she was putting her soul into in case anything happened to her."

Whoa. Her soul? I guess Bill's sister had even nuttier ideas than Bill. My tongue itched to ask what had happened to her, but I didn't. Bill made a circle with a finger and thumb from each hand and put it over his heart, other fingers spread. "I guarantee you, if Liv sees this thing and you tell her the story, it will be better than any costume. It's *this* big, silver, a fat fucking red jewel in the middle like blood. Crazy symbols on it. They almost make your eyes hurt. She puts it on, says Julia's name after you get her motor running, and then she can spend the rest of the night screwing you as my sister's horny ghost."

Even though the hair on the back of my neck felt like I had beer foam in it, I shook my head. "I dunno. I don't think she'll be all that impressed by me asking her to role-play some ghost sex. We role-play every week at the game, and her characters are always sex-obsessed, and we, ah ..." always have fantastic sex after a game where her necromancer gets really nasty "... anyway, I don't think that's such a big stretch. Not like what she keeps asking me to do."

He sat back, his head down so his eyes were kind of shadowy. "You'll think different when you see this necklace. It's the real deal, bro. Spooky. I promise. And you don't tell her you want to role-play. You tell her you're going to put the necklace on her and she's going to be possessed. Act like you believe it and like you're kind of scared. Trust me, that part won't be hard. The whole thing will work like a charm."

Never listen to Bill's ideas.

I scratched my head for a minute. Why was I even talking about this?

"I guess it won't hurt for you to show me the thing and let me decide once I've seen it."

Bill smiled and tapped his empty glass to mine.

"That's the spirit."

CHAPTER TWO

So Liv got home from her yoga class and my heart was going like a pack of wolves just chased me up ten flights of stairs.

"Hi," she said, meeting me halfway from the kitchen, where I'd been waiting, wrapping me up in a hug and kissing me. She'd been living with me almost a year at this point, and we still open-mouth kissed for absurd amounts of time whenever one of us got home. She kind of hums when she's kissing. I know the kiss is almost over when the humming stops. This time she stopped and pulled her face back and opened her eyes and said, "You taste like beer toothpaste."

Goddammit, now I have to tell her I was at Able Schnabel's, and she'll ask with who, and I'll have to say Bill, and she'll know the necklace was his idea, and that will be the end of that.

Somehow, I forced my instinctively truthful mouth to say, "How was class?"

"Eh," she said, releasing one of her arms from around me to put her hand on my cheek. Her eyes, deeper brown than the Car Theft Dark, wandered across my face, and like always I felt like pinching myself over the way she smiled while she was looking at me. "I don't think yoga's the one."

Liv had spent the last six months trying to find a new activity to get into. Despite having absorbed a boatload of great taste from Uncle Nate, she was still fifteen years behind me, experience-wise, and I was way ahead in the tally of, "What? You've never heard/listened to/watched _____? Whoa. You've got to check this out." She figured if she picked up a completely new interest and then turned me on to it, the score would be evened out a little. But that meant finding something she liked *and* she thought I would like.

"I mean, it's okay," Liv went on as she slipped out of my arms and headed for the kitchen, "but every time Ilya tells me to blank my mind and

7

concentrate on my breathing, I imagine I'm setting up for my trench run, or I whisper, 'Remember your failure in the cave.' Then instead of getting my breathing straight, I'm holding back from giggling the whole time."

"Ha," I said. "Yeah, I think even if you master that one, I'm going to crack up whenever we try it together."

I hung back in the living room, listened to her open the refrigerator door, heard her get something out.

"So what have you been up to? Besides beer and brushing your teeth, I mean."

I cleared my throat disgruntledly. "You know, this and that ..."

The sound of her swallowing reached my ears. Part of me wanted to keep talking to blot it out, part of me wanted to go around the corner and watch her standing in front of the open refrigerator drinking straight from the carton of orange juice. Her perfect jaw tilted up, her long slender dark neck oscillating slowly as each mouthful coursed down through it. She would have used a glass if I'd gone straight into the kitchen with her, but then I would have felt bad about making her.

The fridge whiffled shut and Liv came back out and kissed me again, briefly, a peck of citrus with just a dart of tongue. She was still smiling.

"I love you."

My throat felt dry and my face kind of flushed. "I love you too."

"Can you live with yoga sweat, or do you want me to shower before we get in bed and mess up the sheets?"

You're supposed to be brave tonight, I told myself. *Adventurous. Showing your daringly dirty side.*

"I, uh, can live with yoga sweat." Oh yeah, that sounded like the courage of Hercules. "In fact ..."

A fire sparked in her eyes. "Mm, yes?"

"Well, this is weird ..."

The fire heated, curling her lips up. With her whole face, she asked me to go on, so I did.

"I have something to show you."

* * *

The first time I had sex with Liv, I was terrified.

She'd joined my Thursday night RPG group a month earlier. We'd bumped into each other at the Saturday matinee the week she'd played her fourth or fifth session with us. Then we'd been out on exactly three dates: one that ended with an awkward wave goodbye as she walked up the steps of her apartment building; one that ended with her grabbing me and kissing me on her stoop; and the big one, when she'd kissed me the same way only to break off after a minute and say, "Oh my god, Tim. Come inside with me."

Despite being a geek, and shy, and OCD, I'd had an okay number of girlfriends and what I thought was a pretty good amount of sex up until that point. With the first couple of girls, I got borderline anxiety attacks when the time came to cross the carnal line. But a few heartbreaks made me cynical enough to switch to one-night stands for a while, and somewhere along the way the evidence began to pile on that I was above median quality in the sex department. Once I healed up and went back to romance, heat and desire always swamped whatever first-time-sex jitters might show up.

But not with Liv.

By the time I met her, I'd taken maybe a dozen different women to bed, three of them medium- to long-term girlfriends, two of them live-ins. All of them were in the four-to-six range, except for one seven-and-a-half who did a mediocre job the next morning pretending that I wasn't a beer-goggle mistake. More importantly, all of them were "good enoughs." The girlfriends were nice enough but a little too boring, or interesting enough but a little too bitchy, or funny enough but a little too cheating on me. The one-night stands were all horny enough to be willing and not too sleazy or gross to get me turned on. If things had gone a little differently – especially with the seven-and-a-half – any one of them might have wound up married to me and living a life of tepid romantic stagnation.

Liv, though, was not a "good enough." Liv was a "no way in hell am I good enough for *this*." She was not a six, or a seven-and-a-half, or a nine. She was a make-Bo-Derek-blink-and-say-"Oh, so *that's* what a ten looks like." She was comic books, Star Wars, glam rock trivia, tabletop roleplaying games, and even on the basis of just two pieces of evidence, pretty much the best kisser in the entire world.

And she was *nice*. Crazy nice. Kind. And funny.

So when she said, "Oh my God, Tim. Come inside with me," I almost panicked and ran. I'd been thinking about her whenever I jerked off for the last month. Between the Saturday movie and our first real date, I told myself she'd only agreed to go out with me out of pity, or to keep things from being awkward at the RPG group. Between our first and second dates, I told myself that because she was nice, she was humoring me, but that asking her out that second time had been pushing it, and she would find some way to let me down easy by the end of the night. Between our first kiss that night and our third date, I told myself that I would wake up at any moment and realize it had all been a dream.

And between her asking me in and me saying, "Okay," I knew, with papal infallibility, that letting her see me naked would lay bare every pathetic inadequacy of my body, mind, and soul, and that her reaction would finally prove to me the utter worthlessness of my existence.

The only reason I agreed was that I simply couldn't tell her, "No."

In her bedroom a few minutes later, as she undressed me after undressing herself, I shook so uncontrollably at her touch that she grinned her enormous tropical grin at me and said, "You're like a chihuahua in an icebox! Tim ... this isn't your first time, is it?"

I will never know where my mouth got the words that it said next. My brain would never, ever have considered saying them.

But my lips opened, and what tumbled out was, "No. It's just my first time with someone I could love forever."

The grin dissolved from her face, slowly metamorphosing into something else – so slowly that I had time to be sure it would change into twenty different things. A flat slit of disappointment. A slack-mouthed cough of disgust and shock. A tiny, sad frown full of soulful pity. A grimace. A laugh. Wide-eyed terror. Contempt. But as I stood there waiting, it didn't turn into anything. Her face just went gradually blanker and blanker until her entire being disappeared into an inscrutable stare.

Then she bit her lip and a tear rolled from one of her eyes and she said, "Mine too."

* * *

So when I say that the second-most anxious moment of our relationship was showing her Bill's dead-sister-ghost medallion, I'm not talking about being just slightly nervous.

"Whoa. It's heavy," she said, testing its feel in her hand. "And it's ... cold. And weird. What is it?"

It's one of Bill's bad ideas.

It's what happens when I'm too freaked out by germs to do you in the butt.

It's something I needed several beers in me to make me dumb enough to try.

"It's me being more adventurous."

"Mm-hmm," she said, stepping in closer and putting her free hand on my chest. I smelled the lingering scent of deodorant and exertion in her yoga outfit. "Tell me more."

I had to break eye contact to keep from gushing out the whole truth – talking to Bill, him making the suggestion, him giving me the amulet, me hoping it would help put off the point when she'd ask me a third time for anal sex. Luckily, that wicked crimson jewel did a good job pulling your attention, and I turned my face to look at it.

"So ... you know, at the game ..." The gem twinkled darkly at me, goading me on. "You keep humping zombies and ghouls and shit."

She laughed and simultaneously lowered her eyebrows in curiosity. "Sure. I love seeing you squirm when I do that stuff. But what's –"

"It turns me on."

I looked up at her when I said it, and the most wonderful spark of surprise ran across her face.

"You didn't know?"

She kissed me. "I knew. I just didn't think you'd tell me."

I made a little wave with the necklace. "Well. I've been thinking I need to ... man up a little. That's what this is for."

"Tim." A chiding look pooched her lower lip out. "You know you're plenty manly for me."

"I do," I said, straightening my shoulders a bit. "I mean, you've told me before, and I believe you. But maybe I need to start believing it more myself. Doing something about it. You've had two different necromancer characters roaming dungeons all over Greg's empire, and I get all dry throated every time one starts bonking something undead, and I've been too chicken to say anything about it to you. So I went and got this."

Her eyes went to the medallion as I held it up between us, a weighty ring of silver circumscribing a nine-pointed star centered on that deep, blood-colored stone.

"It's a zombie-summoning necklace?" A playful laugh hid itself in her voice as she spoke.

"No," I said. "It's got a ghost in it."

"A ghost?"

Nod. "To possess you. So that I can ... fuck it, while it's in you."

"Oooh." Her arms went around my neck and she brought her nose in not quite touching mine. "Tim wants Liv to play ghost for him?"

Holy crap. This is really working. And not only was the plan playing out, but Liv's body against mine, and her breath warm and soft across the lower part of my face, and that sultry, low voice she went into when she wanted to be super-sexy – it all had me rock hard before I even noticed what was happening.

Forcing myself to play it cool, I shook my head. "Don't say you're going to be pretending. You're going to *be* a ghost. Dominated by a spirit –"

"A *horny* spirit."

"Yeah ..." Fuck, she was so hot. "A spirit that's going to take you over and get what it wants."

"Shit, this is *great*," Liv said, pushing off from me with a hand in the center of my chest and bouncing over toward the bed. "Tell me where you got it. What kind of ghost it is. What it wants me to do."

She stripped off her skin-tight yoga tank, then the sports bra underneath it. I struggled to think of a story, trying to figure out how to keep Bill out of it and distracted by her perfect dark breasts bobbing loose, each begging for a hand to cup it, a palm to rub the already stiffening nipples.

"Oh, let me guess," she said, seeing me staring. "You went in this strange shop downtown that you'd never seen before, and it was full of all this weird, mystical, creepy shit ..." The tights were off now too, leaving her in nothing but sunshine-yellow panties. "...and the owner's this guy about a thousand years old, and you tell him you're looking for something special for me ..." Her index fingers dipped into the waistband of the panties and then snapped back out again. She leaned away and rolled her pelvis at me, hands gliding up the swell of her belly, pink nails of her fingers all pointing along her curves toward the mound hidden inside that lemony fabric. "Do you want to do this part?"

"Yes," I said, moving over, tossing the necklace onto the bedspread. Kneeling in front of her. "You're, uh, dead on so far. What do you think happened next?"

"Hmmmm," she said, one finger to her chin as I tugged the cotton covering down from her waist, past her tight-curled bush, and then free of her crotch – sliding along her thighs, dropping past her ankles to cover her feet. "I think ..." Her hips tick-tocked gently as she stepped out of the panties. "...he suggests this and that ... none of it's good enough for me ... he goes in the back ..." I moved one hand up the outside of her right thigh, the other up its inner curve – leaned my face in, nose almost to her pubic hair. (There is a weird story behind the fact that women's crotches are immune to my germ phobia.) She smelled intense from working out and not having showered since the night before, thickly tangy, yeasty, slightly sweet. Her breathing hopped up its pace. "...yadda yadda ... blah blah ... ominous warning that you didn't quite listen to ..." My left hand reached her crotch and my right went around to the curve of her butt. She leaned gently back, the upper edge of the mattress catching her just above the hamstrings. "Can I sit down and angle things a little better?"

"Sure." She eased lower and lower and farther back until her ass was perched at the precipice of the bed, her legs spread wide to either side of me, her elbows supporting her upper body. "You're getting the story right too, except that I don't remember an ominous warning."

A perfect laugh came out of her as she watched me closing in on her exposed nethers. I hovered, an inch away, caressing her with hot air from my open mouth.

"Not much more to tell," she said, wetting her lips and watching me. "You got the the necklace suspiciously cheap, you left. It was foggy, right? And halfway down the street you looked back and the shop had vanished. But you didn't go back to check that ... it was probably just the fog, and you really wanted to get home and fuck me. Is that pretty close?"

I shrugged. Then I dove.

"Oh. Mmm ... yes ..."

Liv does this thing sometimes when I make out with her genitals. She flattens her hands and pats them lightly against each side of her lower belly, sort of randomly at first, right-left, right-right, left-right-left. The closer I get her to orgasm, the faster she pats, and the more rhythmically, until she reaches this galloping sound. Pretty soon after that, she just grabs my head with both hands and groans her way to climax. A few mouth-fucks into our relationship, I discovered that the longer I could get her to maintain that gallop, the harder she would come and the louder she would be when she got there.

This time, though, I had barely gotten a taste of her when the patting stopped and she said, "Wait, wait. I'm supposed to put the necklace on, right?"

To be honest, the smell of her and the flavor of her and the wet warm flesh of her against my lips had already put the whole ghost thing out of my head. It took a certain amount of willpower to remember what I was supposed to be up to and pull away to set things up.

"Not yet," I said, looking up from the trembling flower of her femininity to those eyes, so dark and flooded with enthusiasm. "I mean, you can put it on if you want to, but I have to get you primed first for it to work. When you're close, I get into position, and you say her name as I go in."

"She's got a name?"

"Julia," I said, running a fingertip around the wet and swelling lips before my face.

"Who was she? I mean, I should know something about her before she ... takes over, right?"

My finger kept circling, and she wiggled with it. "This goth chick who got into all kinds of weird mysticism and shit. Kind of mean, with a temper. She decided she wanted to be a wicked witch. One of the creepy old books she found described this ritual to put your soul into an object so it wouldn't go to the other side if you bought the farm. A cement truck knocked her off her motorscooter just a couple weeks after she used the ritual on the medallion, so now she needs someone to link to so that she can keep enjoying the living world."

"Fuck, that's hot," Liv breathed. One hand came down to take hold of my finger and ease it away from her privates. "You'd better get your clothes off – I'm going to be ready for you to hit it really quick."

I rocked back to my heels and stood, kicking my shoes off as she twisted to pick up the necklace. As I shucked my clothes, she tilted the silver circle back and forth, staring into the gem and the inscribed lines of the star.

"Wow. This thing is really goddamn freaky."

I was getting my shirt over my head as she said that. When I looked at her again, her eyes remained wide and fixed on that red jewel.

"Yeah, B— the old man said it was the real deal."

Liv's eyes came up to mine, and a daring smile stole across her face as she slipped the chain over her head, settled the cold, shining metal between her breasts.

"And you really want to have sex with a ghost?" she asked, crawling backwards onto the bed. I bent down and crawled on after her.

"Yes."

With a pile of pillows behind her, she crooked her legs at the knees, broadened the V between her thighs, rotated her pelvis to invite my mouth back into her crotch.

I closed my eyes, slid into place, finding my way by the deepening scent, settling in to kiss, probe, suck.

The pattering hadn't even gotten halfway to gallop when she whispered, "Now, Tim. I'm ready."

As I moved up along her amazing, soft, dusky form, I realized that my heart was galloping even if her belly-drumming wasn't. I stopped for a second when I got to the medallion. The jewel seemed to quiver in time with my pulse, as if its color came from my blood shooting through my veins. I blinked the thought away, slid farther up, looked into Liv's eyes. She got a hand between us and took hold of me.

Wow, she's really hot for it.

I was too, and I bent to kiss her as my hips pressed forward and down. She put her free hand on my forehead, gently reminding me to leave her lips free. With her other hand, she rubbed my tip against the wet and wonderful crease that separated the outer world from the miracle of her vagina.

She breathed more than spoke: "I'm ready to say her name."

I swallowed, smiled a little nervously, and went in with a steady, slow push.

Penetration. Liv closed her eyes.

"*Julia.*"

* * *

So, Liv is very active during sex. If it's slow and sweet, she caresses, whispering or cooing. If it's hot and heavy, she drives, grinds, lets me know from deep in her throat how much she's liking it. She gets these looks of joy or sensuous appetite or uncontrolled, animalistic reflex to pleasure. She's never still or blank. Even in the afterglow, one thumb will be tracing little circles on my shoulder-blade, and a soft expression of peace and satisfaction will lie across her face.

Which means I was completely thrown when she spoke the ghost name and went slack underneath me. Head to toe. Face, throat, chest, arms, legs totally motionless, except for her abdomen slowly rising and falling under mine as she breathed.

"Liv?"

She didn't respond – or she did, but only with a faint, hollow sound on

14

her next outward breath. "...uuhhhhhhhhh..."

"Liv?"

Nothing. It was so unlike her that I got a creeping worry all through my chest. I reached up, intending to pat her cheek – then stopped myself. *She's not supposed to be acting like herself, dumbass. Get back in character before you go limp and blow the whole thing.*

I gave a hesitant push down and forward, pressing our crotches tighter, working myself deeper in.

"Uh ... Julia?"

"...hhhhhhh..."

She's playing it, I told myself firmly. *Go with the flow.*

Her body remained loose-limbed, motionless. But she felt *really* good, and I could either screw the whole thing up by pulling out and saying *Liv, Liv,* until she responded and I looked like a complete chicken – or I could appreciate the fact that she was being really cool and creative with her end of the role-play.

I eased and reapplied my pressure, moving just a hair inside her.

Christ, that's good.

"Julia ... are, uh, you there?"

Another faint sound in her breath. I stroked again, a little more surely this time.

"Julia?"

"...hhhhhooohh?..." Had her lips moved?

I worked up my courage and gave her an out-in with half the length of my shaft.

For sure, her mouth twitched.

"...who..."

Oh my god, Liv, that's beautiful.

Stroke. "My name is –"

"...where am..."

Stroke. "You're in –"

"...so dark..."

I stopped.

"Can you hear me?"

Nothing for a moment, then, tonelessly, "so dark...what's happening..."

"I'm, uh ... I'm having sex with you."

Silence.

"Liv? Julia?"

"...am i dead...?"

Still motionless, my cock stiffened powerfully inside her. *Shit, she is such a fucking genius.*

"Yes. My girlfriend Liv is wearing your necklace."

"...holy...fuck..."

I swung out and in. "Can you feel me?"

"...it really...*worked*...but i'm dead? fuck..."

"What do I do?"

"...some kind of...dumbass?...pound me...you fucker..."

"Hey," I said, frowning. Wait. *Bill did say she was kind of a bitch. But I didn't tell ... no, I guess I did say she wanted to be a wicked witch.* "Okay. Okay, you want it hard then?"

"...yes, sheezus...fuck me back from the dark, dammit..."

She'd said all this barely moving her lips, still doing absolutely nothing to move her body. I knew perfectly well that Liv was a great role-player, but this was brilliant.

"If that's how it works, I guess that's how it works. Get yourself ready."

Lifting up from my elbows to my hands, arms fully extended, I looked down on her. Vacant. No hint of animation. I pulled back, then drove deep and hard, enough to shake the bed, send her breasts up and back in a flesh wave that rolled the medallion like a lifeboat on a gentle sea.

"...yes..."

Again, and then again.

"...Yes..." Her chin tilted just slightly with the word.

This was very weird territory for me. Don't get me wrong – Liv's asked plenty of times for me to give it to her hard. But never without her giving back. Feeling her around me while seeing her laid out beneath me, completely passive, I just couldn't jump right in and start slamming away. So I worked up to it, beginning with a slow but powerful back and forth, watching her, listening to her as I gradually picked things up.

"Yes," she growled as I got myself into second gear. The muscles of her brow contracted. Her teeth clenched. "Yes. Hnnh, yes – what's your name?"

"Tim."

Her shoulders moved. Her arms kind of flopped.

"Fuck me, Tim. *Now.*"

I went to third gear.

"Yesssss..." She seemed to have gotten control of her hips, and they started to work with me, timing and controlling how much pressure I was putting on her.

Something was changing inside her vagina. It felt slicker, stronger, tighter around and along my shaft as I oscillated in and out.

Her fingers worked, flexed.

"Yeah, uhh, yeah, *that.*"

Fourth gear. Liv's hands flew up to my biceps, dug the fingers in, scraped up and over my shoulders to my back.

"Shit. Fuck. Tim. Cock!"

Beads of sweat sprung up across my chest, started to roll downward. I stared at her face as I chuffed and steam-trained into her – those eyes still tightly shut, lips strained back from her flawless white teeth, jaw clenched atop the corded sinews of her neck.

Suddenly, I was getting close.

"Oh god, L—*Julia*, Uhh..."

Her legs hooked around me, heels pulling me in tighter.

"GhhHuh ... not yet – fucker – *come* on, *get* me there!"

Arms shaking, I smacked myself into her as best I could, plunging, feeling, hearing her liquid kiss around me. My rhythm had gone all bonkers and I couldn't get enough air into my lungs.

"Julia—*ahh*—Julia—"

"Not...*yet*...so...close..."

Orgasm roared toward me on jet engines. I was the little jumpsuit guy in front of its wheels, trying to hold back it by waving my orange-coned flashlights.

"Julia, fuck, Julia—*Liv*!"

"YES!!!"

Everything exploded. Fluid ecstasy bolted up from my scrotum and prostate, gushed the length of my cock, geysered out inside of her. Her back came off the bed in a whip-crack parabola, her legs and arms constricting as she lurched up against me. Her head tilted back on her neck, mouth wide in an erotic roar.

And her eyes shot open.

And they were green.

"*WHAT THE FUCK?!?*"

I don't mean green pupils. I mean solid, key-lime pie green.

Glowing.

"AHH!" she cried. Green mist floated up from her mouth with the sound. "AHHH! YESSSS!"

If I could have jumped off of her, I would have – her arms and legs were iron. Her back stayed arched; I kept coming – squirting, spasming – there was no stopping that. But terror kicked every sexual thought from my head.

"Liv! Liv, what the hell?"

She dropped back to the mattress. Limp as she'd been when it all started. The glowing eyes fluttered closed with a sigh.

"Jesus!" I was out of her and off her in a second, grabbing the necklace to jerk it from her neck in another second. It clattered against the wall. I scuttered up to kneel by her head. "Liv, sweetie, please, oh my god, please..."

A few careful, horrified pats on the cheek later, her eyes flittered opened.

Brown again, but unfocused.

Then blinking.

Then, with whites showing all round the irises, locking onto my panting face.

"Tim, holy *shit* ..."

I grabbed her hand and squeezed it between both of mine. "Are you all right? Liv, are you okay?"

"Ahah ..." Her mouth hung open. I felt her fingers tighten around mine. "Ahah...oh. Whoa."

Bill. I am going to fucking kill that bastard.

"Liv, I am sorry, I had no idea –"

"Tim..." She lifted her other arm, fumbled the hand across my lips. "Tim, it was real."

"Believe me, I saw. I'm sorry, honey –"

"Tim, I was coming the whole time."

Now it was my turn to blink.

"What?"

Her voice stayed hushed and low. "I was in here. I could see you, hear you, sort of feel what you were doing, even though I couldn't say anything or move. But it didn't matter, because the second I said her name, I was coming, as hard as I've ever come in my life."

"That's...I mean, uh..." The whole time?

"It was fucking incredible."

"Aren't you...jeez, I was *terrified*."

She drifted her head side to side. "It felt too good for me to be scared. God, I wish you could –"

"Oh, no," I said. "I don't care how good it was, you couldn't get me within a mile of that thing now that I know it's real."

Her eyes took in my face. Her hand moved up to my cheek.

"Tim, I wasn't afraid. I don't think we need to be afraid of her. I could...I don't know, *sense* her."

"Well, you didn't see the green glowing eyes. I think maybe you were sensing her with orgasm goggles."

She laughed. The sound poked and pushed at my fear and made it warm up, slink away, or half away.

"You're so funny," she said. "But you know what this means, don't you? It's *real*. The afterlife. Spirits. Ghosts. I don't know, I guess even *magic*."

I sat there beside her, both of us naked, her dark hand in between my pale ones. Some kind of thrill or chill ran through me, because she was right: something supernatural had just happened in our bed. The world would never look quite the same again.

Only I don't think it made as big a change for me as for Liv. Every time I ever looked at her, I knew there was magic.

I opened my mouth to say that, because I needed her to know it.

But another voice spoke up before I could get the words out.

"Yeah, magic's real. But let me tell you, it's a good-news, bad-news kind of thing."

Both of us turned our heads.

There in the corner where the necklace had fallen, Julia stood looking at us with eerie green eyes.

CHAPTER THREE

Julia didn't cast a shadow on the wall behind her, and the textured off-white paint showed through her skin just enough to prove that she wasn't some living person who'd cleverly snuck in while Liv and I were distracted. Although come to think of it, if someone had been pulling a trick on us I think they would have found a better-looking girl to play the ghost's part. Maybe somebody with kind of a late-teen Christina Ricci/Angelina Jolie vibe going on. Instead, this person (ex-person?) I found myself looking at had a doughy, maybe even stocky figure, a too-round face and a too-shallow chin. From her right shoulder, an oversized tattoo of a dragon or some sort of monster-bat sent a loop of its tail curling down around her breast. (And turned its head around her shoulder to her back, which was why I couldn't tell exactly what it was.) If the breast had been shaped a little more like Liv's and a little less like a dumpling, it might have been a good effect. Or if the tattoo had been really well-drawn instead of half-assed and badly proportioned. Her stringy, dyed-black hair hung to her shoulders, shading to purple at the ends. Her eye-shadow was way overdone too, though that was hard to notice because the green-glowing eyes kind of distracted you.

In other words, she looked like one of those goth chicks who becomes a goth chick to prove how little of a fuck she gives about life and the world when really she's just pissed that no one wants to ask her out. And the fact that she looked mid-twenties and was still goth-chicking it probably said something about her too.

While I was taking all this in, Julia just stood there staring or glaring at us, I couldn't really tell. I didn't say anything because she looked mean. Sure, the fact of her being a ghost might have had something to do with my hesitation, but it was the meanness that really locked my tongue. I scooted a little forward and around Liv to put myself between the two of them.

"Do we get to say whether we want the good news or bad news first?" Liv asked, sitting up and putting one arm gently around me from behind. The warmth of her chest against my back took some of the edge off my freaked-outedness.

Julia laughed, short and loud. "No, I'll just tell you. The good news is, magic is real and you don't just *pfft!* and then rot when you die. The bad news is, it doesn't solve a goddamn thing. People still suck, still disappoint you, still screw you over when you're depending on them. How fucking long was I in that medallion?"

A couple of years, Bill had said.

"I'm not exactly sure."

"Well, it was way longer than it should have taken my brother to find some bimbo and screw her in order to let me out." She looked around the room. "Shit, I would kill for a cigarette. Not smokers?"

"No," Liv and I both said at the same time. Then Liv went on, "Could you pick one up and smoke it if we had one?"

Julia's round face came back to us, losing some of its goth-bitch certainty. "No, I'd have to...I mean, you'd have to smoke it for me. With the necklace on."

"Not happening," I said, shifting more directly between her and Liv. I felt Liv's fingers give a calming squeeze where her hand lay across my chest.

The blank green eyes made it hard to really gauge Julia's expression, and her hollow, echo-ey voice didn't carry emotions normally either. But I thought she seemed worried when she said, "But ... you called me. I'm fucked if you won't ... you know, share with me."

Head shaking, I said, "I'm sorry, but Liv's not –"

The arm around me tightened in a hug before I could finish.

"We didn't think the necklace was real," Liv said. "We were just using it as a prop."

"But you said my name."

"Yes, but that's all we really know about you, and we didn't even know that was real. If I'm going to ... help you again I need –"

I started in her grasp, shocked that there might be any kind of "if" to be discussed. "Liv, you're not going to –"

She squeezed me again. "Honey, shh. I told you, I felt her inside me. I'm a little weirded out, but I'm not really scared. If she can reassure us, let us get to know her, maybe I could ..."

The very thought made me shudder, and I know she felt it. But I was the one who'd gotten us into this, and it was her body, not mine. I certainly didn't have the right to tell her what she could or couldn't do with herself, now that I'd fucked up and put a ghost in her.

Trying not to let my voice shake, I asked Julia, "Okay then, so – what's the deal here? How does this work?"

The ghost tucked her upper lip behind her lower one for a second, then said, "I guess, *if* the books I got the ceremony from were right, I'm really stuck depending on you two. I can show up like this –" She waved black-polished nails down to indicate her see-through body. "– but only to my host and the one who brought me into her."

The word *host* made me shiver again. "Uh, let's find something else to call my girlfriend, all right? 'Host' creeps me out."

Her snub nose crinkled. "Christ, I don't know. She's the host. It's the only word the book used."

"Well, we're going to use something else."

"Symbiote?" Liv asked.

I craned my neck to look at her over my shoulder. "Ugh, worse! Are we trying to name a straight-to-DVD horror flick?"

"Is this really important for us to settle right now?" asked Julia.

"If it's important to Tim, it's important to me," said Liv. Something in her voice and the way she held me as she spoke settled me down inside. Partly.

"I guess if you can talk around it, we don't need a word this second."

"Receptacle."

"Liv! Ew!"

"*So,*" Julia said, "you can see and hear me, but nobody else can. And I have to stay close to the necklace. And I can't take Liv over unless –"

"No, no, there's not going to be any 'taking over' either. Call it something else."

"*Rrrhh!*" she growled. "Inhabit. Control. Borrow –"

"There," I said, jabbing a finger toward her. "Borrow. That's right. Not that I'm saying we're going to let you, yet."

"And I can be the lender," Liv said, her tone more helpful than I liked.

"What-*ever.*" Julia's fists clenched and unclenched. Her chest tightened as she did it, and the dragon's tail looked like it was squeezing her tit. "I can't ... *borrow* the *lender*'s body unless she puts the necklace on. I'm at your fucking mercy."

"For how long?"

She paused for a second. "A truck hit me before I finished researching that part."

"The setup doesn't sound like a very good deal," Liv said. "Why would you put yourself in that position? When you were alive, I mean?"

The ghost looked away. "Maybe I wasn't thinking it through all that well." Then she looked back. "That's basically it. Put the necklace on, I can borrow your body. Take it off, all I can do is hang around like this, not able to pick anything up or touch anything or basically do shit."

"And ..." Liv searched a minute for words. Which she didn't do very often. Which worried me. "Will I ... come like that? Every time you're in control? Sorry, Tim – borrowing?"

I'd stiffened in her arms at those words. Embarrassingly, I realized I was also stiffening down below, in full view of our supernatural party-crasher. No, she wasn't really a party-crasher – we'd invited her. I guess a guest who was already past her welcome. From my point of view.

Julia shrugged. "I kind of skimmed the parts that said what it would be like for the h*h*—lender. We won't know unless we try."

Liv wrapped her other arm around me and pressed her body tight to my back. Her lips at my ear whispered, "Tim, it was *so* good."

I felt helpless. My cock stood straight out from my groin, partly from Liv snugged up against me, partly from her breath in my ear and on my neck – and although it should have revolted me, partly from Julia's pudgy naked ghost body in front of me.

"How do we know you're not lying? That you won't take her over and make it permanent as soon as she puts the necklace back on."

"I don't know. Shit," Julia said, waving her arms. "I guess you'd have to find those books and read for yourself."

"Where are they?" Should I hope she'd say Bill had them or that she'd say she had no idea? "Did you have them when you...you know?"

She shook her head. "I borrowed them. Which – you might not like the fee the guy charged me for access. But I can tell you where he is if you want."

I took a few deep breaths. My erection stayed stubbornly alert.

"Tim, I believe her."

Oh shit.

"Honey, we've barely had half a conversation with her. You can't see a goddamn thing in her eyes, they've got no pupils. How can you trust her?"

She shrugged, the motion sliding her breasts ever so slightly upward along my back. "I don't know if I really *trust* her. But I believe her. Does that make any sense?"

No, it did not.

"Then what do you want to do?"

"Let me put the necklace back on. Just for a minute, to see what happens. You can yank it straight off if you get worried."

The look of hope on Julia's face ground away at the cold rock in my stomach. She was young, younger than Liv, and she'd grabbed at something weird because the regular world alienated her – or ignored her – and now, if she'd been telling the truth, she was in a pretty piss-poor situation where any hope of a physical existence depended on us.

"Okay," I said, shaking my head. "Okay."

* * *

Putting the necklace on did not send Liv into orgasms. In fact, it didn't do anything. She just shrugged and said, "Still here."

Making contact with Julia didn't do it either.

"Wow." Shaking her head as her outstretched hand passed through the ghost's.

Next, Julia moved fully up onto the bed with us, kneeling in the same position as Liv, right next to her. Each one of them looked at the other, Liv with a sort of amazement and Julia with a depressed frown. Lined up side by side, the two couldn't have contrasted more, and the contrast couldn't have been much less flattering to Bill's dead sister. Julia must have been a full head shorter, but obviously weighed more – or had in life. Her figure bulged fleshily where Liv's curved in and out. Her breasts hung floppy and small instead of standing proud. I could almost see her trying to keep from making a face until she said, "Are you ready?" and straightened and looked ahead when Liv nodded.

Julia shifted sideways on her knees, and then there she was, superimposed over or around Liv's body. Her face hovered halfway down Liv's neck.

"This is so freaky," Liv said, looking down at their overlapping forms, then running her hands along the solid apple-butter-brown of her own skin without any resistance from the spots where Julia's pale ghost-flesh stuck farther out.

"I'm going to take control now, okay? Uh, start 'borrowing,' I mean."

As Liv opened her mouth, I scooted closer and got a hand on the chain of the necklace.

"Just for a second," I said. "Then come back out."

"Yeah, yeah," Julia replied, in a tone I didn't really like. But she vanished before I could say anything about it.

Liv's arms came up in front of her face, turning her hands to let her look at their backs and palms. Her posture barely shifted, but I knew immediately that it wasn't her moving the body.

"Okay, that's enough," I said.

My girlfriend's beautiful face scowled at me, and her familiar voice said, "Sure."

And then Julia split out from her.

Liv wavered a second before recovering and putting a hand over her heart. "We-ird."

"You're all right?"

She nodded, breathing fast. But she looked more excited than scared.

"No orgasms?"

"Huh-uh. Everything just went sort of distant. Like in a dream, or like I was down a tunnel or behind a camera with the edges all blurred."

"The orgasm might have been a one-time thing," Julia said, though she didn't sound as though she believed it. "Something to do with the bonding process."

I opened my mouth with a tongue-load of skepticism at the ready, but Liv spoke before I could.

"Let's find out."

My ears went back like they wanted to hide from those words.

"Do you really *want* to find out?"

There's a look she gives me when I've said something dumb, where her eyes stare right into mine and her eyebrows sort of curl in a wave one direction and her mouth curls in a wave the other. It's normally hilarious but in this case it made me uncomfortable.

"Tim, have you ever had a five minute orgasm? *Yes*, I want to find out."

I sighed and looked from her to our ghost guest. If I'd known Julia at all, I'm pretty sure I could have told whether she was looking blasé or just trying really hard to look blasé. But from where I sat at that moment, I had no idea.

I looked back at Liv. "You're saying ... you want me to have sex with her again."

"Well, you'd be having sex with both of us. If it worked like the first time."

"But she'd be the one actually moving your body to fuck me, and you're okay with that?"

She laughed. That laugh, those teeth – god, I couldn't help being embarrassed that the situation amused me less than it did her. "Tim, are you worried I'm going to be mad about you cheating on me with my own body?"

I shrugged, a little helplessly.

Liv took my hand in hers, placed it against her stomach, moved it up to the medallion between her breasts. "When the guilt gets too much for you, take it off and ask me if I'm still okay sharing you and my body with our ghost."

Then, still looking me in the eye, she reached down and encircled my dick, one-handed, stiffening it back to full erection with a touch. Not that it had drooped by more than a quarter through all of these experiments, however appalled I was to stay turned on in this situation.

"Someone," she said, giving me a squeeze, "is less worried about this than you are."

My cheeks felt like coals. All but unwillingly, I said, "Okay. Do I need to, you know, get you going again first?"

She grinned and slid her hand along and then off my cock – very, very slowly. "Honey, I am about as going as going gets."

I leaned forward, trying to get a kiss of reassurance. But Liv fell to her back on the mattress, legs spreading and arms going out from her sides.

"Get in me," she said, the tone coming from deep in her throat. "Her first, then you."

If Julia weren't already gliding over and down, I would have hesitated. As it was, though, I had no choice. If I waited even a second or two after Liv's expression disappeared and Julia's took over, I knew I would lose my nerve. With the ghost's doughy, translucent nakedness overlaying itself on Liv's, I got quickly into position and fumbled the tip of my dick between her legs to find her slit, and the second Julia disappeared and Liv's back arched, I pushed in.

My first thought was, *Holy shit.* Liv was right about being ready. She parted around me glossy and slick and tight – as sweet as I could ever remember her feeling. Pressed all the way in, I held myself in place a moment, blinking, lips open in surprise.

"Good?"

I looked down, and Julia looked up at me. They were Liv's brown eyes, but – something mocking darted them across my face, sardonic, judgmental.

"Yeah, sure," I said. Then, with my face burning because I couldn't help trying to be polite, I added, "Um, how about you?"

She shrugged, mouth still in a wry twist. "I like having a cock in me, and Liv definitely warmed the place up for me. But one stroke doesn't exactly rock my world. How about you get going?"

I grimaced. "Uh, yeah. All right."

It took a real force of will to move my penis in and out of my girlfriend. Or, the first time it did.

"Jesus," I couldn't help but say.

Julia used Liv's mouth to laugh at me. But it wasn't Liv's laugh. Kind of a thin-lipped snicker. Still, her hips rolled and she played her inner flesh along me before I could take too much offense, and suddenly I was humping her full-tilt.

"How the fuck ... does this feel so good?" I grunted as Julia enfolded me in Liv's arms and legs.

"Do you ask her this many questions? Because I'd just as soon you shut up and screw me." She lifted up as if to kiss me, but I kept my lips tight and dropped my face in against Liv's dark neck. I didn't need to feel her tongue moving past my teeth like a stranger's, probing my mouth in an unfamiliar intrusion.

I should stop and take the necklace off, I thought. *Ask Liv if things are okay. Holy crap, this feels good.*

Julia growled in my ear as I thrust up into her hard and fast. "Yeah! That's it, yeah, *cram* it in me. *Bang* it, tap that *cunt.*"

I felt terrible that I couldn't get myself to stop. Julia spewed accelerating vulgarities, louder and cruder with every thrust. What if Liv was in there, unable to move or say anything, aghast at how much I was enjoying sex with someone else, groaning and jamming harder with every smut-mouthed encouragement Julia gave me?

But I was already really close. And the reverse was almost as mortifying – what if I pulled the necklace loose and Liv asked me why the hell I'd stopped?

"Jab it in there, you prick! Gush your nasty all up inside us!"

If I could have formed a complete sentence, I would have growled at her to cut the fuck-talk out. Maybe said something about how distracting it was. But I really didn't have that kind of coherence at the moment – or even the coherence to realize I plainly wasn't *that* distracted.

Instead, all I could do to express my displeasure was ram her with everything I had.

"*UH!*" I grunted, a syllable for each of the three most brutal thrusts I'd ever sunk into a woman. "*Uh!* FUCK!"

And that did it. Shut Julia up, opened my floodgates. I clutched Liv's body and moaned against her neck as storm-front waves of pleasure surged through and out of me. The ghost inside my girlfriend was making a long *Nnngggggg* sound and doing her best to squeeze permanent indentations into me with Liv's arms and legs. She held me so fiercely it ground the medallion between us into my chest.

As the third contraction squirted a weakening streamer of cum deep into Liv's belly, I had an overwhelming compulsion to give the last of my climax to her, not to Julia. With a wrench, I got my hand between us in time with a fourth shallow throb, and flipped the medallion up and over her head just as the last quivers spilled out of me. I managed one more tremor inside her, hoped she could feel it.

Looking at her face, I found a major case of nerves creeping in with the recession of my orgasm. Somehow, over my pounding heart, I managed to gasp out, "God, Liv, it was so good. Are you okay?"

She nodded weakly, eyes closed. One hand went to her forehead, palm up.

"Same again ..." she breathed. "Coming the whole time."

Despite the freakishness of the situation, despite my distrust of Julia, despite my worry at how drained Liv sounded, I couldn't help but feel ... proud? No, happy ... that my beautiful, beloved dark woman had the most satiated look that I had ever seen on a female face.

I kissed the curve of her jaw. She shuddered and laughed, pushing limply at me with the hand she'd placed on her forehead.

"No ... don't. Too much ..."

That laugh coming out of her – even exhausted – and the curl of her mouth not quite strong enough to be a smile ... it made me glow. I had done something for her that took her beyond mortal pleasure. I don't think

I could have felt any better if I'd been the one coming for the entire however many minutes of sex.

And then, grating across the moment: "So I guess no one's going to ask how it was for *me*?"

I raised my head. Liv opened her eyes and craned her neck. Standing out of the bed right where the necklace had fallen, Julia had her hands on her hips and her face in a sarcastic squint. The wedge of her brown pubic hair and the curve of her mound stood just above the topsheet, as though she were wading cunt-deep through our mattress. Reflexively, I readied a jab about her carpet not matching her drapes.

But Liv's voice, open and sincere, beat me to it. "How *was* it for you, Julia? I know it can't have been as unbelievable as it was for me, but ... Tim's really good, isn't he?"

The ghost looked down at her. One pale cheek twitched as the sharp expression lost its edge.

"It was ... yeah, it was fine."

Liv reached out to touch the other woman's hip, but her hand only passed through. Her fingers flinched back, but if anything her face looked more determined.

"Come on, it was better than fine, wasn't it? All those things you were saying –"

"Okay, it was good." The ghost looked away.

"What's wrong?"

Weirdly, Julia took a deep breath in and out. *Do ghosts even* need *to breathe?*

"It ... wasn't as good as the first time." Her round face turned back to us. I'd swear it looked hurt. "The first time, he thought I was you, pretending. This time I could see he was scared of me. I mean, you did great, Tim. It's just – have you ever had sex with someone and they were terrified of you?"

Now Liv laughed, loud and unexpected, making Julia flinch. Then she lifted her hands and eyes to my face.

"The best sex I ever had was with someone who was terrified of me. But I guess the *very* best part of it was the moment something clicked in him and he stopped being afraid, and you didn't get that, did you?"

"No."

The word had a surly edge, and an awkward silence squatted down on the bed with the three of us.

Then Julia straightened up, her jaded facade reappearing. "I came, though. I came really hard, and what else is sex really good for, right?"

In that second, I felt as sorry for Julia as I'd felt angry and fearful of her before. But I didn't have anything to say, and apparently neither did Liv; her hand rubbed along my rib-cage at the same moment I gave her shoulder a wistful squeeze.

The ghost tossed her black-and-purple hair.

"So. What are we going to do now?"

* * *

"Tim and I need to have sex," Liv said. "By ourselves."

Despite having come twice already, the second time not that long ago, my cock surged within Liv's pussy. She slapped me on the ass. "Not yet."

Julia backed away, ending up half-in and half-out of the wall behind the bed's headboard. "Sure. I get it."

Liv's head shook. "No you don't. It's not to exclude you or talk about you behind your back while we fuck. We just need to know that we're still us before we go any further with you."

My dick was back to rock hard. *My god, I love you, Liv. What in the world did I ever do to deserve this?*

"Is that okay? Can we ... I guess, take the necklace in the other room and let you hang out there?"

Julia folded her arms across her little dumpling breasts.

"Is there a TV?"

"Sure. Tim, can you go put it on for her while I take a stop in the bathroom?"

I really hated the idea of separating from her right now – she felt so warm and real beneath me and around me. And even worse, I hated the idea of leading Julia into the other room with my erection waving around in front of me. But I also wanted to get Liv alone, and there wasn't any other way to do it.

"Yeah. No problem."

Sighing, I withdrew and crawled off the bed, picking up the necklace as I went.

"Come on," I told Julia. "Through here."

I led her into the hall. Behind us came the sound of the mattress springing back into shape as Liv got off it to go to the bathroom. Thankfully, I had mostly softened up by the time we made it to the living room.

It took some skimming through the channels before Julia settled on something – one of the Spanish-language stations showing what I guessed were Mexican soap operas.

"You know Spanish?" I asked.

She shook her head. "I just like trying to figure out what they're saying, pick out the words that sound like English ones."

"Cognates," I said.

"Fuck you."

"Jeez, you don't have to be –"

29

"I'm just kidding. Are you always this much of a tight-ass?"

I tried not to scowl. "Yes."

She turned her face back to the television, blank green eyes revealing nothing. "Okay. Go bone your girlfriend while I bone up on my fucking cognates."

Liv sat cross-legged on the bed when I returned, hands on the mattress behind her to support her languidly reclining upper body. I shut the door.

"This is not how ghosts are in the movies," I said.

"Shh." With a tilt of her head, she beckoned me over. I went. By the time I reached the bed, she'd uncrossed her legs and settled farther back, on her elbows now. "I need you to make love to me."

I didn't need any encouragement, and she shushed me again when I opened my mouth to ask a question, and soon we were touching each other, kissing each other, sliding gently together toward a peak completely different from the one I'd hit with Julia just a few minutes earlier. Liv's orgasm was quiet, tight-lipped, ending with just a little whimper to let me know it had passed. I came a few seconds later and not much louder.

After a bit of stillness and breathing in each other's ears, I said, "I guess that probably doesn't compare so much to five minutes of solid coming."

"You're dumb," she said, caressing my jaw with one hand while nibbling at my opposite earlobe. "I wouldn't trade this for an hour of wearing that necklace."

"But you were worried you might." I lifted up and looked her in the eyes. "Isn't that why we had to do this?"

Liv nodded ever so slightly. "I wish you could feel it, Tim. I wish I could give that to you. It's good enough to be kind of scary. But I'm not scared now. I'm not going to lose myself, not when I have you to make me feel like this."

"What are we going to do?" I asked, half-reassured and half-bewildered that this beautiful woman kept saying these things to me, day after day and month after month. Somehow even the improbability of a pudgy goth ghost watching telenovelas on the TV in the other room couldn't make me think that this world held anything stranger than someone like Liv loving someone like me. "I mean, my head is spinning from how good it's been tonight – everything. But I don't – I can't –"

She put a hand to my lips. "What we're *not* going to do is make any kind of decision right now." Her laugh floated me away from my doubts for a moment. "I would be *crazy* to think I'm in any shape to use my brain the rest of tonight. And I bet you're even worse. I can see those shaky-chihuahua jitters in your eyes."

"*Please* don't call me a chihuahua," I said.

But she laughed again, and I would let her call me a chihuahua all she wanted for that laugh. "So what we're going to do is, one of us is going to go out and tell Julia that we're sleeping on it.

"Well, I'm not going by myself," I said. "If you want to come with me, I'd be happy to –"

"No, I'll do it," she said, smiling.

"Now? Do you want me to let you up?"

She raised her head and scraped her gorgeous white teeth gently across my chin. "Not quite yet."

CHAPTER FOUR

The first six weeks after Liv moved in, I woke up two or three times every night in a sweat, positive I had just come out of a beautiful but crazy dream and that the mattress next to me was going to be empty. Every time, I would lie there tense and blinking, hearing her breathe just inches away, wanting to curl up against her and physically reassure myself that the sound was real. Eventually I would drop back off, only to have the same thing repeat a few hours later.

Then one night when I jolted awake yet again, instead of just breathing, Liv reached over and touched my hand and said, "You're going to get used to me being here at some point, aren't you? I mean, we could get a king bed if you need more space, if you'd be more comfortable."

I couldn't find anything to say, so I just scooted in close to her with her hand in mine, and I went back to sleep faster than any time since she moved in. After that I didn't wake up in the middle of the night, ever, unless I needed to pee.

Until Julia showed up.

"Boy, were you restless last night," Liv said when she came out of the master bath the next morning and saw me awake.

"Shit." I sat up and rubbed a hand through my hair, looked at the clock. Five twelve a.m., only a little before the alarm would go off if we'd set it, which I'd forgotten to. "Sorry. I hope I didn't wake you up too much."

She shook her head, walked to the bed and sat down next to me, her perfect body still naked, still smelling faintly of the night before.

"I couldn't sleep either. Holy crap, Tim, we've got a ghost in our house. It's fucking crazy."

I nodded blearily toward the bedroom door, not thick enough to keep the television out, but thick enough you couldn't tell if the words were still in Spanish. "Go out there yet?"

"Huh-uh." She put her forehead against my shoulder and scratched my back in slow, lazy circles the way she does when we're talking and she's thinking. "I don't know if I'm more worried she'll be there or she'll be gone."

I squirmed a little. "It'd worry you if she was gone?"

"Yeah, because we might have imagined it."

"Both of us?"

She laughed. "Would both of us imagining a ghost be harder to believe than there actually *being* a ghost?"

"I guess not."

We sat there a little longer, then I said, "Uh, I have to get up and piss."

With a pat on the back, she leaned away and released me. "And you need a shower. And I need one too. *And* I'm hungry for breakfast."

I got out from under the sheets, stood up, stretched. "We could ... save time and shower together."

A curved flash of those teeth, and she leaned to push me away with both hands on my ass. "That would *not* end up saving time. You go, I'm going to poke my head out and tell ... her, that we're getting ready."

I pissed, then showered, then left the water running while Liv switched out with me. After shaving, I texted my boss that I needed a personal day for something urgent that had come up. Liv was substitute teaching, so unless they contacted her out of desperation, she could skip by just not calling in to the district office.

Breakfast was weird.

* * *

Julia sat in the chair opposite mine at our square kitchen table, still naked, the amulet in front of her instead of a plate. And when I say "sat," it was more like she'd been superimposed over the chair by way of cheesy 1970s blue-screen technology, because it couldn't actually support her, so she basically just hovered on it with her legs bent to *look* like she was sitting. And you could see the chair back through her.

"Ugh," she moaned with one hand on her forehead: her right hand, which raised her breast and made the dragon twitch the tip of its tail. "Why the hell couldn't you guys have been smokers?"

"Sorry," Liv said, bringing the skillet of scrambled eggs over to spatula a heap onto our two plates. I had made the toast (using tongs) and poured us juice and milk. "Do ghosts get nicotine withdrawal?"

The dead goth shook her head. "No. But that's my breakfast – cigarettes and coffee. *Was* my breakfast. And a smoke would just be really good right now."

I looked at her pudgy body, thinking she didn't exactly look like someone who subsisted on tobacco. Apparently, I looked too long, or frowned or something.

"I said breakfast, not three meals a day. A fucking pint of Ben and Jerry's was my dinner, okay?"

"Sorry."

To avoid her green-eyed glare, I focused on my plate, buttering and jellying a piece of toast while Liv put the skillet back on the stove and explained what we both did and that we were taking the day off to get our heads around this.

"...get to know each other a little, figure out as much as there is to figure out about how –"

"Dude, are you eating your toast with a *fork*?"

I looked up from slicing my toast. Liv had joined us at the table. Her expression was a little more amused than I would have liked, but she stepped in to defend me before I could open my red-cheeked face to speak up myself.

"That's just how he does it. I think it's cute."

"Whatever. Kind of freakish from where I'm sitting, but I guess I don't have much business talking."

"No, you don't," I said, jabbing a square of toast with my fork and stuffing it in my mouth before I could say anything surlier. Liv put a hand over mine.

To Julia, she said, "I don't think *any* of us has any business judging the others right now. We're strangers, but we're going to be living – well, staying together, until we get this sorted out, and we need to get off on a good foot."

The ghost crinkled her nose. "I guess." Then she jerked her chin at me. "Sorry. I'm not exactly good with people. Sometimes I rub everybody the wrong way."

"Don't worry about it," Liv said, her hand giving mine a squeeze. "I'm pretty sure I can teach you how to rub Tim the right way."

* * *

We had sex two more times that day – against my better judgment, but Liv is hard to turn down when she gets horny, and something about Julia's translucent, constantly naked body made it even more difficult for me to say no than normal.

The first time was about an hour after breakfast, when Julia had wrapped up a brief story-of-my-life for us. Rich girl. Inattentive parents. Socially awkward. Bad-influence older brother. (At that point, she mentioned Bill's name and I had to admit where I'd gotten the necklace. I sort of expected Liv to get mad, but she just rolled her eyes and said, "Of course. Bill. How did I not predict that?") Weight problems. Late bloomer. Dumpy tits when they finally came in. Mutually dissatisfying attempt at lesbian sex with her best friend. Complete failure at becoming a high-school blow-job slut trying to get guys' attentions by offering head. (The combination of a small mouth, overwhelming gag instinct, and total inexperience did her in at that one.) Eventual default to the school's reject collection, where she finally found a boyfriend and got turned onto the occult by him before he dumped her to date a high-performing autistic girl.

At this point, although I felt really sorry for Julia and her crappy life, I was mostly thinking, *Great, we're getting to the occult stuff. Now maybe she'll tell us what's really going on.*

But Liv was apparently thinking something else, maybe because she's so nice, or maybe because she doesn't have the same OCD boundaries I do. Instead of following up on the mysticism angle, she said, "Wow. I wish I'd been brave enough to try having sex with my best friend in high school. I guarantee you if we'd been at the same school, that part wouldn't have ended up being a bummer."

It took Julia a second to respond. Several different expressions collided on her face first, and then it resumed its normal jaded look.

"Yeah, right. I mean, thanks for being nice, but number one, you wouldn't ever have been hanging out in my clique at school, and number two, I obviously sucked at it, even worse than Shelli did."

Liv didn't flinch. "Well, number one, I have never been embarrassed about guiding my partner the right direction in bed, and number two, I totally would have been in your clique. I hated all the jocks and popular kids. None of them like the things I liked, and they picked on all the kids who did."

"Uh-huh. I'm supposed to believe you hung out with nerds all through high school and college and none of them snapped you up before cradle-robbing Tim here came along?"

"Hey!"

"Look, no offense, but you've got to be what, thirty-five? I'm not judging, it just seems like a geek who had access to somebody like Liv here would have locked her in with a ring at his first chance. *If* she was really hanging out with them, and not looking for a mister conventional stability type."

My face was burning by now, but Liv just cracked up.

"You really *aren't* a people person, are you?" she asked. "I'm not with Tim because he's conventional, because he's not. And I'm not with him because he's stable, because he's a weird kind of stable. I'm with him because he's special. And for your information, he's probably a bigger nerd than anybody you knew in high school."

Julia looked back and forth between us like somehow the knowledge didn't sit well with her.

"We are ... *way* off topic here," I said.

"Right," Liv responded. "We were talking about high school lesbian sex."

"No, we were –"

"And I'm betting if that didn't go well and the blow-jobbing didn't go well and the black-magic boyfriend was a shmo, you've never been properly eaten out, have you?"

I could see where this was headed, although it didn't look like Julia could.

"Because Tim is awesome at it, and I think I'm ready for a break from talking."

"Oh," said Julia, sitting up a little straighter. "*Oh*, okay."

* * *

When I was in high school, my aunt and uncle went on a very bumpy downhill ride toward their divorce – I mean boulders-in-the-middle-of-the-road bumpy, neighbors-calling-the-police bumpy. So on nights when things got really bad, my cousin Danny would come over and ask my folks if he could stay with us, and of course my folks said yes. You might imagine that with a home-life like that, Danny wasn't the most balanced of kids, and you'd be right. Most of the time, he could be all right, but it humiliated him to have to show up at our place on his bike, and he didn't like being alone in his humiliation.

As luck would have it, Danny had an OCD cousin who could be mortified at the drop of a hat, so there was no need to be alone at all.

Now, I could tell a whole lot of stories about the things Danny snuck into my lunchbox for me to discover in the middle of the school cafeteria with maybe a million people looking. (Believe it or not, the worst were the cookies. You can't use utensils to eat cookies, and if I didn't want to look like a freak, I had to sit there with my skin crawling while I tried to wolf them down as fast as I could.) I could also tell a lot of stories about the glee he took describing all the things I wasn't going to be able to do in the unlikely event that I became sexually active. ("How are you even going to get a girl excited? You can't finger her, you sure won't be able to lick her.") And there are stories about the various objects and substances he would put in my bed while I slept so that I would wake up next to them or under them and go bug-ass hysterical.

But at this point I'm just going to mention the one prank from that last category that didn't go the way Danny expected.

He'd spent the whole evening talking to me and my older sister Lisme about this fight his dad and mom had been having. I always squirmed through these stories because I had to listen and be sympathetic even though they inevitably worked their way toward some obscene revelation that brought my dinner up against the back of my tongue. In this case, Danny's mom had apparently responded to every one of his father's shouted insults with a complaint about how she couldn't get her own husband to go down on her. My face stayed flushed the whole time, as he repeated my aunt's detailed descriptions of the parched state her vagina had been in for years, so dry that even my uncle's purportedly tiny penis couldn't go in without rasping like sandpaper, and what a cowardly, selfish brute it was that wouldn't tongue his own wife into readiness for his all-too-brief sexual performances.

Lisme didn't make things any better. She had a wicked streak too, and kept asking him to repeat things for the sake of my discomfort.

Finally, I couldn't take it any more, and I told them both to fuck off and went to bed. But my room sat just off the upstairs den where we'd been talking, and I could hear them giggling and snorting over my embarrassment for an eternity before I dropped off.

Fortunately or unfortunately, I fell asleep before they hatched their plan. Lisme would tell me later that it was all Danny's idea, but I never believed her.

At some point in the night, Lisme rubbed herself to an orgasm or several through the fabric of her panties, then took them off and gave them to Danny, who snuck into my room and draped them over my slumbering face. They probably expected me to leap up and scream, or to inhale the cloth into my mouth and choke on pussy fumes. But for whatever reason, the damp crotch of Lisme's panties over my nose and mouth didn't pull me out of my sleep, and eventually they got tired of watching me snore through their mischief and went off to their own beds — or to the den couch in Danny's case.

It would be crazy for me to claim that I remember every dream I had that night. Supposedly you only remember the very last dream you have before waking up, if you remember anything at all. But I have these vivid recollections of scene upon scene, dream upon dream: working in a bakery, where the dough swelled up and enfolded me as I kneaded it; getting into a wrestling match with Lisme when she tried to pull me out of the mess, which for some reason I didn't want her to do; having sex with a frog while I was looking at it under a microscope where its flowing egg-mass lubricated the way for my dick to slide in and out; lying with my head in some girl's lap, which was also a bowl of seasoned pasta, eating cookies with my fingers and licking the cookie juice off of them after every one; putting in a hot, sweaty shift in a donut shop where I had to fill the cream pastries by coming into them ...

I woke up in the middle of ejaculating at that last image. But at first I didn't realize I'd stopped dreaming, because my face felt swaddled in cotton and in the rich, yeasty, greasy smell of the donut shop. As my cock slopped thick runnels of semen out into my pajamas, though, my eyes blinked open and my eyelashes brushed against something right in front of them and I took a deep breath that sucked Lisme's panty-crotch flat against my open mouth, and I came awake to an immediate, complete understanding.

And I didn't gag or screech or claw the underwear from my face, even though I knew what it was and whose it was and why it smelled the way it smelled.

Because the end of every other wet dream I'd ever had was cold spew making my pajamas cling to my leg as I tried to get out of bed before any soaked through to the sheets. The end of every other wet dream was joyful physical paradise disappearing with mocking laughter as I hobbled to the bathroom feeling ashamed and degraded, praying no one else happened out into the hallway while I was between my bedroom and the toilet.

But the end of this wet dream wasn't the end. The scent that had hung thick in the air of the donut shop and the bakery, that had wafted up from the girl's spicy pasta lap, that had replaced the formaldehyde stink of frog preservative – it didn't go away. It stayed. It was real. And it was incredible.

And that's why even though I can't eat pizza with my fingers, I have no problem planting my face in a girl's crotch and tasting bodily fluids while nose deep in pubic hair.

* * *

So about half an hour after Liv made her suggestion, the three of us were lying on our backs in the bed, Liv next to me, Julia on the far side of her, all of us slowly shaking off an orgasmic stupor.

"Holy. Fucking. Hell."

"Told ... you ..." Liv gasped. As before, when the necklace came off, it left her quivering and limp – maybe worse this time than the other two, because she'd had the thing on for maybe fifteen minutes of cunninglingus and then another ten of intercourse, in the form of Julia riding me cowgirl into a mutual explosion of ecstasy. The sex was fantastic, some of the best I've ever felt, and only the fact that Liv's body kept saying things that Liv would never say caused it to last as long as it did.

"Where did you learn to *do* that?" Julia asked hollowly.

"I've kind of had an obsession since high school," I said. "So I was pretty decent by the time I met Liv, and she's full of good pointers."

"...definitely nothing like ... being full ... of a good pointer, haha ..."

I laughed too, but Julia didn't. Nor did she make a smart-ass remark. Rising up on one elbow, I looked over to find her staring at the ceiling. Although I say we were all on the bed, she actually floated half-on and half-off the edge, undisturbed by the lack of support against gravity. The joy of fornication had faded from her face. Part of me wanted her to look that way: unhappy, distant, detached from us. But a bigger part of me squirmed. As much as I *didn't* want to feel for her – because I didn't trust her – I'd basically had sex with this woman twice now and heard her life story, and there wasn't any doubt in my mind that she was desperate to connect with someone.

After a minute of internal wrestling, I asked her, "Are you okay?"

"No," she said flatly. "I'm shitty. You two are something else. You care about each other, and you're even nice to me when this ought to be scaring the crap out of you. I'm never going to fit in with that – I'm a fucking mess. Sooner or later you're going to want to get rid of me. I'm pretty sure *you* already do, Tim."

"Uh ... I'm not good at – adjusting. But, you know, who knows what's going to happen down the line."

"You're a terrible liar."

"Yeah. Sorry. But look, this is obviously great for Liv, and I would try to get used to just about anything for her, so, really, if she wants to give you a chance ..."

We both looked at Liv's sleek brown form between us. That was her cue to be positive and sweet and optimistic about the situation. But instead she put both hands over her eyes.

"Liv?" I settled my right palm gently onto her stomach. She reached down to stroke my forearm, opening her eyes but not turning them toward either me or the ghost beside her.

"I'm ... a little worried that it's *too* good."

Julia's face went miserable.

"I'm not saying for sure," Liv went on, turning toward her and putting a reassuring hand out gently but uselessly through the fleshless specter. "But – it's like a drug, coming for that long. I'm scared I'll get addicted to it. It's almost scarier than you being a ghost."

"We need to know more," I said. "You said yourself you didn't learn everything about the medallion or how to get out of it. If we're really all stuck together, then we're really all stuck together, and we'll have to find a way to make it work. But we shouldn't get all down before we're sure about what's what."

"Right," Liv said, a little more upbeat. "You should tell us what you can, and then maybe we can find a solution that works for everybody. And maybe while we're looking for the solution, we'll all get more comfortable and less worried about things."

Julia still frowned, but she nodded slowly, and she told us what she knew.

Or most of what she knew.

Maybe.

* * *

After several years of digging and searching and working her way into steadily creepier and legitimately magical circles, she'd bought the medallion and rented several books that came with it. Her source, a guy who claimed to be a 200-year-old warlock, charged her ten years of life for each week she kept the books.

"I figured that meant I'd kick off at sixty instead of seventy, but apparently I was due to be fucked over by the Grim Reaper a lot younger than I expected."

It had taken her eight days to learn the rituals that activated the necklace. The first couple of days had been a laugh, with Julia giddy about the possibility that the books and necklace might be real, but suspecting the warlock was just a freak and would try to get in her pants when she brought everything back. But the further she delved into the books, and the more she held and stared into the medallion, the more real everything became.

"There was a crapload left to read by day eight, but I couldn't make myself wait, especially since I'd started to believe the dude was leveling with me and I was taking years off my life every day I kept studying. So I did the ritual to bond my soul to the gem, and when I hit the end and *felt* it, really felt something being sucked out of me and into the amulet, I just about shit myself. I panicked and rushed the books straight back to him, and he laughed and made a mark on my forehead with a grease pencil and told me if I washed it off in less than an hour, it would take my whole life instead of just the ten years."

She barely slept the next five days, madly going back over every source she had and grilling every contact she knew to try to find out exactly what she'd done to herself. By the time the truck hit her less than a week later, this is all she had supposedly learned:

Once she died, the medallion would hold her soul until bonded to a –

"Lender. See? I remembered."

The "lender" would be her only connection to life. With the necklace on, the lender could be possessed at Julia's whim, but without it, all she could do was hover around, invisible to everyone but the two people who had brought her out of entrapment in the gem.

Destroying the medallion would release Julia's soul from the gem and automatically transfer it into the lender's body, permanently. If and when the lender subsequently died, the ghost would be stuck haunting the immediate vicinity of the corpse for eternity.

The books she'd borrowed supposedly held additional rituals that could break the bond and allow the spirit to roam free and possess whoever she liked. But every source she consulted lacked the details for the rites, and when she went back to the warlock, he'd raised his book-lending rate to ten years per day.

"Turns out I should have taken him up on that, right? Joke would have been on him."

Not desperate enough to pay the higher fee, or at least not yet, she'd dug up a couple of additional leads through Internet chat rooms, and was on her way to one of them when the truck ran a red light and trash-compacted her.

By the end of all this, I didn't know what to think. Should I be terrified that she might try to get the necklace destroyed so she could take Liv's body? Or should I trust her because she was honest enough to reveal that scary possibility to us? Should I feel reassured that she'd be eternally screwed once the body died, if she did take Liv over? Or should I suspect that she'd just go back to the warlock and burn up some of Liv's decades trying to buy a way out of that predicament? And should I ask what those last couple of leads were, so we could chase them down and try to fix this whole mess? Or should I be terrified of getting any deeper into the occult than we already were?

I teetered back and forth like that through her whole story, and when she was done, I felt too off-balance to even pick a question to ask.

"So ..." We were still in bed, naked, which didn't exactly help my conversational ease. But there had to be *something* I could say. "... I hope it didn't, uh, hurt too bad."

She looked at me like she was trying to decide whether to be grateful or sarcastic. It had sounded lame even to me, so I almost hoped for sarcastic.

"You know how everybody's always saying you should wear a helmet on a motorbike or scooter? Well, if I'm reincarnated or something someday, fuck that shit. I had ribs sticking out everywhere and poking through lungs, ruptured guts spilled all around me, but thank you, helmet, my brain did not get bashed in when it hit the concrete, so I got to scream and gurgle until I bled out or drowned in my own blood or whatever finally made it go black."

"Oh. Sorry."

She shrugged. Liv rubbed my arm.

"On the plus side," Julia said, like she suddenly realized she was pooping the party, "the next thing I felt after that was somebody fucking me, which was a lot better way to wake up than the way I went out."

Great, I thought, feeling the blood wash up through my face. *Now I'm embarrassed* and *queasy.*

"So what do we do, then?" Liv asked. "I don't like the sound of that warlock, but, no offense, I'd really like to ... not be in this position. Where were the other places you were going?"

"This isn't my first choice either, believe me. But we're screwed on those two leads. I was driving to meet this tarot chick at a coffee shop. No idea where she lived. And I had the other place written down. A bookstore with a weird name. I don't remember the address."

That seemed conveniently inconvenient. But I didn't say so.

Thankfully, before the silence got too long my stomach growled really loudly and I looked at the alarm clock. Morning had raced us by. It was almost noon.

"I guess I'm hungry," I said.

"Me too." Liv gave my bicep a squeeze and slid out from under the covers to stand up. "Maybe lunch will give us some ideas."

Julia didn't say anything. I didn't try to figure out what was going on behind her green eyes.

* * *

That night we fucked again, which was probably a bad idea. But after lunch, we spent the rest of the day at the computer trying to see if Julia's old chat-room logins could get us anywhere. But everyone online now seemed to be what she called "wizard wannabes and fantasy fucktards." Evidently the authentic occult crowd migrated to new sites every few months as hangers-on took over too much of the conversation. We ordered pizza for dinner, and Liv let Julia eat a slice when we saw how she kept staring at it. Then more surfing the supernatural sex-net.

Nothing.

Except post after post and chat-room after forum after blog of occult fetishists who, like Julia, focused on the erotic end of the magical spectrum.

And the stuff our ghost guide thought looked most promising always seemed to get really, really graphic before something clued Julia in that we'd run up against another fake.

"Good grief," Liv said as she clicked to close the last window. "My eyes are crossed and I'm moist as a towelette. How are we ever supposed to find the real stuff in all this magic porn?"

Julia shrugged, looking defeated. "Honestly? I've been tapped out for like two hours now. All the real stuff has moved on since I died, obviously."

"Two hours?" I'd had an uncomfortable boner on and off for almost exactly that long. "Why didn't you just say so?"

She shrugged again and looked away.

Pushing back from the computer desk, Liv stood and kissed me on the cheek. "Come on, Tim. She was trying, and I'm sure she didn't want to let us down."

Or she was wild-goose-chasing us and deliberately getting our juices going.

"Look," Liv went on, "maybe we need to just call it a night on this and ... unwind."

Uh-oh. Part of me said this had been Julia's plan all along. But another part of me – also known as the penis – didn't really care by that point.

"You guys can leave me out here if you want to," Julia said, with her face still turned away and her shoulders slumped. Goddamn if I didn't feel guilty about wanting to take her up on that. She'd spent the whole day guiding us through this stuff, and even though I didn't completely trust her, it had somehow turned into a team effort, and her cynical jokes at the endless parade of online weirdoes had made things a lot more tolerable.

I looked at Liv with my "whatever you want" face.

"How about," she said to Julia, "if, mm, Tim and I just let you watch most of the way through? And then you can 'borrow' me right at the end, after he's gotten me there a couple of times. I don't want to completely shut you out, I just don't know if I can handle another ten minutes of orgasm again."

The ghost looked from her to me and back again, made a shrug with her lips instead of her shoulders, and said, "Okay."

* * *

I *hate* to be watched doing *anything*.

Liv doesn't really know this about me, because she's mostly an exception. I have a hard time peeing with her in the bathroom, and I make her leave and shut the door if I'm taking a dump. But in general, she's so beautiful and the idea of her being interested in me is so perpetually amazing that I can suppress my instinct to wince when she's hanging out, keeping her eyes on me while I'm cooking or reading or at the computer. I even let her look over my shoulder. The way she smells and the warmth of her body and breath push the crawly self-consciousness into a back corner of my mind.

Which means Liv was already naked and climbing into bed by the time I got my shoes and socks off. Julia had preceded her – no clothes to take off, so she just walked through the mattress to stand in the middle of my pillow, watching my girlfriend crawl toward her across the sheets.

"Jesus. How the hell do you get a body like that?"

"It's all luck," Liv said, standing on her knees and looking down at her breasts as she gave them a little lift with her hands. "I don't deserve any of the credit, except that I swim at the health club a couple times a week. I wish I could tell you my secret."

Julia shrugged and looked down at her own body, gnurling one side of her mouth up. "Not like I could do anything about it now. I'm stuck in this lumpy dump the rest of eternity, it looks like."

"Oh, you're not that bad. Tim, if you didn't have me, you'd fuck her, wouldn't you?"

"Uh, sure." Pulling my belt off slowly.

"Tell her something nice about her body."

Christ. "I don't know. I like the Y where your thighs come together. Is that okay? I'd definitely go down on that if we were dating."

I wouldn't expect a ghost to blush, and Julia's skin didn't change color. But if the expression she wore said anything, her face would have been as red as mine at that moment, if she'd been alive.

"Come on, honey, you can do better than that. Hey, and you can undress faster than that too. What are you doing, the world's least enthusiastic strip-tease?"

"Sorry," I said, cheeks burning even hotter as I fumbled with my button and fly. "I guess your boobs are kind of growing on me too. They're not that big, but they're ... different."

"Wow," the ghost said flatly. "That's really going straight to my head."

Liv laughed. "I know what he means. I'd put my hands on them right now if I could."

I had both thumbs inside the waistbands of my shorts and briefs, but hadn't quite worked up the nerve to push them down.

"Do it," I said. Not only did it sound hot, but it would take the focus off me as I finished getting out of my clothes. "I mean, pretend."

Liv raised one eyebrow at me and turned back to Julia, who looked uncomfortable at Liv's hands coming up, palms toward her.

"Can I?"

"I guess. Sure."

I got my shorts off as Liv cupped her dark hands over the slightly droopy, conical non-flesh of Julia's breasts. Liv's got pretty big hands, and Julia had pretty small knockers, so I could see nothing of the ghostly tits as my girlfriend rotated her wrists and mimicked a gentle nipple caress.

"Mm-hm, these are nice."

Julia snorted, but it looked to me as though her mouth wanted to throw off its jaded twist and smile.

"Girl, where were you when I was in high school?" Liv asked, squeezing enough that her fingers dipped into those incorporeal breasts, but not enough for them to go through and be visible inside. Julia was definitely working to keep her expression flat now.

I slipped out of my shirt. Both of them were looking at Julia's chest, at Liv's fingers pretending to knead there. I not only had a good view of that, but a great view of Liv's taut, smooth back and incredible ass, along with a hint of her lips at the V made by her thighs. That little glimpse told me exactly where I wanted to be, so I walked over and slid onto the mattress with them, rolling face-up behind Liv and then worming my way slowly under her until my shoulders hit the soles of her feet and her already-glistening crotch hovered directly above my face.

Liv glanced down from her ghost-breast groping and smiled at me. I saw her hands waver through Julia's chest, then I took hold of her by the hips and encouraged her gently downward. Contact, soft and wet, savory and heady. My lips found their nether partners; my tongue flicked in.

"ooh…"

She went back to fondling our phantom while I got to work. It's always incredibly hot for me when Liv sits on my face, and this time there was the added stimulus of what I slowly realized was my first threesome. I'd never really expected to have a ménage a trois, but I guess I should have predicted that if I was going to, it wasn't going to be a remotely normal one.

There was no way to tell from the tilt of Julia's head whether her blank, blank eyes were focused on Liv's hands, Liv's chest, or my face, half-covered by my girlfriend's slow-rocking groin. A little creeped out by that, I shut my eyes and disappeared into a sightless, womb-like world of oral sex, where Liv's perfect, responsive pudenda glided in sync with the caresses of my mouth. I could taste and smell her pleasure flowing, hear it build within her breath. Her hips quickened their pace surprisingly soon, and when she started to gasp, I knew she was close.

And then she rose up and off of my lips, crawling backward over my chest, her eyes wide and hungry when I opened my own to look up at them.

"I'm going to sit on you and come now," she said. Then she turned her eyes to Julia. "And I want you to sit on his face while I'm doing it."

Before I could object to that idea, Liv had her hand on me, then her crease kissing my tip, and then her place of wonder opening up around me, enfolding me as she sat firmly down.

"Jesus, Liv," I gasped.

Julia moved forward on her knees, mouth squished dubiously to one side. Her lower legs passed through my shoulders and biceps instead of lifting over them. Her face turned down to see if she'd gotten into place.

"Okay, so … still like how it looks down there?"

Liv was firmly grinding her pubis against mine, making it not exactly easy to think of an answer. So I just said, or actually kind of gulped out, "Yes."

She had a puffier mound than Liv, and her labia dangled farther out, one side slightly longer than the other. The hood of her clit nestled deeper in her mons, peeking out just enough for me to spot it. She kept looking at me. If she'd been solid, I wouldn't have known that, because my eyes were fully under her crotch. But her ghostly translucence let me meet her gaze through the curves and creases of her genitalia.

"What's so great about it?"

"It's got personality," I said. "I really wish I could put my lips on it and feel you."

Her hips wiggled, while Liv's continued to press down and ease forward, then back.

"Make believe," Liv said. Her voice had gone all husky.

Feeling *extremely* awkward about it, I lifted my head up and opened my lips right where they would have connected with Julia's crotch, if it had been real. Even knowing she had no physical substance, I almost flinched back when my mouth passed into her without resistance. No smell, no taste, no sensation of any kind.

"*Yes,*" Liv said. "Eat her up."

Her pace quickened. Even though burying my face in Julia's cunt gave me no satisfaction whatsoever, I made myself lick and slurp as if her flesh could be kissed.

"Mm, oh yes, Tim."

"Shit, Liv," Julia said. "Look at you *go*. They don't even make porn this good. Fuck, *ride* that cock, would you?"

I don't think Liv needed any encouragement. Her lower spine undulated sweetly and with ever-greater speed, rubbing her clit against me, milking my shaft all the way to the root. I waited for the squeaking sound that would tell me she'd hit her first orgasm.

But it didn't come, and everything was kind of falling apart for me.

"Come on, Tim, jam it up in her. Yes, fuck you two, fuck!"

I kept up my pointless cunninglingus because I could see Liv staring at what I was doing, her eyes drinking it in as her lips snarled over clenched teeth. "Ah! MM, Ah!"

I met her pressure, pushing up with my hips. Ordinarily, I'd be nearing the edge myself, and if I wasn't careful, that first squeak would push me over. But the emptiness of Julia's groin, her crude sex-talk, and the transparency of her body intruded too much.

"*Fuck*, I want a piece of that."

Fierce concentration tightened Liv's face.

She's not feeling it either.

"*Hnn,* nh, *nh* ..."

"So fucking sexy. Goddamn, I wish I had a body right now. Work it, Tim! Come on, bring her off."

Liv leaned forward, still riding me fast. Her right hand landed against the mattress practically in my armpit. I thought she was about to come right down through Julia's abdomen and kiss me.

But instead, her other hand stretched out to grab the medallion where it lay near the head of the bed.

"I don't know what's wrong," she panted, still fucking me hard. "So close, but I just can't ... is it all right if I ...?"

"Uh. Sure. Sure, yeah," I said. My ass fell back down into the mattress, but Liv didn't seem to notice, just sitting a little deeper to make up for it. As she fumbled with the necklace's chain, Julia moved quickly into her space and turned around, mimicking her stance.

The medallion fell down between Liv's breasts, and she was gone.

"Oh, fuck, she was right about being close!" Julia started banging down hard with Liv's hips. "Yes, fuck!"

Her pace was all wrong. Her posture told me this was a completely different person having sex with me than a second before.

So it really bothered me that the pussy around my cock was suddenly absolute paradise.

"Almost there ... almost there ... shit, roll me over and hammer it into me!"

I did what she asked, flipping us, levering myself up, turning my hips into piston-drivers. Liv's body became a writhing tempest of orgasm beneath me.

"*AAHH! GOHHHHD!*"

I barely got two more thrusts in before I erupted right along with her, groaning helplessly at the power of my ejaculation. Just like each of the other times, the sensation overwhelmed me, rolled back and forth through my body like thunder, went on and on in a series of diminishing echoes. When it was done, I barely had the presence of mind to grab the amulet and fumble it up and over Liv's head.

Panting, I kissed her slack mouth. She moved her lips in response, but only a little. So I lifted up, waiting to see if her eyes would open. Even the rise and fall of her chest struck me as limp – vacant.

"Hon, are you all right?"

"Uhh." One of her arms twitched, as though she had no energy for more than that. "Too good again. We shouldn't have done that."

Which is exactly what I'd thought ahead of time. *Goddammit, why didn't I say something?*

"I'm sorry, honey. I should have –"

Her head tossed weakly back and forth. "Uh-uh. My fault. But I can't deal with this. Not on a regular basis. I dunno, maybe we can put the amulet in a drawer and get it out once or twice a month."

From the corner of my eye, I glimpsed something – movement: Julia, standing and drifting ghostily backwards from the bed.

"Um, *you* wouldn't be stuck in the drawer, right? You could still hang out, watch TV, talk to us ..."

"Yeah," she said, then turned away.

Liv still hadn't opened her eyes. "I'm sorry, Julia. It's just –" Now she turned her head and looked over at the ghost. "–when I couldn't come with Tim, when I gave up so easy and wanted the necklace – I just can't have that. If we can make it work where you can be an 'also,' that will be okay. But you can't be an 'instead of.'"

"No, right, I understand."

Two of us had trouble falling asleep that night.

The third haunted the living room, watching soap operas again.

CHAPTER FIVE

That was Thursday.

We had called the guys and told them we were skipping the Thursday night RPG session, mostly because gaming was the last thing our minds, but slightly because Bill would be there, and neither Liv nor I had any idea how we would manage to deal with him in our current situation.

Friday went okay, though it was awkward. Liv stayed home again; I went in and counted beans with my financial software, cutting out early when my boss made a 3:00 head-start on the weekend. Liv and Julia had done more net surfing, but with no better results.

"I kind of wish she wasn't growing on me," Liv said as I changed out of my work clothes and into shorts and a t-shirt. Even more than usual, I felt self-conscious about her standing there, watching. But also even more than usual, I really, really, really wanted her near me and really, really needed the way her face warmed up as her eyes stayed on me. Not with sexual heat: with something better.

"She's growing on you?"

"Stop it. Don't pretend you don't feel sorry for her too. I saw the look on your face last night when she heard me say we needed to put the necklace up."

"Okay. She's not horrible." As a last step, I stripped off my dress socks and tossed them in the hamper. "She's got a sense of humor, and you're right, I can't help feeling some sympathy."

There was also something about seeing someone casually naked for hours on end that fueled a strong sense of connection. Subconsciously, I guess my brain associated female nakedness with closeness. But I didn't want to bring up nudity at the moment.

"Maybe ..." I moved toward Liv where she stood in the door of our walk-in closet. She didn't step aside to let me out. "Maybe that's okay.

49

Maybe if we get to be friends with her, she'll have an easier time ... not having a body."

Not being able to touch or feel anything. Not being able to eat.

Liv put her arms out, and I stepped into them. She touched her soft, round nose to mine

"Or maybe we can just make it work long enough to figure out how to disconnect the two of us."

As she held me, I silently hoped she was right.

At dinner, Julia asked – meekly – if she could have a bite or two of Liv's spaghetti and meatballs. We let her, but I insisted on standing behind her and holding the necklace until she was done.

Liv went to bed early, excusing herself when she almost nodded off halfway through a movie on HBO. Julia and I finished watching, then made an awkward attempt at conversation about it. She hated the whole thing – a chick flick with a beautiful, delightful female lead unsettled by the suave, handsome love interest who meets her during the off-season at a beachside resort town. The combination of pretty people and conventionality didn't sit well with her. To be honest, though, I hadn't been focused enough to remember half the scenes Julia complained about, and I went in to join Liv not too long after that.

In my dreams that night, I ran along the wintery beach after Julia, calling her by the chick-flick heroine's name. But I wasn't the love interest; I was Liv, or in her body possessing her through the medallion, and when I caught up to chick-flick Julia and grabbed her in my arms to tumble to the sand, we were both suddenly in Catholic schoolgirl uniforms, Julia's looking adorably alluring on her plump little body. Then the beach became a princess bed, swaddling us in its thick sandy comforter as we hiked up each other's plaid skirts to bury our faces in the panties underneath. Julia's crotch strained tight against the cotton fabric, its outlines shaped exactly like what I'd seen earlier that evening.

I woke up just before I could experience my subconscious mind's idea of the female orgasm.

Beside me, Liv stirred in her sleep but didn't wake. I lay there for a while, wanting to put a hand between her legs and coax her out of slumberland. But I worried that it would be selfish and shallow of me, or that she'd be too tired to want to respond, and I'd only deprive her of her rest. So I closed my eyes and waited for my erection to subside and hoped my dream would pick up where it left off.

You know, the way dreams never do.

* * *

Saturday morning my boss called me on my cell phone. For some damn reason, she'd decided to stop by the office and found that a bunch of reports I was supposed to do hadn't been done, which made her make a checklist of a bunch of other stuff she realized she wanted done, which included a Powerpoint for a client meeting she had Tuesday, which reminded her that everything she'd planned to do on Tuesday needed to get done on Monday, which meant that most of the stuff she wanted done Monday had to get done today, because she "wouldn't want to make you work on Sunday."

I fumed at myself, because if I'd stayed till five or six on Friday instead of cutting out early, I could have begged off and said I had a personal crisis to deal with, and she would have sounded disappointed but would have done everything herself, because she's a workaholic and doesn't really understand that not everybody else is too. But since I'd skipped early, and since I knew she knew it, I was stuck. So I told Liv and went in.

I called home a couple of times while churning through my work. The first time, everything was the same. The second time, everything was the same. The third time, Liv didn't pick up. I shrugged about that, but fifteen minutes later she didn't pick up the fourth time either.

That was around four o'clock.

She might be out in the yard. Left her phone charging or something. We've been stuck inside since Wednesday, she probably needed some sun.

By four-thirty I'd finished all the most critical shit on Jinnie's list, and Liv still wasn't answering, so I went home.

A note on the kitchen table said, "Tim, Liv's letting me borrow her to go talk to my parents. Might take a while, they will probably be freaked out. Julia."

Fucking shit. You lying undead bitch.

If it had been real, the note would have been from Liv. She would never have put the necklace on with me gone and just trusted Julia to explain things. Never.

Would she?

Fingers jittering against my phone's screen, I called Bill. He didn't pick up, but ten minutes later he called me back.

"Yeah?"

"Bill, where do your parents live?"

"My parents? What?"

I could hear traffic in the background, almost indecipherable under that crackling sound that told me he had his car window down.

"Bill, Julia left a note saying she was taking Liv to talk to her parents."

Crackle. Honking. Dopplered engines. Crackle.

"Bill!"

"Fuck me, dude, sorry. I sort of thought it might work, but not really. Shit, Julia?"

"*Where* are your parents?"

"Uh, my dad's been dead six years. Mom is in assisted living – dementia."

"So she was lying."

"Uhh ... *Hey, watch it, you fucking asshole!*" Very loud, prolonged honk. "Jesus damn! Look, I dunno. Mom was still in the house when Julia kicked it. Trying to remember if Gary had divorced her yet ... she might have said 'parents' if she was thinking Gary was still in the picture. Crap, I don't know, I wasn't really talking with any of them then."

"Okay." I made myself take several deep breaths. "Okay, so, where *did* they live?"

"Florida. This suburb of Orlando called Winter Park."

I just stood there. I'd taken the car to work, and we only have one – our place is just a few blocks from the metro. Obviously, they weren't traveling all the way to Florida on public transportation. Maybe I could find some of Liv's credit card statements, call and ask if there'd been a plane ticket charged today.

Without a pin or a passcode? They're not going to tell you a damn thing. And it's all a fucking lie anyway.

More deep breaths, and then I asked Bill, "Do you know where she got the necklace? She said there was this warlock guy –"

"Huh-uh. She called me crying about it a couple days before the accident. Said if anything happened to her, I had to get the amulet and what I had to do with it. I blew her off because she's fucking crazy, but somebody had to clean out her apartment after that truck fucked her up, and when I found the amulet, it kind of ... zapped me or something. I could tell it was real and she was in there."

"What *exactly* did she tell you to do with it?"

"Uh ... put it on some chick and say her name when I started to fuck her. Then Julia would possess her and take it from there."

"And instead, you pawned it off on me and Liv? What the hell, Bill!"

"Look, Julia was not my favorite person and I hadn't really talked to her in a while, but she was still my sister. Would you fuck your sister?"

"Leave my sister out of this!" I recognized a hysterical tone in my voice and tried to calm down. Somehow I'd ended up in the living room pacing in circles around the couch. I didn't even remember putting the note down or leaving the kitchen.

"Anyway ... I figured you and Liv are so, uh, *active*, a couple dozen times would be nothing, and then you'd be done with her."

I stopped pacing.

"What do you mean, a couple dozen times?"

"She didn't tell you?"

"Would I be asking if she'd told me?"

"Chill, dude. Sorry." A police car chirped somewhere. Bill went silent for a second, then said, "Okay, that's not me. So ... Julia said she didn't have good information about how to fix being stuck to the amulet. Wherever she'd got it, they didn't know or wouldn't tell her or something. But she found a description online that sounded sort of like it might be the same magic she had used, and it said the solution was for the ghost to possess the host and sort of ... suck up the juices from a bunch of sex. After it had enough, it could break free and go do whatever it wanted."

Oh my god. What has she taken Liv to do?

"You said a couple dozen times ... how many exactly?"

"Well, that was the problem. It was in a poem or some kind of shit like that, translated from another language and all fucked up with allegory and mythological references. Something about so many moons worth of this and so many touches of so-and-so god's elbow ... Julia thought it was a few dozen. Twenty-something? Sixty-something? I dunno."

"You don't know." I had my face in one hand by now. "So what *do* you know, Bill?"

I couldn't hear him shrug, but I could imagine that casual *eh, whatever* lift of his shoulders. "That's about it, really."

"You're sure."

"Yeah, dude, I'd totally tell you if there was anything else."

"Okay, Bill." I believed him, but I kept trying to think of some other question, something that might jog his memory. Nothing occurred to me.

"Oh, hey, but listen –" The words and Bill's tone shot a charge of hope through me. Then he went on: "You guys missed the most kick-ass session at the game Thursday night. Greg had us –"

I hung up.

Fucking Bill.

* * *

I can put two plus two together. And two plus two in this case equaled maybe sixty times the amulet needed Julia to have sex, spread out to once or twice a month if Julia took Liv at her word from last night, meaning it might take five years for us to pile up the necessary amount of intercourse, and that was assuming we didn't quit letting the ghost borrow Liv's body for sex entirely.

So instead of explaining things to us and saying she didn't want to wait that long, Julia decided to take matters into her own hands and speed things up.

She had to have tricked Liv into putting on the necklace. "Just for some cookies" or something.

And if she'd tricked Liv and taken her body out trawling for sex, she almost certainly wasn't going to come back until she'd hit her goal. We'd never trust her again. Her chance would be gone.

Jesus, what is she going to do?

My first thought was to jump in the car and drive around to every nightclub in town to see if she was out trying to pick up guys that way. But that would be useless. Too many clubs, and hitting up strangers for one-night stands wouldn't provide enough volume. It would take her months to finish, and while it was bad enough thinking of Liv being missing for months, her body being used to have sex with different guys every night, Julia was probably smart enough to know I would put out a missing persons report, and her credit cards would be traced, and she'd get caught.

Which meant she had to get it done even faster than that – which literally made me sick to my stomach.

After vomiting into the toilet and then desperately cleaning up, I called Bill again and asked him where the biggest streetwalking districts were in town. Bill's got good enough looks and enough of a dating record that I didn't think he'd go out picking up hookers himself, but it seemed like the kind of information he would know, and he did.

I spent the rest of the night driving up and down the grossest, scariest streets I've ever seen, looking for Liv and having to fend away offers from dissolute women and overmade transvestites who ranged from skin-crawlingly unclean to ripely voluptuous and sleek. After a while, I started asking every strumpet who propositioned me if s/he'd seen anyone of Liv's description, and after another while I even started giving the nicer ones my number and offering a hundred-dollar reward if they saw her and helped me find her. I could change the number later – my only concern at the moment was finding Liv.

By three a.m., I'd gotten half a dozen callbacks about tall, short-haired black hookers. Four of the callers were pissed when I got there and told them they'd found the wrong woman, and for some reason I felt guilty enough about wasting their time and browbeaten enough by their anger that I gave them twenty bucks each even for the bad information. The other two calls were by the same sweet little hispanic girl, who refused to take any money and looked genuinely distraught each time I pulled up and it wasn't Liv she pointed out. If I'd had any spare brain cells to devote to it, I would have been depressed at the thought of such a nice-seeming young woman selling herself on the street. But that would have to wait for later – my increasingly panicked need to find my girlfriend blotted everything else out.

And then at 3:14, Liv called.

When I saw her number, I actually dropped the phone and had to screech the car to a stop in the middle of the street. Thankfully, there wasn't another car in sight – nor, at the moment, any prostitutes to walk over and bend down by my window as I fumbled in the floorboards for the ringing cell phone.

Stay on the line, stay on the line, don't hang up ...

"Liv! Liv, honey, where are you?"

At first I heard nothing ... then a sound I slowly identified as shaky breathing.

"... Tim ... help me ..."

Then nothing again.

"Liv!"

Fumbling sounds. A male voice, sounding concerned: "Hello? Is this the boyfriend?"

"Yes! Who the hell are you?"

"Man, listen, you'd better come pick her up. I don't think she can really talk."

"*Where?*"

"Epsilon house. Epsilon Mu Upsilon, on Branhauser, the east side of campus. You know how to get here?"

"I have GPS. Don't you let anything happen to her. I will pull your throat out if anything happens to her."

"Okay, no, I get it. Just come pick her up."

* * *

I was lucky not to crash the car on the way to Branhauser. Also lucky not to run into any cops, since I'm pretty sure I did about twice the speed limit down every street I drove on. Standing on the porch of the tall, Victorian house that my GPS led me to, I simultaneously pounded the door and rang the bell until a nervous-looking guy in a sweater vest opened it. The look on my face appeared to unravel him even more.

"Uh, Tim, I guess? Come on, she's upstairs."

The frat kid led me up to the second floor, both of us dodging empty disposable cups and a couple of beer puddles along the way. He kept twitching his eyes back toward me, pretty obviously scared I'd either change my mind and bolt, or pull out a badge and a walkie-talkie and say I was calling in for a paddy wagon. The place smelled like college party – sweat and perfume and cologne and beer and a hint of weed in there somewhere. A glance at the living room as we climbed the stairs looked like a set from "Animal House" got sick and threw up.

We passed another uneasy-looking kid on our way down the second-floor hall. When I was in college, these guys would have been named Brad or Chip and I would have hated their guts. But for some reason tonight I thought they seemed like nice guys, clean-cut and young and healthy and worried that something might have gone wrong with one of their guests. Maybe they'd grown up with less blockheady names than Brad and Chip, and that had made the difference.

My guide pointed anxiously toward an open door and said, "She's in that one."

I moved a little faster walking past him because I didn't like the fact that he didn't want to go in first. Then I heard Liv moan from behind the door before I could quite see in, and I bolted through like I'd been cattle-prodded.

"Uhhhhh..."

And two steps into the room, I stopped like I'd been double-cattle-prodded. I was vaguely aware of having a lower jaw, and that I was trying to do something with it, maybe something to do with making a sound of some kind. But nothing came out.

"Look, uh, this was all completely, uh, consensual," said Bradchip from the doorway. "She was totally into it, I mean totally, until the last guys finished up and somebody took that necklace off her to look at it."

The smell of sex filled the room so thick I felt like I was swimming through it. A queen bed had been stripped down to the topsheet and moved to the middle of the room. Liv made an asymmetric diagonal across it, her molasses-brown limbs splayed into awkward, exhausted positions, her head lolled to one side just inches from a noticeably used condom. She gleamed with sweat all over, and amidst the perspiration sheen ran zigzags of shiny blibs and globs, spattering her breasts and her neck and one side of her face. Even from where I stood, I could see the cum seeping out of her vagina, pooling in a dark wet spot between her legs.

"Oh my fucking god, Liv."

She shifted a little at the sound of my voice, and I could see her eyes blink. Then her whole body shook. "...hhh...tim...ah, ah, uhuhuhuhhhhguhuh."

My legs unfroze and I stumbled to the side of the bed, stepping on not one but two sloppy, deflated rubbers along the way.

"Liv. Liv. Liv ..." She focused on me as I knelt and tried to get my hands to move toward her on the spooge-drenched sheet.

"...tim...help...hh..."

A glint of red pulled my eyes off of hers – the jewel at the center of Julia's medallion, a little farther off from Liv's face than the spent condom.

"You fucking *bitch*," I told the thing, then grabbed it up in one hand.

"Dude, fuck, what are you doing?" Bradchip squawked. I heard him take a step closer behind me and I threw a glance at him. Every inch of his face said he thought I was about to lift the medallion and brain Liv with it.

"No, no, I wasn't talking to her." I waved a hand at him. He didn't look reassured. I didn't give a shit, turned back to Liv. Using one edge of the medallion, I scraped the condom off the bed so it wasn't right there between us. "Liv, honey, what do you need me to do?"

"nnhhh...still coming," she quavered. "jesus god, tim ... fuck ... get me ... hmnhh ... get me dressed ... home ..."

I stood up and looked at the reeking, greasy mess they had made of her, cum in the tight curls of her hair – on her head and at her pubes. "Goddamn, how many of you guys *were* there?"

Bradchip twisted his feet a little before he answered. "Look, I wasn't counting, in fact, I was downstairs most of the time. I couldn't tell you."

"Fuck." I shrugged. "I don't know. I guess, at least some of them used rubbers."

"Uh. Yeah ..."

"What?"

"Nothing."

"What?"

"They were complaining they'd run out by around eleven o'clock."

I wanted to shout at him, *Jesus, couldn't you tell she wasn't in her right mind?* But instead I closed my eyes, took a few deep breaths before opening them again. "Do you have a towel or something?"

He got one, and I gritted my teeth and used it to wipe most of the semen trails and dribbles off. Liv trembled and made tiny orgasmic groans with every touch. By the time I tossed the towel on the floor, it was sopping with more cum than I had ever seen in one place. *And there's more on the bed, and more in those condoms and more ... inside ...*

I kept swallowing against the urge to puke and somehow managed to get Liv into a robe Bradchip found and offered me. Trying to dress her in the jeans and shirt she'd worn here would have been a nightmare – even slipping her arms through the sleeves of the robe made her spasm. Once I had her covered, the college kid and I each took one of her arms around our shoulders and lifted her upright. She didn't support any of her weight on her legs – they just twitched and jerked.

"...tim..." she whispered.

I bent my head close in to hers. "It's all right, Liv. Everything's all right."

"...tim, I'm so sorry...I never should have trusted her. I never should have..."

"Hush. We'll be home in a little bit and everything will be fine."

With a moderate amount of difficulty, Bradchip and I maneuvered her down the stairs, through the front door, along the walk, and into the car. He grew visibly more relieved with every step of the trip, until the act of releasing Liv's arm lifted some vast weight from him and freed him up to talk as I positioned her in the passenger seat and lifted her feet from the pavement into the car.

"Look, I don't know what's going on, but I'm really sorry. If you'd asked me to point out the most lucid person at the party when she came in the door, I would have said her. Are you going to call the cops? I swear, we all thought she was just looking to go wild and have some fun."

Liv whimpered as I stretched her seatbelt across her and fastened it. I took the necklace out of my pocket and tossed it in the back seat, along with Liv's clothes, which I'd had slung over one shoulder. Satisfied that I'd gotten her safely in place and as comfortable as possible, I straightened up and looked at Bradchip.

"Did you have sex with her?"

He went billiard-ball red. "I'm sorry, I'd never seen anything like that. It was early on, when there were still condoms —"

I shook my head to shut him up. "Just ... next time, don't. Okay? I mean, if there's a next time, with some other girl, tell everybody they shouldn't. No matter how much she seems to want it. Nobody should get the idea that this kind of thing happens, or is okay. Something's wrong, even if she seems to be having fun, something's wrong with a girl who's letting herself get drilled by dozens of guys without protection."

"Yeah. I get that," he said with a genuine-seeming nod. The kid was definitely shaken up, which made me feel ... well, not *better*, but less sick.

"Thanks for helping her call me."

"Yes," he said. "Absolutely."

I saw him make a decision, and he stuck out his hand. Without much other choice, I shook it, then closed Liv's door, went round to my side, got in. He'd already made it back to the front door by the time I got my keys in the ignition. My palm should have been itching for me to get the hand sanitizer from the glove compartment and cleanse away that handshake.

But I started the car instead.

It just seemed more important to get Liv away from there.

* * *

About halfway home, Liv came around enough to talk.

"Tim?"

I glanced over. She had her head back against the headrest and her eyes closed.

"Yeah, honey, I'm here. How are you?"

"Super-angry. I am so angry, Tim."

"Me too."

"No, not like this."

We stopped at a light. I turned and looked at her — she hadn't moved. Everything about her and the situation made me want to pull her into my arms and hold her, except that I didn't know if she was still physically sensitive, or if she'd be able to stand the touch of a man right then.

"It's exactly how you should feel. I mean, she basically got you gang-raped –"

Her head shook slightly. "Those guys weren't raping me, Tim. Julia's the only one who did anything I didn't want. I was screaming inside from the moment I realized she was taking me out of the house. And I kept screaming all the way to that party. But once the sex started, I wouldn't have stopped it for anything in the world." A ripple of anger went through her voice. "It was *great*, Tim. It was – I couldn't have stopped it. I wouldn't have taken the necklace off even if Julia let me. I *never* wanted it to stop. If I could go back right now, I would."

I had a sinkhole in my guts. Someone honked – the light was green. I got the car moving.

How long did it take Julia to find the party? How long were they there? It had to have been five or six hours. Five or six hours of solid orgasm. No wonder she could barely move or talk when I got to her.

"Tell me what I can do, Liv."

"You can't –" Her voice caught, and she had to start again. "There's nothing you can do. I love you more than anything in the world, but I don't know if there's ever going to be a point in you touching me again. Any time I think of sex, I'm going to be thinking of *that*. Of Julia turning me into – and then of – oh my god, it was so *inhumanly* good." From deep in her throat, a choked squealing sound swelled. She hunched over in her seat, fists, eyelids, teeth clenched. "*RRRHhhh!* I *want* it again, Tim. I want it *so bad*."

I was crying by this point. And when we reached the next light, a sobbing made me turn my head. But it wasn't Liv.

It was Julia, sitting in the back seat, ghost tears running down her ghost face.

She looked about six or seven months pregnant.

CHAPTER SIX

"*What in the holy hell, Julia?*"

She didn't answer me, at least not right away. As soon as the light went green, I pulled through the intersection and swerved to the side of the road. In the back seat, Julia had her hands over her face, crying uncontrollably, her voice nothing but hysterical sobs. Beside me, Liv remained curled in a knot, but now mashed the palms of her hands against her ears.

"Why didn't you tell us? I talked to Bill – were you planning this shit the whole time you've been here?"

She shook her head, groaning.

"Goddamn, if you weren't a ghost, I'd climb back there and beat the shit out of you!"

Through her hands, she said, "I wish – wish you *could.*"

I don't think I ever heard anyone sound that wretched, not even in an overacted chick flick like the one we'd watched the night before. My whole body burned with adrenaline, but uselessly, and the sick grief in Julia's voice squelched my anger just enough for me to realize that, no, I wouldn't have beaten the shit out of her even if I could. And knowing I wouldn't made me feel even more impotent and frustrated. Her despair was like a wet sock in the face.

"*Please,*" Liv said. "Can we just go home?"

"Shit. I'm sorry, honey, I –"

"Just take me home."

I drove on. We went several blocks without saying anything, but Julia was blubbering in the back the whole way.

Finally, Liv growled and said, "Julia, would you *shut up?*"

"Huh...ahuh – I'll try."

"Shut up! You don't have any *right* to be crying."

"I know, I'm terrible, I was just so scared that you and Tim wouldn't –"

60

"*Shut up!*"

A few more blocks of crying, quieter now, coming from both of them.

"I hate you," Liv said, her head leaning against the passenger window.

"I know," Julia moaned. "You should. I can't believe I did that – no, I can, because I'm a shitty person. You were helping me, and I just got scared you wouldn't keep helping me, and shit Julia came out. I want to die."

Liv laughed – a nasty, sharp thing instead of her normal laugh. "Didn't solve anything the first time you did it."

"No, I mean I want to be wiped away. If – when we find some way, if it needs a sacrifice, if I can, I'll do it. If there's some way I can stop being, to fix it, I will."

Liv went back to crying. "No, don't say that."

"But I *will*."

Now Liv turned around to grimace at the pale, miserable specter in our back seat. "*No.* Stop saying that. Just shut up about it, okay? Because I would take you up on it. If I could, right now, I would. And I don't want to be that person. It would just be trading one part of my soul for another."

"But I want to *fix* it. You have to believe me – I want to fix it."

"Well you can't." Her voice went cold. "And maybe that's your punishment: you have to live forever knowing you can't fix what you did to me."

Silence for a full block, not even any crying. Finally, Liv turned and leaned back in her seat again, and stayed there unmoving until we got home.

* * *

I helped Liv wash and scrub and rinse and wash again for maybe an hour when we got home. She mostly just lay there in the tub, which meant hell for my knees and my back, leaning over with the loofah and going through an entire bottle of body wash. I didn't really feel it, though – or I felt it, but felt like I deserved it for leaving her alone with Julia and that necklace.

After I'd drained the tub a third time and started refilling it, Liv took my hand and rested her cheek against my forearm. It was at a terrible angle and uncomfortable as hell, but I kept my arm in place and just tried to shift to minimize the pain.

"I'm sorry, Tim," she breathed. She didn't move her head, so I knew she wasn't talking about my arm.

"Sorry? Good god, honey what are you sorry about?"

"I let myself be ruined."

"That's ridiculous. You're not ruined."

"I am." She looked up at me with those eyes, those wide, richly lidded eyes of far, savannah-scanning brown. "I still want to go back. I want to take that necklace and have them all over me again and in me from both ends and – and if the party wasn't broken up already, I'd be begging you to take me back."

"No you wouldn't." I put the loofah down and brought my free hand around to her cheek. "You wouldn't, because you know how I would feel about that, and you wouldn't let me feel that way. Just like you're not asking me to let you put the necklace on right now and have me fuck you. You're not ruined, Liv. You're still you."

"No I'm not. I hate her, Tim. I hate her so much. I've never hated anyone like this in my life. I want to kill her."

"But you wouldn't. You said you would, in the car. You're mad and you're hurt enough to *think* you would, but when the moment came, you'd back down."

"What makes you so sure?"

"Because I can imagine a real person backing down. And there's not any real person better than you, Liv. There's just not."

She reached up with both hands and put the palms wet against my cheeks. "Sure there is. There's you."

I shook my head. "No, and do you know why? Because I'm not sure I'll be able to forgive her, and I think you will."

Her hands dropped away and she blinked wide enough for the whites to show all the way around her irises. "Tim, I'd have to be a *saint*. Now you're just projecting on me."

"No. I heard it in your voice. The thought of her destroying herself terrified you. I don't know what she said to get you to put the necklace on while I was gone, but I'd bet my life you listened because you had started to care about her. You started to care, and that's not something you can stop. If she gives you a chance, if she *lets* you, you'll forgive her. It's just how you are."

With a squeak of her skin against the porcelain, she twisted up out of the tub and wrapped her arms around me, dripping wet and shivering.

"Don't ever leave me, Tim. Please don't ever leave me."

I held her with everything I had.

"Why would I do that? How could I ever do that?"

Eventually she let go and we got her out of the tub and dried her off.

* * *

We slept until well after noon the next day. Or, Liv slept until well after noon, while I kept jerking awake every hour or so, terrified she might have disappeared with the necklace again – or worse, cut her wrists in the bathtub or something awful like that. But she stayed under as if she'd been … well, as if she'd been through six or eight hours of nonstop strenuous physical activity in the form of better sex than any human being has ever had. And every time I woke up, it took me longer to fall back asleep, because that peaceful oblivion of pure exhaustion on her face reminded me of what had happened to her, and I couldn't wring the disgusting images out of my mine – my beautiful, perfect girlfriend surrounded by masturbating frat kids all leering and waiting their turn for a chance to shoot their wads down her throat or up her cunt while their pals groped her and came on her and –

When she finally woke up, it was about the greatest relief of my life.

She shifted first, and groaned and stretched a little in her sleep. Then she sniffled and rubbed her nose and opened one eye at a time.

"Tim."

"Hi. How are you?"

"I'm okay. But I don't know how long it will last before I start thinking about ... everything."

"Do you want me to get you some breakfast?"

She nodded. I kissed her forehead, got out of bed, went into the kitchen – shutting the bedroom door behind me to keep a barrier between Liv and Julia.

The ghost lay where I'd left her hours earlier, curled up on her side over the necklace, which I'd dropped in the center of the living room. Her pregnancy disturbed me for some reason or several reasons I couldn't define, along with *one* reason I could: it made her much hotter. Her little dumpling breasts had filled in and plumpened. Her doughy stomach now swelled round and taut in front of her. Pregnant women have never been a thing of mine, but for some reason it worked wonders for Julia – at a time when I probably *least* wanted her to be attractive.

She didn't move or say anything as I walked past her into the kitchen. And she still hadn't moved when I finished making Liv's breakfast – toaster-heated frozen waffles, a glass of milk, and the carton of orange juice. So on my way back to the bedroom I stopped.

"Julia. Listen, we're going to find that goddamn bookstore today. We're going to find it, and we're going to get started fixing this thing."

Without getting up, she looked at me and said. "We searched. We searched everything in town, bookstores, occult stores, fortune tellers – it wasn't any of those."

"Then they must not be on the web. But it doesn't matter, because we're *going* to find it. And then you're going to hope none of those guys gave her anything."

Her head lifted a little. "No ... Tim, they couldn't. The whole point of doing it was – I put this ectoplasmic sheaf around them, when they were ... and it absorbs all the vital essence." She pushed herself up on an elbow, looked down at her swollen belly and put her hands there. "That's why I'm like this. Each bit of reproductive energy I absorb gets me closer to rebirthing myself, as a free spirit. Nothing gets through the sheaf but inert goo. It couldn't make her pregnant or infect her with anything."

"Oh." I looked down at the tray of food, wondering if I could trust her and be relieved – and also just getting my eyes off her fertile-looking body. "I guess that's ... something."

She bit her lip. "And I want you to know, I told them 'no' whenever anybody tried to, uh, put it in her butt. I could have made a sheaf there too, but I didn't know if she'd ever done that. Anal sex."

"Shit, do *not* talk to me about Liv and anal sex," I said.

Looking down, she mumbled, "Sorry."

I took the breakfast tray into the bedroom.

* * *

Liv felt better after breakfast – maybe because I let her drink straight from the juice carton without saying anything and without turning my face away. She didn't exactly smile at that, but I thought I caught a hint of her normal glow as she watched me watching her while she wiped her mouth with one thumb.

It turned out I was right about the bookstore. We borrowed a tattered Yellow Pages from Mrs. Carlisle down the street, a borderline hoarder but very nice old lady whose house I could not walk into. Liv went in with her, though, and came out carrying the phone directory.

Julia found the listing right away – the fourth one down in the specialty books section. Twenty minutes later we parked at a meter half a block down the street from the address. I had a nervous time getting out on the street side of the car. The traffic wasn't heavy, but the road was practically as narrow as an alleyway, tight-packed with old brick buildings to either side and a strip of sidewalk no wider than a trashcan.

"I hope they're open Sundays," Liv said, though her flat tone didn't *sound* like hope was on her mind. Although it wasn't cold, she'd layered up in a t-shirt, a thin hoodie, and jeans, and her hands stayed in the jacket pockets, arms straight, shoulders pinched. "I still think we should have called first."

I kept just ahead of her on the walk from the car, wishing she had a little more energy in her step, or that the sidewalk weren't so microscopic. My feet wanted to run down the block and kick in the door, and it would have been easier to restrain myself if I'd been able to hold Liv's hand as we went. "Everybody's open Sundays nowadays. I'm thinking someone who runs an occult bookstore isn't going to be a real churchy type – and we needed to get out of the house, don't you think?"

Her shoulders shrugged even tighter.

Julia floated along behind us, head down, apparently too depressed to bother with walking. I had the necklace in my pocket, and either it dragged her along or she didn't really have to move her ghost feet to get around. A few other people strolled along in sight, some window-shopping across the street, a couple more standing at the crosswalk signal for the next intersection ahead. They paid us absolutely no mind, proving Julia right about being invisible. But I still expected a scream any second, followed by the whole street turning our way to stare and point.

We reached the store. A frosted window no wider than our plasma TV carried the sign, stenciled in black:

Amused Books
Gio R. Gioenne, Proprietor

There weren't any hours listed, not there or on the rickety-looking door. The door had a dust-fouled window through which I could see hints of shadowy bookshelves inside, but I couldn't tell if the interior was dim from the lights being shut off or just intrinsically gloomy.

I turned the knob and pulled. After sticking a second, the door swung open.

"I guess they don't have Sundays off, then," I said, trying to smile at Liv. She tried to smile back, but did an even worse job than I think I did. We went in.

New bookstores are a favorite of mine. I love books, the places are usually kept in careful, precise order, and they want you to check out what you're buying, so the lights are always bright. Used bookstores have diametrically opposite characteristics, and this one oppressed me more than most, packed thick with the crushing smell of age-rotted paper, jumbled and disarrayed, the lighting a mere nod to the notion that customers might want to see their hands in front of their faces. As my eyes adjusted and let me penetrate the murk and whorls of dust, mis-matched ranks of randomly placed bookshelves revealed themselves. More often than not, they held their books stacked flat instead of standing upright, and wherever free space could be seen, odd bits of knick-knackery stood in between the stacks.

Liv put a hand gently on my shoulder, so I walked in. With no sign of anyone around, I hadn't much choice but to move deeper into the maze-like recesses. The whole place made me want to sneeze. Worse, as I drew even with the closest bookshelf, I almost jumped out of my shoes at sight of a rat scaling one of the Jenga stacks of books.

"It's a carving," Liv said, and I realized immediately that she was right. Not even the curling tail moved by a hair.

Relaxing a little, I walked forward and said, "Hello?"

More rat figurines populated the shelves to either side, scattered here and there in different positions and freakishly lifelike. If they hadn't creeped me out so much, I might have stopped to admire the details. They looked like soapstone or white marble.

"Hello?" I asked again. I could see a back wall over some of the shelves ahead, but heard absolutely nothing.

Then I came into a five-way intersection between several shelf-aisles, and I almost screamed, because someone was there, not a foot to my right. Actually, I think I did scream – but just a little, and the dense air of the store and muffling heaps of books swallowed the sound up.

"Can I help you?"

She was a she, and she had a breathy, whispery voice that made me think of a hypnotist. Very tall – taller than Liv, taller than me. She wore a tunic-style dress, slate-grey, with sleeves that came down just past her wrists and a high-necked top of some kind that rose out of the dress all the way to her jawline. I swear to god she had a wimple hiding her hair.

Who the hell wears a wimple? And who the hell wears sunglasses in a place this dark? Is she blind?

They were huge, wraparound glasses too. She could have been wearing a whole other pair of glasses underneath them.

"Um. We have an unusual problem, that we heard you might be able to help us with some information on."

Liv came up next to me, and Julia floated around where she could see, ending up half-in and half-out of a bookshelf on my left flank.

"Tell her it's about a tantric soul medallion," the ghost said.

"They don't have to – I can see and hear you."

"Okay," I said. "That's kind of scary."

She looked me up and down. At first, I thought her complexion was incredibly clean, smooth, and pale. But as I watched her examine me, I realized that she had an impenetrable layer of powdery makeup on.

Shit. I hope she's not a fucking vampire or something.

Despite not being able to see her eyes, I felt like they stopped at my crotch as she raised her head. Even once the sunglasses pointed straight at my face, I would have bet money she was eying my groin. And even though I couldn't tell a damn thing about her figure, or much of her face, and even though she might be a fucking vampire, I realized I was starting to get hard.

Why the hell is that happening?

Then she turned to Liv and everything went back to normal. Well, everything in my pants did.

"You're the host?"

Liv nodded, wide-eyed.

To Julia: "And you look not that far from rebirthing. Why is there a problem?"

"I –" said Liv, only to stop and start again. "I can't –"

"Liv can't have any more sex," Julia finished for her. "We have to break the bond without any more sex. Even if it means I have to be destroyed or something."

"*No.*" Liv's voice firmed up and her jaw set. "That's not what we're going to do, and I don't want to hear anything else like that, Julia." She looked at the strange shopkeeper. "Is there a way? Can you help us?"

"There are several ways." The sunglasses scanned from each of us to the next. "I could indeed destroy the ghost, which would be easiest and would have been my default a long time ago."

"I said we're not doing that."

"Of course not. But if she is not destroyed in this realm, and if you will not let her use you for sex in this realm, then the next easier method would be for you all to cross over, where he –" The face turned my way again. "– could finish filling her out directly."

I stood there blinking for a second.

"There are *so* many things about that sentence I don't like."

CHAPTER SEVEN

"Why don't we continue this discussion over tea in my workshop downstairs," she said, not making it a question as she moved past us toward the front door. "Give me a moment to lock up."

I didn't the sound of that any better than the bit about "crossing over" and "filling" Julia out "directly." Like I wasn't already uncomfortable enough without being locked in and ushered down to a basement completely out of view of the windows and street. But Liv seemed prepared to wait, quiet as she watched the woman – Gioenne? – glide away through the crooked aisles to the door.

"At least we know this place is for real," she said.

"Yeah." I glanced at Julia, who met my gaze, which wasn't what I wanted, which made me even more uncomfortable. From somewhere out of sight at the front of the store came a deadbolt's *klatch!* loud enough that I thought I felt it in my teeth.

The shopkeeper returned.

"Now then, follow me."

She moved deeper into the store, to a back corner where a narrow, doorless frame opened onto an equally narrow, rail-less stair lit by bare bulbs that I'm guessing rated twenty watts at most. The stair turned back on itself four times before it reached bottom, I swear a much longer trip than a single floor below ground level.

"You may call me 'M,'" the shopkeeper said, leaving the stairway for a long room.

I tried to fool my feet into walking after her by being conversational. "Uh ... like Em? Short for Emily?"

"No."

Inside the room, she pointed us to a small sitting area, then walked past it, between two tables heaped with candles and unidentifiable, bottled organic curios, finally reaching a kitchenette that occupied one of the two far corners – the other corner being a seamless, bare slab of stone six or eight feet on a side. "Sit. I will start the tea."

"You don't really need to bother on our account," I said, edging toward the sitting area, where narrow-legged chairs and a couch waited beneath moth-eaten embroidery. Liv took my arm and squeezed it, and with a sigh I moved more directly to sit. The two of us settled in on the couch, Julia on an adjacent, high-winged chair. A coffee table before us held a brass toad the size of a crock-pot, its mouth open and filled with Jolly Rancher candies.

"It's not on your account," M said in her hiss-whisper, opening a cupboard to rummage inside. "I enjoy the smell. Now – your names?"

We told her.

She ran water into a teakettle. "And how would you rank your knowledge of mortality and proto-lives and afterlives?"

"Right, that would be zero. Four days ago I was pretty much a complete agnostic."

Liv nodded along with that. Julia gave a shrug.

"Before I got pasted by a cement truck, I would have said maybe three out of ten. Now I guess if they're zeroes, I'm a half. Maybe a one, just for being a ghost and knowing what that feels like."

M left the kettle on to boil and made her way back across the room to us. I became awkwardly aware of the fact that I didn't know where the light was coming from, and looking around and over my shoulders I got no better idea. I did see, though, that the stairwell took another bend after the one that deposited us here, heading farther down into darkness with a more rough-hewn look to it, as though it had been carved directly from the bedrock. Above that shadowy mouth, a round silver shield had been hung – gleaming everywhere but its center, where a stain or patch of tarnish rendered it unreflective. When I looked back, M had settled into a chair across from us, face pointed our general direction but the black sunglasses making the exact angle of her gaze impossible to figure out.

"If the sum of your knowledge is the operation of a tantric soul medallion and the experience of incorporeality, then you are perhaps one one-hundredth. Possibly you other two are even less than zero, since I would rank incorrect knowledge on a negative scale."

"That's kind of why we're here," I said, trying to keep a scowl off my face. Liv rubbed my shoulder.

"It's not my intention to denigrate you. I am old – very old – and out of ten I would rank myself a four. The point is to make sure you have a realistic understanding of how little you know. I can help you cross over, to a safe location, and once there you will simply have to complete the gestation of Julia's rebirth, destroy the amulet, and return. But if you become curious and decide to explore while you are there, you will get out of your depths very, very quickly. Do you understand?"

"Yes."

"Yes, but ..."

M's face turned toward Julia.

"It's not enough for us to just break the bond. We have to fix Liv too. She and Tim need to be able to have a normal sex life once I'm gone. Otherwise all I've done is left them up shit creek."

"Hmm."

The teakettle whistled. Our host rose and returned to the kitchenette.

Liv sat up straighter to peer across the room. "Will I eventually get over it? Knowing what it's like to be fucked while possessed and wearing that amulet?"

"No."

I felt her stiffen, but M went on as she filled a porcelain teapot and added an infuser that glinted silver from across the room.

"There are, however, ways to remove it from your memory. If you're crossing over anyway, the best would be some Wine of Forgetting. But acquiring it will mean a journey much more complex than just skipping across, fornicating until Julia delivers herself, and skipping back. Are you prepared for that?"

"I'm pretty sure we're not," I said. "But we'll do it anyway. I'll go by myself if it's dangerous."

Liv's hand tightened around my arm. "No you won't."

Bearing a tea tray, the shopkeeper returned again.

"It would be impossible anyway. The wine can only be given to a mortal by a citizen of the Dionysian Fields." Artfully, the powder-faced woman poured out two cups of tea and stirred a spoonful of what looked like honey into each. "If Julia rebirths herself there, she will qualify. So she must go, and once on the other side, the two of them will not be able to stray more than a few yards from one another until the bond is sundered."

Julia sat forward a little. "Dionysian Fields doesn't sound bad."

"We'll do it," I repeated. "What do we need to do to get started?"

M reached across the coffee table to set a cup before me and another before Liv.

"To get started," she said in her sough of a voice, "requires a discussion of price."

* * *

So here's my moral stance on prostitution. It's wrong for you to be involved in if you think it's wrong, and it's wrong if the person on the other end of the transaction thinks it's wrong. Other than that, it's pretty much no one else's business. But driving around the red-light district the previous night had kind of strained that stance – I'd seen a lot of cynical, heartless eyes in oceans of eyeshadow, a lot of used-up faces, a lot of overdone poses thrusting out breasts and butts that threatened to split the seams of the clothes that held them. It was gross, and I couldn't help thinking that most of those women hadn't been that way when they'd fallen into their profession. And I couldn't help wondering what I would see ten years from now if I bumped into the nice hispanic girl who'd tried so sincerely to help find Liv. It seemed like maybe you just shouldn't let that happen to people, even if they'd chosen it for themselves and thought they were okay with it.

As it turned out, though, I wasn't done having my prostitution opinions tested.

* * *

"Sex," I said, when our sunglassed hostess explained what she wanted. "That seems kind of ..."

"Yes?"

Gross. Creepy. Disgusting. Insulting to Liv.

"Inexpensive?" My stomach featherweighted its way around the ring with my other innards, none of them able to lay a glove on each other, waiting for the bell to return to their corners. "I mean, is there a catch? Are you going to suck my soul out through my penis or something?"

She whispered something I didn't quite catch, and after a second I decided it had been a laugh.

"No. And if you weren't as you are –" A long-fingered hand, powdered like her face, waved from me to Liv. "– I would name something else. But I am not loved, and I do not love, and if I take your seed, given out of love for her, it will let me feel for a little while something that I am denied."

"So you want me to have sex with you, and that's it?"

"There is an alternative price, but I promise you, you do not want to pay it."

Beside me, Liv held tight to my hand, saying nothing aloud but everything through the pressure of her fingers. She didn't want me to have sex with this woman, and she didn't want me to do anything I didn't want to do, and I had the choice to turn M's offer down and leave if I wanted to. But her grip still said, *Please*, as loud as if she'd been shouting it through a megaphone. And really, I didn't need her to ask at all.

Sometimes, though, I can make my mind up and not be ready to have it made up. When Liv and I first bumped into each other at that Saturday matinee, I knew I was going to ask her out for real after maybe two minutes of talking to her while we waited for the trailers to start. But I didn't ask her before the movie, and I didn't ask her when the lights came up after the credits, or as we were walking out through the lobby or as I was holding the door for her on the way outside. I didn't even ask her as we pulled up in front of her building, because I'd offered her a ride home, because she'd walked to the theater, because it was just a couple of blocks from her apartment. Instead, I push-buttoned the window down right after she'd shut the door and asked her at the last possible moment, with her turned and leaning down to put her head into the window. And it wasn't normal nervousness or fear of rejection. I knew she was going to say yes.

My head just took that long to get used to the idea of a world where she would say yes.

So I picked up my teacup one-handed and looked into it like I didn't already know my answer. I hadn't sipped any of it yet – I wasn't sure I could trust it, or whatever thick treacle the shopkeeper had stirred in. I certainly didn't know why I should trust her freaky supernatural ass not to suck my blood or bite my dick off with vagina teeth once I got inside of her. But I blew on the tea and took a slurp of it, and it was sweet and fragrant and strong and too hot by a lot. I had a hard time swallowing, and was blinking at the pain when I looked back up into M's opaque sunglasses.

"Sure, okay. I'll do it," I said, squeezing Liv's fingers back. "What, ah, where ..."

Our hostess stood up and stripped the sash from around her waist in a single economical motion.

"Here, and now." Without waiting for me to react, she bent and pulled the wimple from her head, tossed it aside, and began drawing her dress up and off.

"Wait," I said, almost spilling my tea as I put it down. "Right here? With Liv and Julia watch –"

Under the dress, M was pale and grey, her skin strangely textured and glinting slightly in the sourceless light that filled the room. Under the wimple, she was bald, her whole scalp pebbled with round scars about the diameter of a fingertip. When she pulled her shirt over her head next, she had no breasts, no nipples, no bellybutton, and no body hair of any kind. Only her powdered face and hands still looked human. I couldn't really see her genitals between her legs – possibly because I was deliberately keeping my eyes from focusing there.

"Not with Liv watching," she said, tossing her shirt aside and re-settling her sunglasses across the bridge of her nose. They'd come askew when she took off the shirt, and I'd gotten a glimpse of one closed, dark-grey eyelid with no lashes along its seam and no eyebrow above it. "With you watching Liv. With you seeing her, and feeling what you feel for her, as you enter me and fountain your bliss and love into my womb."

This is fucked up. She is totally not human. Good lord, I am looking at something that is not human, and I'm supposed to have sex with it. About nine-tenths of me could have bolted to the door and run out into the street yelling like a crazy person at that moment.

But Liv's hand in mine kept me grounded, or something else did, because I didn't get out of my seat.

And as I sat there, I realized I was completely rock hard.

"Julia does not have to remain, if you would rather carry her medallion around the bend of the stairs before we begin."

I looked at our pregnant ghost sitting wide-eyed with her arms crossed tight over her breasts, and for some reason I felt sure she was just as freaked-out and scared as I was.

"No," I said. "What the hell, I'm about to fuck a complete stranger. She's at least seen me naked and had sex with me a couple of times before." *And she at least used to be human.*

"Good. Stand, then, and undress."

Letting go of Liv's hand, I got awkwardly to my feet and fumbled at the buckle of my belt. M stepped over to the coffee table, lifted one end of it, and dragged it aside, leaving nothing but a bare stretch of oriental carpet between her chair and the couch. While I kicked off my shoes and scraped my jeans down past my hips, she came closer, put a hand on my shoulder, and gently directed me farther from the couch until she could step between me, and it, and Liv.

Fuck. Those are scales. That explained the strange texture and glossy sheen of M's grey skin. Up close, her muscles rippled beneath thousands or millions of tiny, flawlessly overlapping scales. She also had a finger-thick scar encircling her whole neck, and another that ran as a seam across her throat, along her jawline, and up and over the crest of her skull, as though her face had been transplanted onto her. But it hadn't – at this distance, even her thick white makeup didn't conceal the scaly texture of the skin underneath, a perfect match for the naked grey hide around it.

"What – happened to you?" Liv asked. She put a hand to her own sleek brown throat as she stared at M's.

"A serious misfortune followed by ... reconstructive procedures. Move there, to the end of the couch."

I had my shirt off by now, nothing but my briefs left to remove. Liv shifted into the corner of the sofa where M had pointed, and the grey woman knelt and leaned forward onto the cushions, angling herself so that her head faced Liv and her slim, flattish ass pointed toward me. I closed my eyes for a second, took a deep breath, and yanked my underwear down, freeing maybe the hardest erection I've ever had to swing up and point straight out from my groin.

"Okay," I said, not very steadily. "Is, uh, everybody ready?"

"Go ahead, honey. It's fine. You're good."

I opened my eyes to find Liv looking into them, and suddenly it was easy to kneel down behind the long, slender form presenting its narrow rump to me. I put my hands out and made contact. M's flesh felt cool and dry and smooth and plainly scaly, as though I'd taken hold of a pair of coiled anacondas instead of a pair of buttocks. My breathing had gone incredibly fast, in a strange, frenzied, panicked arousal.

I'm really going to do this, I thought, still looking Liv in the eyes, their brown depths pouring concern and encouragement into me. *I'm about to fuck whatever this thing is. What the hell is* this *going to feel like?*

A shiver went through me, and I forced myself to look down as I took hold of my shaft and guided the tip of my cock toward –

I stopped.

"There's only one hole back here."

M's head twisted on her neck to look at me, the angle unnatural. "It's a cloaca."

"Uh ... you mean, everything comes out there?"

She laughed her windblown-sand laugh. "No, dear. Nothing comes out. I don't eat or drink."

"But that's where everything would come out if you did."

"Yes."

"And what's that other price you mentioned?"

"I get to cut off the head of your penis."

"Shit," Julia said in a low voice. "Guys let you do that? What do you use them for?"

"Nothing. I just have a thing for cutting off men's little heads. Personal issues."

How the fuck am I still hard?

"Go on," M said. "I'll make sure things get to the right place inside."

"Tim, you don't have to –"

Liv's voice put some kind of determination into my spine. Before she could even finish, I bit my lip and leaned quickly down and forward, sliding myself straight into the pouchy, everted opening between M's ass cheeks.

"Ahhhhhh," she said. Her back arched, her pelvis rolled up to take me deeper.

"Holy shit," I gasped. The scales or whatever lined her interior tube welcomed me inside almost frictionlessly, and as soon as I reached full penetration, powerful muscles constricted tight and rolled along my shaft in waves. This creature was fucking me as hard as I've ever been fucked, and neither of us was even moving. *"Oh my god what the hell holy fuck."*

"Hhhhhh." Her spine contracted, pulled her ass forward and her squeezing urogenital tunnel almost all the way off me. Then she shoved back and the hole swallowed me to the root again. *"Look at her."*

My eyes worked hard to focus – the whole room had blurred with that lunge of her hips. But then Liv was there, and I was falling into her pupils, absorbed by her face, where I could see in her trembling lip and the tracks of her tears every emotion she felt: fear and worry and love and pride and hope – and a sympathetic joy at seeing me experience such uncontrollable physical pleasure. At some point, I realized I had my hands on M's waist and was pounding rapidly into her in time with her bucking ass and the rhythmic rippling of her cloacal muscles. But even though my eyes saw these things and my body sensed them, there was really only Liv and the vision of what she felt for me.

And suddenly the scaled creature attached to me milked a stunning, throbbing ejaculation from my genitals and I cried out Liv's name and spasmed and clutched at M orgasmically.

"God. Damn," Julia said, just before I dropped panting to my back on the oriental rug. "That was the hottest fucking thing I have ever seen."

I just stared up at the ceiling for a while, unable to move. Then, finally, I groaned and hoisted myself half up on one arm.

M remained in about the same position, rump still lifted high, legs trembling. But her head had fallen forward into Liv's lap, where she lay making a faint cooing noise. And with that phenomenal climax settling away into memory, I remembered what she had said: "I am not loved, and I do not love."

And whatever she was, as I saw Liv hesitantly stroke that scarred and knobbed scalp, I felt very, very sorry for the woman.

* * *

After a few minutes, M came down from whatever high my orgasm had given her, stood up, dressed matter-of-factly, went over to the stone slab opposite the kitchenette, and started working on something that I assumed I had just paid for by whoring myself.

I'm not sure how long I lay on the floor staring up at her ceiling, trying to figure if my opinion of prostitution had just turned itself around. There was no denying that M had just used me for her own sexual satisfaction, in a purely financial bargain. That ought to have made me feel something – cheap or dirty or demeaned – but the sex had been *so* good, and while I had no evidence that my scaly partner in intercourse valued or respected me as a person – in any way – seeing her lying gratified in Liv's lap had created a definite emotional connection in *me*.

Maybe my nice hispanic streetwalker would feel this way several times a night after satisfying a client, and maybe that would keep her from degrading into one of the soul-soiled women I'd found myself talking to while searching for Liv.

But while I didn't feel bad about selling myself, I did feel bad about something else. And the longer I lay there, the worse the feeling got.

Finally, I sat up and looked at the most important person in my life, who sat watching me as if I hadn't just committed infidelity with a reptile before her very eyes.

"Liv," I said. "I'm sorry." She looked baffled, but I went on before she could say anything. "I'm sorry I didn't fuck you in the ass the first time you asked, or even the second time. I'm sorry I got us into all of this, and instead of doing the thing you wanted, I ended up making you watch me do it to someone else instead."

Her head shook in a narrow, side-to-side vibration, her mouth open and disbelieving. "Tim. What the hell? You just put your dick into some ... alien *butthole* for me, and you're apologizing? Do you think I don't know what a nightmare that was for you to work yourself up to? I mean, it looked like it was pretty good once you got going, but I wish I could show you the terror on your face when she said it was a *cloaca*." She laughed, a dumbfounded laugh about half her normal volume and warmth, but still a sound that pushed away some of my guilt. "Honestly, honey, don't you know how *grateful* I am right now?"

I sat there red-faced trying to think of what to say, but nothing came, and then she slid off the couch to her knees and leaned in to kiss my forehead.

"We're all to blame for this, Tim," she said, locking eyes with me and putting a hand on either side of my face. "You, me, Julia ... fucking *Bill*. Hahaha, *Bill*, what would he say if we told him he got you fucked by some breastless grey who-knows-what with a *cloaca*?"

My diaphragm tried to make me laugh. It didn't quite succeed, but some of the weight came out of my chest.

"Now get your clothes on before your scaly new friend comes back over and gets the hots for you again and makes you give her a second helping."

I nodded and crawled over to my discarded jeans and shirt.

"And Tim?"

"Yes?"

"When this is all done, and I'm fixed ... you're going to fuck me in the butt, and it's going to be your first time. I don't have a cloaca, sweetheart. Whatever she did to you with her thing, I'm going to do something else with mine. Okay?"

I pulled my underwear on quickly, because my cock was suddenly ready to go over and take her up on that right now. But as certain as her voice was, it also had a wistful sound, and her eyes had sorrow in them along with promise, and I knew she was making herself talk about something that she couldn't desire, not yet.

"Okay," I answered her.

By the time I finished dressing, M called us over from her corner.

"We can begin when you are ready."

CHAPTER EIGHT

That long tunnel with the light at the end, the one all those near-death-experience people talk about?

It's a urethra.

I'm not kidding.

M had drawn this weird twisty circle on her stone slab using chalk and I swear to god craft glitter, then made us stand in the middle of it while she lit several different-sized and differently foul-smelling candles.

"Since you'll have to travel to the Dionysian Fields," she'd breathily told us, "I'm sending you to a receiving station. Explain to them that the two of you are alive, and need to accompany Julia to her destination. They will provide you what you need and point you on your way. If you want to get some of Julia's seeding in as you travel, that might be for the best. But she looks to me as if twelve or fourteen inseminations will finish her off, so don't go beyond ten. She must take your final expulsion at the Fields to rebirth there and become a citizen."

"Does it have to be me?" I asked, glancing awkwardly toward Julia, who looked at her feet. "I mean, Dionysian Fields, that sounds like we could find somebody there who would be happy to help out."

"The process requires a living man's seed. You'll be unlikely to run into anyone else qualified, unless you want to pause here and go find someone to accompany you –"

"No, no, that's fine. So we'll be able to ... touch each other? On the other side?"

"Her form will be physical there, yes. Now hold the necklace between you, and all three of you close your eyes."

We did, M said some things in a language that was Greek to me, and then we were somewhere else.

"M?" I asked. No answer, so I opened my eyes. Darkness. I kept hold of

Liv's hands. "Shit, where the hell –"

Dude, don't talk about hell.

"Look, a light."

I felt Liv release one of my hands, and sensed more than saw her point over my shoulder. When I turned, a faraway dime-spot of white hovered in the blackness.

"Dammit, she didn't even tell us how to get *back*."

"Maybe they'll be able to tell us – you, I mean, at this receiving station," Julia said. She sounded distinctly unhappy. I guess it had just hit her that only Liv and I were on a round trip.

So we started walking toward the light. And when we'd gotten it as big as a basketball, things started happening.

The soft floor beneath our feet vibrated, then convulsed. The glow ahead of us pulsed wider and narrower, wider and narrower in time with the waves that threatened to shake us to the ground.

Then a rushing sound came from behind us, and a wall of fluid smacked up against our backs, and we shot toward the rapidly widening circle of light on what felt like a tide of pancake syrup.

Splurt.

The tunnel squirted us out in a high arc. Perfect white clouds and a sky of *holy-shit* blue turned overhead. Sparkling green hills rolled beneath us. We sailed up and over on a slowly turning dollop of off-white ectoplasmic fluid, passing flocks of gold-gleaming birds and silver dandelion seeds as big as my head. As we went, our rotation let us see back the way we'd come – *literally* come, I realized, because directly behind us and pointed along our trail rose an enormous phallic half-arch of pink granite, its far end rooted between two testicular batholiths and its ore-veined length twitching to spit another gobbet of spiritual spoo from its tip, this one along a different trajectory than ours.

Seriously? We've been jizzed into the afterlife?

Thankfully, the ooze surrounding us didn't feel wet or clingy – in fact, it didn't really have any substance at all. Which was a good thing, because otherwise I would have been scrubbing my skin raw for hours trying to get the shit off.

Ahead and below us swelled a tall hill jammed with some kind of monuments and columns in a crown around its top. Rings of wildflowers spread down the sides except where a long, winding stone stairway cut through them and linked the monuments with a wide riverside plaza on the hill's far flank.

We landed amongst the towers in a cushion of our transporting goo, and as soon as our feet touched solidly to the ground, the stuff sloughed aside and evaporated.

* * *

Like a lot of agnostics, I've wondered every once in a while what happens when you die, and what I'd do if I ended up standing ankle deep in cloud-fluff with Saint Peter looking back and forth between me and his stone tablets trying to figure out whether to let me in the gates or put me on the down escalator. Unsurprisingly, I can go kind of overboard on the subject. Based on conversations with Liv and other people who think metaphysics mostly deserves a shrug and the occasional bullshitting session over beer or coffee, agnostics as a group find life-after-death scenarios more abstractly interesting than worth worrying over. But I'm the other kind of agnostic, I guess: the agnostic who worries so much he can't make up his mind. It would suck to tilt into full-blown atheism and end up roasting on a spit while some guy in bat wings uses a pitchfork to test whether I'm done or if I need a few more turns. And it would equally suck to convert to Buddhism and eliminate desire from my life, only to disappear into a black void at the end after missing out on decades of chocolate cake and sex.

And whose feelings would I hurt by choosing to worship or disbelieve in one deity or another? Does atheism make Baby Jesus cry?

As it turned out, for once I didn't have a damn thing to worry about.

* * *

We landed in the middle of a small stone plaza. On all sides, sculptures and free-standing columns and obelisks in a crazy number of designs lay at the ends of colored stone paths radiating out from where we stood. One line of yellow stones led to a stylized fig tree carved of grey stone with a man sitting cross-legged beneath it. Another one, red, paved the way to a huge cross of marble bearing a figure of Jesus, nails through each of his palms and another nail pinning both of his feet. A splinter path from that one, in a slightly different red, led to another cross, made of wood with a painted wooden Jesus who had nails in each foot instead of the economizing two-for-one method. Several small Chinese or Japanese shrines held tiny statues nearby, or yin-yang symbols, or in one case an uncarved block of wood.

Past this grove of random icons, about a dozen small buildings ringed the plaza's edge, each maybe fifteen or twenty feet to a side, none of them in similar architectural styles. Half a dozen or so people wandered around between the buildings and monuments, wearing the same number of different cultural or historical fashions. If someone had shaken up a history book and dumped the contents out on the hilltop, it probably wouldn't have looked any more random.

I looked at Liv to see what she thought. She shrugged. Julia just stared down at her feet, sliding the right one back and forth across the stone beneath it. After a moment of trying to figure out what seemed so strange about her, it dawned on me that the objects behind her no longer showed through her flesh.

She took a few running-in-place steps. "I can feel the ground."

Before I could respond, a woman near one of the Asian shrines shouted something at us in Japanese or maybe Korean. It took me a moment to realize that I had understood her: "You people there! New arrivals! Make way!"

She pointed enthusiastically at something above and behind us. Another giant ectoplasmic cum-wad streaked down from the sky, headed straight at us. As we jumped out of the line of fire, it deposited an old man in the spot where we'd landed. Fingering the front of his hospital gown, he looked around in wonder, then straightened and, paying no attention to us at all, moved creakily toward one of the giant crucifixes.

The Japanese or Korean lady shook her head and turned away muttering.

"Aha," came a voice from another direction – a man in a mime outfit, beret and striped shirt and suspenders and all. "You are not pulled to the totem of your religion? Did you die without faith, or –"

"We're not dead," I said, indicating myself and Liv with a thumb. "I mean, the two of us aren't. She is."

He looked from us to Julia and said, "Aha!" again. Then he said, and I noticed it was in French, "Come with me."

We went with him, past a couple of the religious monuments to a little generic industrial-complex-looking building with a square concrete frame and a shiny front of tinted glass. The mime held the door for us, so we walked into what looked like the customer accounts section of a small credit union: a central aisle with two rows of interlocked metal-and-vinyl waiting seats, and then a couple of cubicles on either side. We could see into the front two cubes – mass-manufactured office furniture in both, one uninhabited, an olive-complected woman in a toga sitting behind the desk in the other.

"I have a couple of live ones here," our Frenchman said. "And a clinger." Holding his hand to one side of his mouth, he whispered, "A clinger is someone who didn't cross over when it was time."

"I'm sorry," Julia said. "I didn't mean to cause so much –"

"Come," the lady in the toga said, reeling at Julia with one hand. "I will provide your orientation." Looking at the mime, the toga woman nodded her head toward the empty cube. "Put them there. I imagine a badger will show up soon."

"A badger? What?"

"Someone who dispenses badges," the mime explained. "You should have a seat and wait."

Liv and I went to the empty cubicle, Julia to sit down opposite the orientation woman's desk. The Frenchman disappeared out the front door. Before I could settle in, I reached the maximum range of the necklace; it tugged toward Julia within my pocket, so I stood back up from chair I'd tried to sit in and scooted it a few inches toward the cubicle door until the medallion settled.

Looking around at the bland, upholstered panels of the workspace, I blew out a long breath.

"Well this isn't where I expected to be a few days ago. Or what I would have expected it to look like if I had."

Liv shook her head. "Me either."

I reached and touched her wrist. She turned her hand over and let me lace my fingers into hers, then squeezed tight. A door opened somewhere toward the back of the building. Footsteps came along the center aisle. I squeezed Liv's hand again and looked at her as the steps approached our cube.

"I guess they don't keep you waiting here."

In the gap between the cubicle panels, an African woman appeared, her hair pulled into a puff-ball at the back of her head. She wore a loose, wide-sleeved white shirt swimming with embroidery at the neckline and a long blue skirt beneath it. One arm folded an office binder up against her chest. She moved past us and circled to the far side of the desk, where she laid the binder flat, sat down, and only then looked up at us.

But she didn't say anything, and I didn't say anything, and Liv didn't say anything either.

I didn't say anything because the woman looked freakishly familiar.

Liv didn't say anything for pretty much the same reason – I could tell, because when I glanced at her she was just staring with her mouth slightly open.

The woman didn't say anything because she had started to cry.

From across the aisle, the muddled sound of Julia's orientation got loud enough or hit some perfect acoustic resonance for me to hear "wah-wah wah-wah mermaid wah-wah," and I thought, *Jesus Christ, this is going to get even weirder before it's over.*

"I've been waiting so long for you to come," said our crying badger, her voice husky and unsteady. I had no idea what language she was speaking.

Obviously something they speak in Ethiopia or Kenya.

"I didn't want it to be so soon, but I still couldn't help hoping – and now here you are, and still *alive*. Can I touch you?"

Liv nodded and moved her chair forward, leaning across the desk. She had tears rolling from her eyes now too, which maybe shouldn't have surprised me but did – she was only a little sentimental about her adoptive parents and I'd never heard her express any feelings at all about her biological ones. Uncle Nate was her family.

But it meant something to her when this woman placed a palm against her cheek.

"Oh, my little Hiwot ..."

They sat like that for long enough that I had to work to keep from fidgeting, even though it was beautiful and I would never have said anything to interrupt the moment. Thankfully, I managed to hold still until the woman lowered her hand and sat back. She looked from Liv to me, then back to Liv.

"My name is Enku. I'm so happy to meet you both. Would you like to share a meal as I give you your badges? We have time; orientation for your friend will take a bit."

Liv nodded. I said, "Sure, of course. I'm, uh, Tim."

"Oh! And I'm Liv. That's – my adoptive parents named me Olivia."

Enku took something from a drawer – a remote control, it looked like. While pushing a few buttons on it, she said, "Yes, they told me. And it's on your badge."

Liv's eyes widened – then widened some more as the cubicle walls rose to the ceiling, backed away, and changed from beige upholstery to pale blue plaster.

"You met them?" she asked, looking around at the room as it transformed into a simple dining area, with wood-framed chairs instead of the commercial furniture we'd been sitting on, and a cloth-covered table instead of a desk.

"It's not coincidence that I'm here for your arrival. Most of us work in the receiving stations every so often, at least until our friends and loved ones have all crossed over and joined us. You feel a kind of a tug sometimes, and you come, and someone you help that day might be an acquaintance, or a public figure you especially admired, or ... your daughter. Or her other parents."

Enku rose and went to a counter that had materialized along the back wall, beneath a bright window. She returned bearing a large platter of food.

"Will I get to see them too?"

Setting the platter down, Liv's mother shook her head and looked apologetic. "They weren't done helping people on the other side. Almost as soon as I explained the option of reincarnation, they decided to take new lives."

Liv nodded slowly. "That sounds like the kind of people Nate said they were ... are, I guess."

"I met him too, very briefly, when he had his heart attack last year. He was very nice."

"Really? He came all the way here? But they said he was only dead a minute or two – why wouldn't he tell me?"

Enku shrugged and smiled. "Some people don't remember. Or don't want everyone around them to think they were just hallucinating. What would you have thought if he told you he'd met me and I said your adopted parents were living new lives right now?"

"Yeah. Nate would have known I wouldn't buy that. Oh! Ethiopian food!"

She had finally looked down at the serving tray, where four or five different mounds of stew-like dishes sat on layers of giant, spongy, I don't know, tortillas? *I* had been staring at the stuff from the moment Enku put it in front of us. One heap was thick and lumpy and yellow. Another looked like lentils. Another had a kind of ruddy brown color and a couple of chicken legs sticking out of it. In and of itself, it didn't look bad. But I remembered what Liv had said about it: you were supposed to use the bread to eat everything.

"You've had it?" Enku asked her, looking pleased.

"No, but my friend Shawna has. She showed me pictures on her phone. That's where I'm from? Nate was never sure."

"Yes, Bahir Dar, in Amhara. Let me get us drinks, too." She almost stepped away, but looked at me and stopped herself. "Oh. Tim, do you need me to get something else for you? You can eat whatever you like."

Liv touched my hand and laughed. "No, he just needs a fork. He doesn't like to eat with his fingers."

I felt my cheeks getting a serious glow on and said, "It's okay. I can ... manage."

"Are you sure?" asked the woman.

"Oh, he's sure – he's sure he wants a fork."

"Liv – I'll deal with it. Maybe you've notice me dealing with some shit the last couple of days? I don't want to be rude."

Enku stepped around to my side of the table and put a hand on my shoulder. Her grip was strong, and her eyes met mine firmly.

"Listen to me. Out of love you have come with my daughter to the land of death. What more do you think you could ever need to prove?"

Stuck for a moment in that gaze, I realized where Liv got her eyes and her ability to say so much with them.

"Okay," I said then. "Yes, I would like a fork, please."

She laughed, and Liv laughed, and very quickly we had wineglasses before us and I had a fork alongside mine, and we made a toast to unexpected meetings and ate and talked.

CHAPTER NINE

Our meal took a few minutes less than Julia's orientation. I spent most of it watching Liv and her mother eat, feeling annoyed at myself and jealous as they tore strips of the big sourdough tortilla (Enku called it *injerna*) to pinch up lentils or chicken stew or whatever the other stuff was by the mouthful. On a fork, the food didn't strike me as all that different from what you'd get in an Indian restaurant, except that the bread added some tanginess and a different texture. But Liv kept saying how terrific everything was, and it was pretty clear she was having a different level of experience than I was.

Maybe that's related to eating with her mother, I told myself. But I knew that wasn't it, because I would bet money I loved Enku as much as or more than Liv did. Liv had spent nine months in the woman's uterus and owed her for some genetics, but I owed her for Liv.

Anyway, the meal was over too soon, and Julia's crash-course in being dead was over too soon after that, and then the four of us walked down the wide stone steps from the hilltop plaza to the riverside below.

Five or six new souls got ejaculated into the afterlife as we went. I found myself distracted every time a new spirit-spurting cum-shot arced down between the towers, but it didn't really matter because the substance of conversation along the way was less important than the sound of Liv's voice and laugh intermingling with her mother's.

"Be well," said Enku, embracing Liv on the bottom step of the stairway. "I want to hear about many more years of life the next time we meet."

Liv kissed her on the cheek. Then it was my turn.

"And you," she said, coming to the edge of the step. I stood one stair lower than her, on the dockside flagstones. "You're older, but I don't want to see you here much before Liv. Stay with her as long as you can."

"Uh, yeah," I said, glancing at her daughter. "That was already my plan."

"Good." She put her lips to my forehead. "Now I must return to finish my work at the station. Fortunate travels to all three of you."

We waved, Julia less enthusiastically than Liv or I. Once Enku rounded the slow curve of the hill, we turned toward the docks.

"So. We're looking for a mermaid symbol," Julia said.

"What," I asked, "are the Dionysian Fields in Atlantis or something?"

"No, but to get there you travel by mermaid."

The plaza stretched maybe as long as a football field around the base of the hill, with a brilliant orange flower carpet to one side and a quietly flowing river to the other. Piers stretched out thirty or forty feet into the current, held up by stone pylons. At the entrance to each pier, mosaic tiles had been laid to form an icon – the one closest to us a swan, the next a turtle, the more distant ones a little hard to make out. A woman in a sari stood at the end of the turtle pier. The rest looked deserted.

"Are they going to carry us?" Liv asked as we walked. "Pull us in rafts or something?"

Julia shrugged. "I didn't get a lot of details. They don't care much for 'clingers' around here – people who don't leave the other side when they're supposed to. My orientation lady was pretty hostile. You guys obviously got a lot better deal."

I could see Liv trying not to smile – Julia's voice had a sullen, envious tone, and Liv's not the kind to rub things in people's faces. But in this case she wasn't very successful.

"That was my mother," she explained, carefully not bubbling. "My birth mother. I'd never met her. Maybe if it had been someone else we would have been treated more like you."

"No," Julia said. "Not only was she mad at me for staying over there, she tried pretty hard to guilt-trip me for dragging the two of you here with me. She wasn't shy about taking sides. When I asked if I could have some clothes, she just laughed at me."

"I'm sorry," Liv said. But I thought I heard an undertone of *serves you right* in her voice, and I couldn't entirely disagree.

At the same time, Julia's naked, pregnant form reminded me that we weren't going to get through this thing with an arm's-length relationship – at least, Julia and I weren't.

"Look, there's the mermaid." I pointed to the symbol two piers away. "I guess that one's us."

We walked the rest of the way in silence, including the trip out to the landing's end. Back the way we'd come, I saw the woman in the sari step from her pier onto the back of an enormous turtle. Julia stood looking impatiently up and down the river. Liv had turned to face the hill, and at one point waved when her mother rounded another spiral curve of the stairway. I waved too.

Sunlight ricocheted brightly off the river's surface. A low breeze ran along the dockside. Everything was very nice.

"Anyway," Julia said, facing away from the river like waiting annoyed her. "The mime guy said you two were getting badges?"

"Yeah." I pulled mine from under my shirt – a flat disk showing planet Earth in blue and green, with a white cutout male figure like you'd see on an airport bathroom. The badge stuck directly to your skin when tucked out of sight, but didn't feel like anything there, and peeled right off if you needed to get it out. "We're supposed to show these if anyone gives us any trouble while we're traveling. And when we want to go home, we just tear them in half."

"Poof," Liv said, fluttering her hands apart. "What about you? The lady must have told you *something* useful, as long as she had you in there."

Julia's head tilted a little and her eyebrows moved. I recognized that she was rolling her eyes – it was just hard to tell since she still had no irises or pupils.

"Most of it was about my options. I could go here, I could go there, I could get reincarnated and remember this life, I could get reincarnated and not remember anything. I kept telling her I just needed to get to the Dionysian Fields, but she said she had to cover the standard destinations. So I got mad and I told her the only place I deserved to go besides the Dionysian Fields would be Hell." I flinched at that, and I saw Liv frown in spite of herself. Julia went on, "But she said there isn't a Hell – the closest she could give me was the heaven for sadomasochists."

"You're not going to go there, are you?" Liv asked.

Julia shook her head and looked down at her rounded belly, both hands on its bare swell. "I have to rebirth in the Dionysian Fields to get you that Wine of Forgetting. Then I'll be stuck there – you don't get to change afterlives unless you reincarnate back to Earth in between."

I couldn't help but follow her gaze down to the fertile globe between her hands, especially with her talking about having to rebirth. M had been pretty clear about what I had to do to help that process along, and at some point one of us would need to bring the subject up.

But it wasn't going to be me, not right then. And if it might have been Julia, a sound of rushing water interrupted any chance of that happening.

* * *

Just to be clear, I fucking hate that "Little Mermaid" movie. I'm not big on Faustian bargain stories to begin with, or on stories about stupid teenagers making bad decisions because they want to be rebels. I made a crapload of bad decisions as a teenager, but selling my voice and my soul to a witch seems to me like the kind of thing your more admirable teenager would identify as not such a great plan. Now, I say this having recently put my dick in a weird reptile-slash-monster-slash-witch to save the love of my life, so maybe I shouldn't point fingers. But even having acquired a new reason to identify with her, I did not want the Little Mermaid giving me a piggyback ride anywhere while her crab and sea cucumber friends sang me show tunes.

Apparently, the powers that be on the other side *really* like "be-careful-what-you-wish-for" scenarios.

The rushing water got loud enough that it could have been dozens or hundreds of Little Mermaids. But it wasn't. As we watched the river, a huge bulge slid midstream around the river-bend toward us – like, nuclear submarine huge. It undulated as it came, sending waves rolling out in its wake to the riverbanks on either side.

I looked around to see if someone else had come down to the docks. *Maybe there's a giant whale pier.* But no, we were the only ones in sight.

About a hundred feet from us, the swell subsided. I mean, it reached a point and came no further, and its trailing bulge shortened and narrowed at that point until it disappeared. The wake continued to propagate toward us, sending river water lapping up almost to the surface of the pier we stood on.

Diving, I thought. My shoulders felt like shrinking down to the ground and my legs felt like scrambling back to the main plaza – the next step in any decent horror or action movie would be for a sea monster to blast straight up from the river in front of us and drown the whole pier in torrents of falling water.

Instead, the glittery surface in front of us let an image sneak through – an upper back and its set of shoulders, thirty feet across at least, easing up through the dark. As the shoulders breached the water, they dragged up a neck too – all the flesh blue – and then a head of long, drenched, black hair. Cascades rushed down from the dark tresses, across the rising shoulders. A pair of hands appeared, overlapping into a table shape, lifting the waterfall curtains of hair, bringing them up and back from an elfin/asian face big enough to take up a billboard. The head lifted, the hands lifted, a set of elbows broke loose from the waves, and the mermaid slicked her hair back away from her face and behind her. The motion also brought a pair of bare blue breasts up just to water level, each one the size of a VW Beetle, with fire-hydrant nipples bobbing in and out of the waterline.

"Hi!" she said. "My name is Bubbles."

For some reason, 'Bubbles' didn't sound ridiculously incongruous in mermaidish or whatever language she spoke.

"Where is it you're going?"

With expectant, pink-coral eyes, she blinked down at us and waited.

"We're trying to get to the Dionysian Fields," Julia said when she found her voice. "But – my orientation lady said you'd only be able to take us as far as the Bogs of Indolence."

"Ooh, the Fields!" said Bubbles. "But ugh! The Bogs!"

Her vast right arm swung out and down toward us, laying her hand palm-up and flush with the end of the pier.

"Should we be worried?" I asked. I can't say I liked the sound of bogs at all.

"Ha-ha," she sing-songed. Her voice had a strangely high pitch for such a large creature. "Worries are for the other side. If you want worries, you'll have to reincarnate."

Liv pointed from me to herself. "We're still alive."

"Oh! Do you have badges?"

I took mine out. Liv did the same with hers.

"Well I'm glad you told me! Wouldn't it be embarrassing if I drowned you and you ended up stuck here instead of going back home!"

"Sure," I said, looking more dubiously at her waiting hand. "That's – yeah, embarrassing, exactly the word I was looking for."

The mermaid laughed again and nodded at her palm. "Come on, then. If we don't get going, the evening storms will catch us for sure."

No one wanted to go first, and even though something manly somewhere within me said I ought to, it took another nod from Bubbles before Julia stepped off, and then Liv. As I joined them, my nose caught a hint of fish and sea salt swimming up from the blue skin underfoot.

Our transportation lifted us gently up and away from the pier. She was good at it – I didn't feel wobbly or off-balance for a second as she brought her hand around until the pinky and heel of it pressed against the tops of her breasts.

"Lean up against me," she said, "so you don't fall over when I lie onto my back."

We did as she asked, and the world tilted, and her hand rose away, and I found myself resting on a wide blue breastbone with the curved valley between her breasts in one direction and her looming, awkwardly tilted face in the other. River water lapped all around, but none of it threatened to slosh up to our position.

"You might be able to guess that it's pretty uncomfortable for me to keep my head up at this angle. While I'm swimming, my ears will be submerged. So if you need to talk to me, you'll either have to shout or stomp a couple of times to get my attention. Don't worry – you're tiny, so you could jump up and down and it wouldn't hurt me. Feel free to wander around, as long as you don't get too near the edges."

The huge coral-colored eyes focused on me. "Boys sometimes like to crawl up onto my breasts and explore. I don't mind – really! But if you want to play with the nipples, hug and squeeze, don't try to be all tender. You're so little, it tickles unless you put some real effort into it. I like being tickled, but you probably don't want me laughing while you're sitting on my boobies with deep water over the side."

I glanced at the soft slopes of her mammaries. "Thanks. I'll stay down here with Julia and Liv for now, though."

"Okay! Then we're going now. Toot, toot!"

Her head lay back, and somewhere beyond the Valley of the Great Blue Breasts her tail flicked, while her hands at her sides twisted easily through the water.

In the space of a couple of breaths, the piers had fallen a hundred feet behind us. A few breaths after that, the curve of the hill hid them entirely.

"So are you going to climb up there?" Liv asked, watching Bubbles' nipples move with the rise and fall of the mermaid's chest. "You know you want to, and it's not like you'll ever have a chance like this again."

My face heated up immediately, so I knew there was no hope of pulling off a lie. "No, I'm not going to. It's, that would be ... undignified. I can't go up there and play on a nipple like it's some kind of hobby horse – and *definitely* not with you two watching."

"Oh," she said. "So you're going to wait and hope you die first so you'll have a chance to ride on her again while I'm not watching?"

"Let's not talk about dying," I said.

She ducked her head. "Okay, I guess that's not as funny as I meant."

Julia stood looking out at the flower-covered hills. The rat-dragon head of her tattoo glared at us from her right shoulder. Glancing away from it took my eyes down across the pudgy curves of her ass.

"Thinking about getting started on, uh, you know?"

"No," I said, looking reflexively away from Julia entirely. Then, as I met Liv's eyes, "Good *god*, no."

Julia turned at that, and I saw her lower lip out and a hurt look in the set of her eyelids.

"Sorry," I said. "I didn't mean – I mean, these are not exactly ... conducive circumstances, you know?"

I felt Liv's finger poke my shoulder. "I don't know that the circumstances are going to get any more conducive, Tim."

Looking from Julia to Liv and back again, I decided that for three people talking about sex, none of us looked very happy.

"Well, there's unconducive, and then there's how am I even going to get it up, right? Because I can't ask you to help, not after what you went through last – not after what you went through."

She looked frustrated. "But it's got to be done or we're wasting our time with this whole trip. If you need help, I'll help."

"I know you're *willing* to help. But you're not *interested*. Are you? Be honest."

"No."

"And I know that, and so if you try to help that's all I'll be thinking about."

"Rrrh!" Julia growled. She had both fists clenched. "Would you two shut up? You're making me feel terrible, and I know I deserve it, but how is this helping any of us? Tim, listen – drop your pants and look at the mermaid's tits, and I will suck you off. Don't pretend those aren't some great fucking tits. You're a guy. There's no way you're going to stay limp with those tits in front of you and a girl's mouth on your cock."

Neither Liv nor I said anything, but our eyes connected, and she gave a single, unenthusiastic nod.

"Christ," I said, undoing my belt. Julia came over and knelt in front of me, her swollen belly nestling down in the crease of her thighs. Despite everything I'd said, my dick was already half hard by the time I got my pants and briefs down. Between the lushness of the dead girl's pregnant abdomen, the hormone-enlarged curves of her dumpling breasts, and the great hills of Bubbles' rack, the circumstances quickly made a liar of me for calling them unconducive.

Julia's little hand wrapped around my shaft, making me harden further and blink. I kept my eyes on the dark-blue pylon of Bubbles' left nipple, swaying atop the ten-foot hummock of her breast.

A pair of lips closed around my tip.

Okay. I guess that's not as bad as it might be.

Julia leaned forward. Her mouth glided around me, inch by inch by – thump. I hit the back of her throat with less than half my cock in, and she quivered and pulled back.

And her teeth scraped me as they retreated.

"Fuck," I said, looking down at her. I suddenly remembered her story about trying to be a blow-job slut in high school. "You weren't kidding when you said you were bad at this, were you?"

She looked like she was about to cry, and I immediately felt terrible.

"I'm sorry. Shit. Look, try again. Just, you know, keep your jaw wide and your cheeks sucked in and use a lot of tongue along the bottom."

"I can give you some pointers," Liv said. "I'm pretty good ..."

That was a total understatement. Liv can deep throat, and I don't let her do it all the time because she says it's uncomfortable, but she likes the noises I make when she does it and I don't always have the willpower to stop her. I felt my cock swell harder just at the thought of her getting Julia to do half of what she could do.

But Julia pulled all the way off and scowled.

"No," she said. "I'm a fucking ghost, right? I can't choke to death, and there's nothing in me to puke out, so there's no reason I can't just get my neck at the right angle and let you ram it all the way in. Come on."

She backed up a little and leaned in, tilting her head and opening her mouth wide.

"Uh, that seems kind of sadistic."

"What – I don't deserve it? Let's go. Fucking do it."

She gaped again. I looked at Liv.

"Do you want to ... I don't know, tell her something about how –"

"No," she said, her face suddenly harder than I'm used to seeing it. "She's right. Go ahead and do it."

What the hell? But even as I was thinking that, I realized that Liv was standing there watching a naked girl trying to suck a cock, and it probably did absolutely nothing inside of her, thanks to what she'd felt while that necklace was making her endlessly orgasm. *Right. Of course she's pissed.*

I turned back to Julia, whose mouth remained wide open. The rest of her face looked angry and impatient.

"Okay ..."

I eased forward. Julia leaned in to meet me. My head slipped in. A little of my shaft ...

Julia grabbed my ass with both hands and thrust her face up to my crotch. I felt the head of my cock penetrate her throat, felt it spasm around me, saw her brows knit and tears stream out of the corners of her eyes. Her whole body tried to thrash, but she kept herself in place with an iron grip on my right butt-cheek. Her other hand let go and grabbed wildly for my wrist, pulling it up and around when she found it to curl my hand against the back of her head.

This is so fucked up.

I worked my fingers into her dyed-black hair and pulled her harder up against me, pressing her nose into my pubic curls and feeling her lips reach the root of my shaft. I could feel her gagging around me, but with her windpipe shut off, she didn't really make much noise.

Getting my nerve up, I eased back just a little and then gave a firm thrust of my hips to drive all the way in again. Julia dragged us together even harder with her hands on my ass.

I couldn't help being horrified – but it also felt really good.

Just go for it, I told myself. *It was her fucking idea, she wants me to, and Liv wants me to, and she does damn well deserve it for what she did – doesn't she?*

My teeth ground together. I put both hands to the sides of her head, drew way back, and rammed deep.

"Oh, *shit,*" I gasped. Julia's throat cramped and convulsed, trying to disgorge my cock, rippling my tip and my first couple of inches with esophageal flesh and the rough back of her tongue. I pulled back and thrust again, and she squirmed but kept hold of my rear, fingers digging in hard.

"Okay – I'm going to – uh – I'm going to go for it –"

It took some fighting against my instincts to rev up and start fucking a crying girl full-on down her throat. But maybe it didn't take as much fighting as I would have wanted.

"Ohmygod," I said, working into a rhythmic cycle of yank-jam-relax, yank-jam-relax. Julia met it as best she could, hands and arms and shoulders pulling when I did. When I got too far out, she made gargling, retching noises, so I mostly stayed deep and kept her clamped against my root except for inch-long thrusts. "God, Julia, that's so good. Fuck, take it, take it —"

Something angry and violent had gotten hold of me. I wasn't just enjoying the feel of my dick sliding into her mouth and throat — I was punishing her. And it felt good. It felt liberating. And the sensations wrapping themselves around my cock ...

Except that a couple of minutes into it, her whole body started trembling uncontrollably, jerking, spasming randomly instead of moving with my tempo. Her hands stayed on my ass, but kind of fluttered and slapped there.

Oh, fuck. I should stop. But she wasn't pushing away, and I was pretty close to coming ... *I should really stop.*

I let go of Julia's head at the same moment Liv grabbed my shoulder and tugged at it.

"Jesus Christ, Tim," she said as I pulled out. "You can't keep —"

"No, I know, I know." My wet, glistening cock waved embarrassingly through the cool air as Julia collapsed onto her side, wheezing and gagging. I got down on my knees and one hand, using the other to brush the tear- and sweat- and snot-slicked hair out of her face. "Julia, are you all right? Are you all right?"

"Uhhh," she groaned, rolling onto her back, eyes closed. "Should have kept going. You close to coming?"

"I was, but you —"

She spread her legs weakly. "Put it in me. Don't want to waste ... all that effort ..."

My hard-on had subsided a little, but it came right back at the sight of her offered cleft. I looked helplessly at Liv.

"Sure," she sighed. "You have to sooner or later."

I wiggled out of my jeans and pulled off my shirt. "Do you want to —" I pointed through the gap between Bubbles' breasts. "—I don't know, go around the corner? You don't have to watch if you don't want to."

She swallowed and took a step back, glancing the direction I pointed. "I don't know, I guess ..."

In front of me, Julia stirred and opened her eyes. She was still crying. "No, Liv, don't. Please. Please stay with us. I just — I need you to not hate me that much."

Liv put her fingers to her wide, dark lips. I saw tears starting in her eyes too. She nodded to Julia and lowered herself to her knees.

"Okay, I kind of need to put this in here, or all the crying is going to shrivel it up."

Liv squeaked out an awkward sound that could sort of be called a laugh. Her hand went over her eyes, and she said, "Yes, go ahead."

Scooting forward, my knees wide beneath Julia's spread thighs, I took her by the hips and pulled her up, angling her, angling myself, until the tip of my cock settled in between the lips of her vagina, and I looked her in the face and saw her nod, and I entered her.

She was a little dry, but not painfully so, and she felt tight and snug once I got all the way in.

"Is that okay?"

"Uh-huh," she said.

I started moving – gently, because she wasn't lubricated enough for anything harder, and I no longer had any wish to be punishing her with sex. She lay her head back and closed her eyes.

I watched her breasts move with my thrusts. I felt her vaginal flesh tugging all around my shaft. It didn't in any way approach the sensation of the brutal oral fucking I'd given her just a few moments before – but all of a sudden, a wonderful orgasm washed over and out of me.

"*Oh*," I said. "Oh. Julia ..."

She hummed for a moment as my cock pulsed inside of her. My hands had fallen to her ripe belly at some point, and now I actually felt it expand by a centimeter or two beneath my palms. "Holy shit."

Liv scooted closer. "Yeah, I saw that too."

I looked at her and reached over to touch her face, brush a tear from the corner of her eye with my thumb.

Julia's hand rose too, to brush the other cheek.

"Thank you, Liv," she said, crying again herself.

Liv took the hand and squeezed it – her expression conflicted and yet beautiful.

Okay, I thought. *Maybe this isn't going to be such a suck-ass chore after all.*

* * *

Pulling out and relaxing onto my back, I looked up at the blue sky, cloudless at the moment but speckled here and there with flying things too high up for me to identify.

Angels? UFOs? Who knows.

I enjoyed my own breathing for a while, and the gentle lifting and lowering of Bubbles' chest underneath me. I could hear water gliding by and not much else.

Except that sometimes you can hear awkwardness, right? And I somehow caught a little bit of that just before Liv said, in a kind of unsure-how-to-make-polite-conversation tone, "So ... did you come?"

"No," Julia responded. "It totally wasn't about that. I never even really got, you know, all the way fired up. It was nice, though. The second part."

"You'll come next time." That made me lift my head, startled that Liv would say such a thing. But with the look on her face, I wasn't surprised at what she told Julia next: "We're not doing any more of that rough shit, okay?"

"Sure. It was pretty awful. I'm not going to ask for that again. But I needed it."

It occurred to me that I no longer saw hills or riverbanks beyond Bubbles' blue flesh – only a wide expanse of rolling water. We must have hit the ocean, or a huge lake, while we were screwing.

"Why?" Liv asked Julia.

"I don't know ... I said I deserved it, but it wasn't because I wanted to be punished. I guess I needed to know how you felt, having something forced into you and made a part of you, something degraded and ugly." I had to flinch at that, although obviously she wasn't really talking about my cock. "I know it's not the same, not by a lot. I just – I thought I should feel used, the way I made you feel. I didn't want to take what I took from you and then turn around and have fun fucking your boyfriend. Especially right in front of you."

"But then you asked me to stay."

The solid green eyes glanced my way, then returned to Liv. "Because you stopped him. You're so good. You didn't want me being treated like that, even as much as you hate me. I'm so awful and you're so good, and right then I just wanted to be near you so much. I didn't want to lie there knowing you were around the corner having to hide from something I got us stuck doing. I didn't want you to be alone. I wanted us to be together. I've screwed both your lives up so bad, and then when you had the chance to make me suffer, neither one of you could do it. If I'd ever had anybody like that in my life before, maybe I wouldn't have gotten into all this witchcraft shit in the first place. And now you're not going to be in my life that much longer, and I – I just – I *so* didn't want you to go."

We sat there watching her through all this, watching her face twist around into different passions like a circus contortionist, watching her hands clench and gesticulate. I don't even know what I felt, but whatever it was, I felt it deep in my chest and my guts.

Julia looked back and forth between us, and her voice broke as she said, "I love you. I love you both, and I know you hate me but I just don't want to lose you. *Please* stay with me until we're done? I mean, really with me, not just however close the amulet makes us stick. Please?"

Liv put her hands in her face, shoulders shaking.

"Crap, Julia," I said. "We don't *hate* you." Scooting over, I rubbed Liv's back with one hand. "Honestly, we don't even know you well enough to hate you. We hate what you *did*. And we're still pissed at what that did to us. But – and I mean, I don't like putting it this way – you're a fucked-up little girl. Nobody ever helped you grow up. We can't hate you for being that way."

"Well then why's she crying like that?"

"Because you *almost* got her to hate you. That's not who she is, but you almost got her to be that way."

"Oh my god, Tim," Liv said, twisting to throw her arms around me and bury her head into my chest. I hugged her back, and I have to say that it felt really, really, really good to know that I knew her that well.

But a loud, high-pitched voice interrupted us before the hug could go on too long.

"Oooh, aren't you little things so adorable!"

We looked up to see Bubbles' head raised again, her pink eyes bright and her wide blue lips smiling.

"I really hate to break things up, but if you'll look ahead of us, you'll see some ugly clouds on the horizon."

Sure enough, far away over the flat pane of the sea, heaps of grey and black fluff had piled up and now mounted higher and higher, sparkling in their depths with flashes of lightning.

"Those are the evening storms," the mermaid said. "I sort of hoped we'd miss them, but it really wasn't very likely, considering how late we set out. They can get really rough – if we want to avoid lightning bolts and waterspouts, we'll have to go under."

I looked around. She didn't seem to have a people purse or scuba gear lying about. "Is there – how are we going to breathe?"

"Well, I'm afraid there's only one place I can put you that I can keep watertight."

The laptop-sized panes of her teeth snagged my eye with glittering pearlescence as she spoke.

"Will we all fit in there?" I asked, noticing that her incisors and canines all looked considerably sharper than a human's.

"Ha! No, silly," she said. "How would I get water across my gills if I put you in my mouth?"

Uh-oh. That's not good.

"I was talking about my uterus."

CHAPTER TEN

Okay, so I am now guaranteed to beat my friends at any "what's the loosest vagina you've ever been in" fish story competition.

Bubbles directed us between her breasts, down past her navel, past the line at her waist where her skin turned to scales, to a slit almost exactly the size of one of those enclosed slides at a waterpark. As we approached, she flexed her abdomen and the slit gapped open.

"Go ahead and hop in," she said. "You'll slide down and around a bend and probably kind of bounce off my cervix. You can't miss it. Just squeeze through and you'll be snug as a babe in the womb. Literally!"

I've never really gotten those jokes about vaginas smelling like fish. But in this case the aroma wafting up from Bubbles' opening really could have been the seafood counter at a supermarket, if you'd smelled it using a woman's panties as a nose filter.

"Wait," I said, trying to think of a question. "There's going to be enough air in there? How will we get back out?"

"Haha, what do you think vagina muscles are for, anyway? It's not just to give you boys a good time! And yeah, it's self-oxygenating. Also ..." The gash's rim puckered momentarily, and then the shadows inside turned faintly green, as if lit from below. "Bioluminescent."

I had picked my clothes up and was still holding them in my hands. "Okay, well – I'm going to volunteer Julia to go first while I get dressed."

"No, you don't want to do *that*. I'm juicing myself up so you don't rub me raw on the way down. Clothes will just defeat the purpose. Plus, they'll be all crusty and vagina-smelly once they dry out. Just bundle them up against your belly and scoot in – from the tail side, not the top side."

"I'm going," Julia said. She put a determined look on her face, walked to the far edge of the hole, dropped to sit with her lower legs dangling in, and then shut her eyes and pushed off and vanished into the dark.

"AAAaaaahhhhh!!!"

The scales underfoot tremored, almost pitching me off balance.

"Mmmmm, nice!" Bubbles said.

Liv put her hands to her belt buckle. "I guess I'll get my clothes off?"

"I'd appreciate it," the mermaid replied – a little breathily.

Leaning down, I called out to Julia through a rising waft of sex-smell and fishing-pier odor. "Are you all right down there?"

"Uh-huh." Her voice came up muted by the fleshy tunnel. "Kind of ... fun, actually. I guess this hole is where I go through to get out of the way ..."

"Yes!" The ground twitched beneath us again. "Yes, that's the one."

My imagination suddenly gave me an image of Julia half-in and half-out of a giant blue sphincter, only her pregnant belly, ass, and legs showing. Thankfully, I had Liv stripping right in front of me so that I wasn't tempted to slide down and try to get a glimpse of the real thing.

It's weird, how quickly you can start missing something. Today was technically still Sunday. Or maybe we'd passed over into early Monday morning. I had last seen Liv naked – voluntarily naked – early Saturday when she was getting into the shower. But the view of her long bare legs easing one-by-one from the grasp of her jeans, and then the appearance of her stomach and bellybutton and bra-clad breasts behind the rising curtain of her t-shirt – it poured an immense relief over me, as if I'd never hoped to see this again.

Dropping her shirt, she saw me looking and turned half away. For a second, I cringed inside, thinking she didn't want me to see her, that the frat-house gang-bang or her destroyed libido made her uncomfortable.

But her face turned over her shoulder, and she said, offering the bra-clasp at the center of her back, "Do you want to get this for me?"

I stepped over quickly and undid the catch.

"Thanks." She peeled the bra loose and then slid her panties down and stepped out of them. Then she bundled everything up in her hoodie and held it to her chest. "You want to go first, or do you want me to?"

Her eyes stayed politely on mine instead of on the waving pole of my erection, which I'd been helpless to repress at the sight of her stripping down. Although she didn't smile, her face looked at ease – grateful, even, to be looking at mine.

"How about ... you go." *That way maybe I'll have a chance to let this thing simmer down before I have to crawl through Bubbles' cervix and be in her womb with you and Julia both naked.*

Now she did smile, just a second, and nodded. I couldn't help watching her back and her bottom as she walked around to the downstream rim of the vagina – not so much because it was sexy as because it was her, pure Liv without anything in the way.

And then she was kneeling and sitting and, with a little squeak, slipping over the side after Julia.

Bubbles hummed again.

From the recesses of the downcurving tunnel, Liv called up, "Ohmygosh. That was crazy. Give me a second and then come on down, Tim. Julia's right – it's fun."

Then I heard her laugh a little, and heard two voices conversing, not quite loud enough for the words to reach me. I went around and sat awkwardly on the soft, curved edge of Bubbles' genital opening. She felt damp and slick behind my heels.

I wonder if she'd like it if I drummed them while I'm waiting. I didn't ask her, though, and I didn't try it. I just sat breathing her musky marine smell and waiting for Liv to give me the all-clear.

"Okay!"

Christ. Here goes.

Bumping forward on my ass, I closed my eyes, straightened out ...

As waterslides go, fifteen or twenty feet is a pretty quick ride – and the slide inside Bubbles was steep. My feet hit and bounced off the rubbery wall of her cervix almost before I realized I was screaming.

" – aah!"

I came to rest on my back, which belatedly recognized the sensation of full-body sex that had rushed along me the whole way down.

I just fucked a mermaid with my spine, I thought.

The light down here filtered out through a basketball-sized gap in Bubbles' cervical disk. Julia and Liv blocked a good bit of it, peeking to watch me sit up dripping ocean-scented pussy juice from my back.

"Wouldn't you *pay* to do that?" asked Julia.

I got to my feet, the muscles all along my backbone twitching uncomfortably. "No. Please tell me it's not so ... lube-y in there on your side."

"It's actually pretty dry," Liv said. "Come on."

I handed her my clothes and tried to figure out how to get through the hole, way narrower than my shoulders and about waist high. Obviously the girls had both done it, though, and I guessed there wasn't much other way than to basically dive in. So I put both hands into the opening and leaned to start pushing through.

As soon as I hit the point where the going got tight, I felt the whole sphincter throb around me.

"This is messed up," I said. But I kept at it until my head and shoulders were inside.

"That's it," Liv said. "Now just kind of push in with both hands and wiggle."

She was still naked, glistening in spots beneath the odd greenish light shed by patches along the chamber walls and floor. She'd set her clothes and mine to the side, and came over to help with her hands around my right bicep.

"Come on," she encouraged me.

Together we applied enough force to pop my hips through the clutching ring of flesh, and I rolled in and landed at her feet.

Bubbles' uterus could have been a mold for casting giant golf balls. Basically spherical, with dimples spaced around the entire surface – I guess that means the golf ball would have bumps, not depressions – the whole thing stretched about twelve feet side-to-side.

It was hot inside. Not quite a human 98.6 degrees, but close enough that I knew I'd be sweating before long.

"Feels like everybody's in!" came Bubbles' voice, distantly. "I'm closing up now!"

Then the sphincter pinched shut.

And then the entire room *very* slowly rolled to one side.

"Oh crap," I said. "What the hell ..."

Julia bumped into me as we all edged in the direction of rotation, like hamsters in a big, blue, fleshy, fish-and-uterus-scented hamster ball. "She must be turning over so she can dive down and swim below the storm."

Sure enough, when we'd gone about a hundred eighty degrees, we changed to a different axis of rotation, until we found ourselves looking up toward the tight-shut cervix at about a forty-five degree angle. Pressure built in my ears and I had to yawn to pop them. Liv put her hands at the corners of her jaw and worked her mouth open and closed too.

But after a bit we leveled out, and everything became steady except for a gentle rocking motion of the entire chamber.

Our clothes lay all around the lower curve of the room (womb). Liv moved to start picking hers up, so I did the same. When I got close, though, she put a hand on my shoulder and gave me a raised eyebrow before darting her eyes meaningfully toward my crotch. My face flushed; through all the sliding and squeezing and rolling around, my erection hadn't gone down a bit.

"I don't think there's going to be an in-flight movie," she said. "Are you sure you want to put that away instead of making some progress on Julia's whatever-she's-doing?"

I looked around at the green-eyed goth girl. She gave an uncomfortable shrug.

"Liv, I don't know ... this is just so weird ..."

"It's weird for me too. But it's not like we can run away from it." Her eyes rolled up and around the globular ceiling. "And it's not like there's anyplace to run to right now even if we tried. Julia, are you okay doing it?"

"Sure. I kind of have to be, right?" She looked away, though, settling her hands on the curve of her abdomen.

Goddammit. Liv's right, and my cock obviously agrees, so why does this have to be so awkward? All right, then, fuck it. Who the hell needs two different women to argue him into having sex?

Sitting down and leaning back on my elbows, I said, "Fine. I give in, so crawl over here and sit on my face."

"What?"

"Liv said you were going to come next time, and this is next time, right?"

Liv didn't seem entirely happy about that, maybe a little chagrinned. But she nodded when Julia looked over at her. "That *is* what I said, I guess."

"So come on. Settle yourself down on my mouth – and with your belly over my nose, not sixty-nine."

"Okayy..."

She walked toward me and I lay back. Her fecund stomach made her ungainly as she maneuvered into place, but she got there, and nestled her brown-curled mound to my mouth. With significant relief, I found her woman smell blotting out Bubbles' sea-life one, and I closed my eyes and felt very grateful as I tasted her.

"Oh." The surprise in her tone made me smile against her vulva. "Oh, that's – *oh*."

I heard Liv sigh, and I had to stop for a second.

"Are you all right, honey?" Julia's pudenda hovered tremblingly above my lips as I spoke.

"Yes. No, go ahead, Tim. I'm just ... a little jealous. Not because you're doing that for her. Because I ought to be wanting a turn when you're done, and I don't. But I like the way you're making her sound."

"Are you sure?" I wished I could see her face, but my visual world at the moment consisted entirely of Julia's thighs and pregnant belly.

"Yes, I'm totally sure. Make her come so hard she screams. You know how."

That sounded pretty sincere.

I returned to Julia's cunt, soft and moist, the clit and labia engorging as my tongue traced along each crease and ridge. Her breathing had quickened substantially.

My hands went up around and along her thighs, then past them to the taut convexity of her belly.

"It's good ... oh, that's good, Liv, you're so lucky ..."

"I know. Tim, you should see her face, it's beautiful."

"*Uhhhh.*" Julia's hips moved, rolling her mound in a circle against my tightly vacuumed lips. As her crotch shifted forward, I got my tongue deep up into her slit – deep enough to make my frenulum regret it, although it was worth the sound I pulled out of her. "*Hh*-guhh-*h* –"

Licking up and out, I fastened onto the hood of her clitoris and concentrated my efforts there, spelling out her name with the tip of my tongue in cunninglingus caligraphy. Liv says she can sometimes make out the letters I'm writing, but I doubt my penmanship is really that good. "Olivia" makes for a good series of repeated motions, though, and it drives her crazy after I've gone through it enough times.

"Fuck ... *me*. Oh god, that's good. Oh god."

She was really humping my mouth now, making it a little hard to stay on target. It didn't seem to matter, though, and after another minute or so, I'd gotten her there.

"Uu*ahh*—ahh—*ohhhh* ... UHH! Shit, *AHHH!*"

Sitting down heavily, Julia throbbed against my mouth, hips writhing. I sort of expected to feel her stomach plump out another few centimeters, as hard as she was coming. But then I remembered that it was my come that did that, not hers.

"*Fuck!* Fuck, Tim, *fuckkkk!*"

Despite the fact that her weight had driven my head deeper down into Bubbles' uterine flesh, I kept my mouth going until she squealed and rolled off of me, curling up and rocking, moaning, panting her way down from climax. I shifted onto my side to watch her. Around us, Bubbles' womb moved like a soft, oceanic crib, rhythmic and comforting.

After a moment Liv knelt behind me and put a hand on my shoulder, rubbing it lightly.

"You are the tongue master, sweetheart."

"Thanks," I said, after wiping my mouth with one thumb. "Um, I guess you still aren't jealous for a turn?"

"No," she sighed. Then she patted my shoulder. "But I'd be happy to see you enjoy yourself. Our little friend there has to be getting impatient by now."

"Kind of. You going to be ready soon, Julia?"

"Ohhhh. I don't know. Still recovering. Give me a minute, all right?"

"Yeah, sure. Take your time."

"But not too much time," Liv said. I put my hand over hers, on my shoulder, and twined our fingers together. Julia remained curled up and motionless.

"So ... If you're, uh, wanting to watch – any requests on how we do it?"

Liv shrugged. "Maybe doggie style? I don't know. Whatever you're going to like most."

"Doggie style sounds pretty good to me I guess. Julia?"

She rolled onto her elbows and knees, resting her forehead on the backs of her hands. "Whatever's going to be quick. Holy cow, that wore me out."

Something about her dumpy little bottom pushed up into the air – and that curve of pregnancy framed by the gap between her legs – sucked away most of the reasoning power in my brain. If I'd worked at it, I could easily have squelched the moment with guilt or discomfort or worry over whether Liv really wanted to see this or was just saying so. But I didn't work at it. I just let myself move in behind Julia, find the right angle, and penetrate her.

"Uhhh..." she said, sounding more like an extra in a zombie movie than in a porn one.

The sex was okay. She had definitely gotten way more warmed up this time than last time, and while her moans started off exhausted instead of aroused, it didn't take long for them to perk up, or for her head to lift a little as she joined in with my movements. Her softness felt good around me, wet and textured.

But better than the sex itself was the dreamy freakishness of it. The purple ends of Julia's dyed hair color-coordinating with Bubbles' blue flesh and green bioluminescence. The mild sea-glide of our living bed, swaying beneath us in a rhythm we fell into time with. The feel of my partner's impregnated belly under my hands, and the fullness of her breasts, now several sizes larger than when I'd first laid eyes on them.

Even the lurid glare of that monstrous tattoo, staring at me from Julia's shoulder. It looked less angry than jealous now, and as I eased in and out of its mistress' slick body, I thought, *That's right, you'd like some of this, wouldn't you? Stuck forever with nothing but a tail-full of tit, knowing you're just a couple feet away from – ohshit –*

Lording it over the tattoo turned out to be the final push I needed. Without any more warning, my brain swam over into the clutch of orgasm, all thoughts but that beautiful, explosive pleasure getting squeezed out of my consciousness. Julia groaned beneath me. Her nipples pressed harder into my palms as the swell of her breasts increased, a millimeter at a time with each throb of my ejaculation into her.

And then the world rocked.

* * *

"What the hell!"

I didn't need Liv's shout to know something bigger than a particularly good orgasm had just happened. Whatever it was almost threw me off my knees, and I popped loose from Julia without intending to.

Just as I recovered my balance, it happened again, and this time Liv stumbled over and fell against the upward-sloping side of the womb.

"I thought she said we were getting down under the storms," Julia complained, rolling onto her bottom.

"Maybe it's a rougher storm than she thought."

Liv settled against the curve of the wall, not trying to regain her feet. "Or maybe a giant squid is trying to eat her."

"Oh crap, don't say that."

The room shuddered again. I sat on my ass like Julia, putting my hands out for support.

"*Fuck* me!" Julia screamed, pointing. "Look!"

I turned to see the disk of Bubbles' cervix bulging inward. A little round gap appeared at the center, releasing a trickle of seawater to run down the wall of the womb.

"Oh my god," Liv said. "Is –"

With a wet, rubbery noise, something the shape of a tulip bulb and the size of a chair forced open Bubbles' sphincter and intruded through.

"Aah!" Liv squawked. "Something is fucking our ride!"

"God*damn*it!" I said. I thought about crab-walking over to kick the thing – I know *I'd* pull out if something inside a girl's vagina started kicking me – but I had no idea whether our mermaid was a willing participant. "Do you think she'd let us get drowned in cum? Should we try to get it out?"

Before anyone could answer, the fat purple cockhead split down three seams and flower-petaled open. The interior pulsed a vivid hot pink, with darker violet lips around a slit in the center.

"Too late." Liv put one hand over her mouth. "It's anchored in now. We'll just have to hope –"

The sex started for real.

Imagine being on a trampoline in an earthquake with the world's largest sound system vibrating a deep bass backbeat all the way into your bones. We got tossed around helplessly as the cervix bulged in and dimpled out around the giant starfished cockhead, each time letting a little gush of water through. A few dozen strokes into it, I realized the dick had found its rhythm, which let me predict and minimize the bouncing. Liv and Julia caught on too, and we managed to keep from knocking skulls.

"I hope he doesn't take as long as you," Liv shouted over the gut-shaking sex-throb.

"I just hope he pulls out!" I shouted back.

The pulsating dick-blossom swelled even larger, its thrusts speeding up.

"Fuck!" Julia cried. "I don't want to drown in mermaid cum!"

Twitching and trembling, the flesh of the cockhead actually glowed, pink light fighting against the green of Bubbles' bio-illumination.

Orgasm.

The slit at the center opened up – wider and wider –

And a football-shaped casing about twice NFL regulation size shot out and stuck to the far wall, clinging there as if it had been glued.

My shoulders and back unflinched. I could see Liv's and Julia's do the same.

"Is that it?" the ghost asked.

I looked from the pearlescent object to the cockhead, now shrinking and folding itself up. "I guess ... maybe mermen prepackage their sperm?"

The giant glans pulled back. The cervix went concave at its tug. I waited nervously, hoping we didn't get flooded with water when the guy withdrew.

Except that he didn't withdraw.

"She's not letting him go," Liv said. And sure enough, I could see the sphincter clenching around the tugging purple bulb. It pulled again, and again, but the cervix only squeezed harder. "Why isn't she letting him go?"

I turned and eyed the pearly casing. I looked up and around at the dimples lining the womb.

"She hasn't come yet."

Just then, the retreating cockhead relented and pushed back in, bulging the disk around it inward, bouncing us all off the ground. I scrambled over and started collecting up my scattered clothes.

"I don't think Bubbles is a she. I think she's a dude and that's an egg, like seahorses."

"Seahorses?" Julia asked, tottering at another thrust.

"The male's the one that gets pregnant," I said. "When that egg-layer makes her come, I bet every dimple in here is going to gush whatever a mermaid uses for semen."

Liv got to the hoodie she'd bundled all her stuff up in. The womb shook with its most violent pounding yet as the trapped not-quite-penis thrust desperately again and again in the merciless grasp of Bubbles' cervix.

Then, just like that, the cockhead popped out, and glistening white fluid drooled from every pore in the hollow globe around us. The floor trembled like a cello string, but without the violence that had rocked it during intercourse. Mostly the semen ran down the walls, a few dribs and drips spattering down on us – less viscous than human cum, and smelling more flowery than bleachy.

By the time it got to my ankles, I was worried.

"Does it look to either of you like it's stopping?"

"No," said Liv. Julia shook her head.

A runnel dripped down and slunk along my eyebrow. I wiped it away with one hand.

"Oh, great," Julia said. "*Now* look what."

On the wall opposite the cervix, that football egg had grown to at least twice its original size. Where the semen-flow hit it, the fluid piled up and rolled across its top – but seemed to get absorbed along the way. Nothing dripped from the casing's underside. As I watched, the thing expanded like a slowly inflating balloon.

"Super. It's a race between choking to death on jism and being crushed by a mermaid egg."

"Maybe we should pop it?" Julia asked.

"With what?"

She shrugged, then wiggled her shoulders and stepped hesitantly toward the growing ovoid. I felt like I ought to join her, not let her approach it by herself. But I didn't have much luck convincing my feet of that, and I stayed where I was, watery ejaculate climbing up my shins as the ghost goth reached her hand out to touch that pearly surface.

"It's soft," she said, pressing her palm flat with the fingers spread. I could see the membrane give around her hand like dough or clay. "Don't think it's going to crush us, not if –"

Then her hand popped through.

"Hey!"

She pulled at it, but the surface had sealed around her wrist, and when she put her other hand on it for leverage, that one popped through too.

Shit. This gets better and better.

I hurried over and caught Julia by the armpits, trying to pull her loose. Liv came too – but our efforts only stretched the ballooning egg outward in our direction.

"It feels like air in there," Julia said. I could see the muscles of her forearms work, as if she were wriggling her fingers or wrists. The egg had gotten big as a car now and showed no signs of stopping. "I can't believe Bubbles would get us killed just so she could fuck some guy. I'm gonna put my head through and see what's in there."

"Holy shit, Julia, we only met her a couple of hours ago. We've had what, five minutes of conversation with her? What makes you think she wouldn't?"

She looked over her shoulder at me. "I just don't think this is that kind of place."

Then she took a deep breath and shoved her face up against the skin of the egg. It bulged around and then enveloped her to the base of her neck.

Liv and I now actively inched backward to keep from being engulfed.

"I was right," came Julia's muffled voice. "It's fine in here."

The cervical side of the womb was approaching fast. Liv looked at me helplessly, her dark face dribbled with milky fluid.

"Should we just go in?"

I kept backing up, glancing behind myself. "Geez, I don't know. It looks like the decision is about to be made for us, but ..."

Julia's elbows and biceps shrugged our hands away, and she dove forward through the casing in slow motion. "Come on, guys. It's dry in here. There's no cum."

Liv rolled her eyes. "All right, I've had enough."

Crossing her arms and squeezing her eyelids shut, she turned her back to the membrane and leaned against it. Julia had already disappeared most of the way through, and now Liv followed her.

That left me by myself in rapidly narrowing space with cum up to my waist – and rising as the volume on my side declined. I grimaced when I realized I'd dropped my clothes to help Julia. *I'm sure not going diving in this goo for them.*

Shuddering, I shut my eyes and pressed into the rubbery surface ahead of me.

CHAPTER ELEVEN

"See?" Julia asked. "It's nice in here. We're going to be fine."

The hair-matting streaks of mercum had vanished from her black-and-purple goth locks. Looking at Liv, I saw that she was dry too, and clean. A couple of pats to my face and stomach said the same was true for me. The membrane had absorbed every drop of Bubbles' semen as we passed through.

From this side, the egg casing looked bluish, and it came to me as I noticed the dark polka-dots in the blue that I was seeing the womb, not the shell. Either the cum had turned it translucent or the pearly surface outside served as a two-way mirror.

"Hey, our clothes." Liv knelt and touched her bundled-up stuff, then opened the hoodie to take things out. "They're dry too. I'm getting dressed."

I didn't need any encouragement to scout around the egg and find my own stuff. My shoes and shirt and jeans all poked partway through the floor. But one sock had fallen out of the shoe, and I could see it trapped between the membrane and the uterine wall, too flat to push into the egg, I guess.

I dressed quickly, looking around with still-frayed nerves. A knobby structure toward one end of the space made me think of a nucleus or a yolk. I was about to point it out when Julia noticed something more important.

"She's dilating."

Sure enough, one pointy end of the football shape had come to rest at the center of the cervix, which now gave way in a series of slow contractions and relaxations. I finished tying my shoe and sat down.

"I bet this is going to get rough again."

"Oh, god," Liv said. She came over and got down next to me. I put my arms around her.

Julia sat down too. Bubbles had already dilated to five or six feet – and things accelerated from there.

Seven feet, eight feet, nine feet, ten ...

And then without warning, the sphincter relaxed completely and we shot out through a flash of blue vagina into darkness.

The egg tumbled upward. It was like being in moon bounce during a hurricane.

We all screamed.

Then everything steadied, and above us, glowing with soft blue markings all along her body, Bubbles smiled down through the darkness: immense, powerful, her black hair flowing and floating away into an ocean of shadow. She brought us up to her lips, indigo in the night sea, and gave our little vessel a reassuring kiss.

"You could have warned us about that!" I shouted.

The mermaid let out a deep whalesong laugh, turned her head upward, and put the great length of her tail to work.

* * *

On the surface, beneath a starry purple sky, Bubbles cradled the egg between her breasts and pinched open a hole for us to crawl through.

"Tell me, really," she said, laughing a more human laugh now, "would you have gone inside me if I'd let you know how you'd be getting out?"

"Hell no," I said, scrambling between her finger and thumb to exit the ovum.

"See? So I saved your life, because the storms would have swept you over and I could never have found you in all the dark and waves and wind."

I couldn't really argue with that, and once we were all out, the mermaid pulled her fingers loose, the egg resealed itself with a snap, and she tossed it over her shoulder into the sea.

"You're just throwing that away?" Julia asked. "Isn't it going to be a baby?"

"Yes, and I *hate* babies." Bubbles made a face. "They're all *grarr* and those sharp baby teeth and bulgy eyes, ew. Let the fish worry about them until they're five or six and ready to start nursing."

I was beginning to understand why M had told us we'd get out of our depths if she didn't send us to the receiving station. The afterlife was a fucked up place.

"Anyway," our mermaid said, shuddering the image of merbabies away, "we're past the storm zone now, so we've got eight or ten hours of smooth swimming until we reach the bogs. Settle yourselves in and relax. I promise I won't have sex with anyone else for the rest of the trip!"

Her head went back down, and we felt the gentle roll of her tail propel us forward.

"I feel like I ought to feel like I need a nap," Liv said. "But I'm not tired at all. Do you think it's just the adrenaline rush, or is it this place?"

"The orientation lady told me you never need to sleep here," Julia answered. "You can if you want. You just settle down and close your eyes and think about resting. The dreams are really good, she said."

"I'll take her word for it." The likelihood of being able to sleep seemed slim to me anyway.

Liv stretched out on her back. "Well, I'm going to give it a try. If you two don't want to join me, you should probably get it on a couple more times while I'm out, right?"

I glanced at Julia. She gave a nod that acknowledged the point but didn't go much beyond that. If her eyes had had pupils, maybe I could have told whether she liked the idea but felt awkward about it, whether she hated the idea but knew it had to be done, or whether her sex drive simply hadn't had a chance to kick back in since our last shot. But her belly had rounded out even further, and her breasts looked very soft and full, underlit by the blue illumination from Bubbles' glow-dotted skin.

"We'll, uh, we'll see how it goes," I told Liv.

But a few minutes later, she was snoring, and a few minutes after that, Julia and I were having sex again, the ghost on top rolling her gravid tummy against mine, while I watched Liv's face, peaceful and perfect under the stars.

* * *

Despite the somewhat gross and definitely unsettling part of the trip spent in Bubbles' uterus, by the time she extended her arm as a bridge for us to debark, I found I could have done with another day or two of travel by mermaid. It wasn't that Julia and I ended up having sex three times in the night, because that felt good but made me emotionally uncomfortable. It was much more the peacefulness of it, the slow passage of a starry night, watching Liv rest, occasionally talking to Bubbles when she would lift her head. She had an odd but attractive sense of humor, and she made me feel like the universe was stranger than I thought but in a good way.

But what made me most reluctant to end our trip by mermaid was the greenish-brown morass of the Bogs of Indolence, stretching flat and gloppy off as far as the eye could see, with only the length of Bubbles' sleek blue arm between us and its glistening muck.

"Are you sure we won't sink in that?" I asked, standing in the hollow where her clavicle met her deltoid.

"Haha, just to your knees or so. Don't put your shoes on or you'll lose them."

Liv scanned the featureless mire beyond the mermaid's hand. "How will we know which direction to go? Are there any landmarks between here and the Fields?"

"Well, at first you'll just walk straight away from the water here. Then you'll probably lose your bearings and wander in circles for a bit. And then eventually, you'll run into one of the bog people, and if you can convince them it's worth the effort, they'll give you directions or call a serpentrain for you."

"I'm not going to ask what that is," I said. The smell coming off of the Bogs didn't strike me as unpleasant or foul – I wouldn't have called it swampy, more earthy. But everything about the look and the name of the place suggested a steeping sump of amoeba-infested water where clouds of gnats or mosquitoes could be expected to swarm you at any moment.

"That's okay," Bubbles said. "I like surprises too!"

"Thank you for the ride," Liv told her. "I kind of wish we'd be coming back the same way so we could see you again."

The great blue lips that could have swallowed any of us whole broke into a smile. "Everybody sees everybody again. The fun is whether you recognize who you're seeing."

I thanked her too, and we walked down her arm to the hand. Julia jumped in with her shoulders all tensed, like someone jumping into a swimming pool when they know it's too early in the season. But she relaxed once her feet disappeared in the mud.

"Huh. It feels kinda good, actually."

Liv took a deep breath and stepped off one foot at a time. After a few experimental steps, sinking a bit deeper with each one, she looked my way and nodded.

"Come on – it's fine. We should get going."

Considering that both of them were already in the muck, I didn't have any way to delay without embarrassing myself. I stepped in, felt the thick, gooey sludge swallow my feet, and once again cursed Bill for ever telling me about that amulet.

"See?" said Bubbles. "Easy as pirates."

Then she was waving. Then she was turning back toward the mouth of the estuary she'd swum up to get here. Then she slid below the surface and was gone.

And there we were, the three of us alone again, nothing obvious in sight for miles. Bubbles knew what she was talking about – the mud came a little short of my knee, hit almost right at Liv's, and lapped a little over Julia's.

"Well this sucks," said the ghost, trying to wade and barely getting anywhere.

Liv glanced at her, mouth crimped. But she didn't say anything.

"Sorry," Julia said. "I'll shut up about it." She put a little more effort into her wading and started making headway.

"So..." I said, waiting for Liv to slog after Julia. "How were the dreams? They live up to Julia's orientation hype?"

She looked down at her mud-swaddled knees. "I don't want to talk about it."

But she took my hand as we got moving, and the tension that stiffened the air between her and Julia got lighter – at least from my perspective. Which was good, because every step through the mud made me feel like I had fifty pounds of weights on. After a seeming half-hour of labor, I cast an eye back over my shoulder and saw the lapping waters of the estuary, maybe sixty feet behind us.

I opened my mouth to say something about being glad we had eternity, since the trip would obviously take it. But Liv spoke first.

"I'm hungry." She rubbed her stomach and looked my way. "Is anybody else hungry?"

"No," Julia said. "Still dead."

Not sure if that was a joke, I said, "I guess I'm a little hungry. Doesn't look like we'll be eating anytime soon."

"Bubbles said we could drown if we fell in the water. I wonder if we could starve too."

"God, I hope we're not in this swamp long enough to find out. I'd really like to get out of here today if we can."

Liv laughed. "I love that you're more worried about how icky the swamp is than about starving to death."

We struggled onward. Although I hadn't ever gotten sleepy the night before, my legs quickly became exhausted. All three of us were huffing and wheezing by the time we got out of sight of the water.

"Break time," Julia gasped after a while, leaning over with her hands on her thighs. She had it the worst of us thanks to her shorter legs. "Woosh. I sure ... hope Bubbles was wrong about us wandering in circles for hours."

"Maybe we should just skip that part," Liv said, "and go straight to looking for one of these bog people."

I turned around a couple of times. Nothing but muck in every direction, except that way out on the horizon behind us lay a thin line of sea. Here and there, the mud piled up into *very* gentle mounds – no more than six inches high that I could see.

"That would be great if there was anything to look for, or at."

"They could be under the surface, like ... mudfish? Maybe we should just holler," Liv suggested.

"Can't holler," Julia said. "Too tired."

I worked up a deep breath, put my hands to my mouth, and shouted, "*Hello!* Hello, is anyone here?"

Nothing.

We got our wind back and moved on.

* * *

"Ow."

The noise came from one of the mounds as I walked along its edge, where my shin hit something solid. The something felt uncomfortably like human flesh, and I tried to jump back, but only succeeded in losing my balance. With both feet held deep in the muck, I fell on my ass and made a gruesome *splat* – gruesome because it was the sound of thick green-brown mud adhering to me from the back of my head all the way down my spine to my butt.

"Oh, for – god *damn* it."

I had a sudden flash of myself as a caveman stuck in the La Brea tar-pits, with the mound revealing itself to be a sabertooth tiger, also stuck, but at least not going to its final resting place with an empty stomach. Thankfully, Liv and Julia hurried over as best they could and helped me up before I could sink in any deeper.

"You okay?" Liv brushed some of the clingy gunk from my back, or tried to. Mostly it just smeared around and tugged at my shirt, thick and heavy. "What happened?"

"There's something in there," I said, pointing at the mound. "Or someone. Hey! Is somebody in there? Can you hear me?"

I didn't get an answer, so I started carefully skirting the low mud-bulge. It was roughly oval, about as long as a body. Near one end, I saw a dimple in the rounded slope. Closer inspection revealed a depression just the right size to hold a nose and mouth.

"Is somebody there?" asked the mouth. Its voice came out soft and with a bit of an exhausted rasp, too quiet to tell if it was a man or woman's.

"I just asked you that. Yes, somebody's here. Is there a whole head in there? Can you sit up?"

"If somebody's there, I can't hear you. My ears are full of mud. Do me a favor and clear away the mud on my eyes, would you?"

"Can't you just –" *Never mind. He can't hear you, remember?*

With my upper lip curling like a poked caterpillar, I reached down and ran a finger from the tip of the nose along its bridge toward myself, making a little trench on the way. Then I gently wiped to each side, lower and lower, until the curve of a couple of eyelids could be seen. The mud cooperated a lot more than I expected, more or less sloughing away as I pushed at it.

"Great," said the mouth. With the nose clear and the brow and eye area showing, it looked pretty male. "Now go ahead and open them for me."

What the hell? Are they glued together by this crap? I reached down a couple of times, but kept pulling my hands back, not wanting to pry open the guy's eyelids and flood his eyes with mud. Also not wanting to touch him any more than I had to.

"Okay, well if you're not going to open them, cover them back up and let me get back to relaxing."

I growled and forced myself to put a fingertip on one eyelid, gingerly increasing the pressure until I could brush the lid open. The eye immediately blinked and squinted, then both eyes squinched tight before opening again. Surprisingly, none of the surrounding slop oozed in; around their brown pupils they stayed completely white.

"Criminy!" said the face, flexing angrily. "You couldn't open them both? Do you know how hard it is to keep just one eye open? Now you've gone and made me work practically every muscle in my face."

"Look, I'm sorry," I said. "I just –"

"Still can't hear you, and if you don't lean over, I can't read your lips either."

Well out of the bog-face's view, Julia said, "This guy's a dick."

"Shh." I glared at her and then bent over the face. Trying to exaggerate my lip movements, I said, "We're sorry about disturbing you, but we need help getting to the Dionysian Fields."

"Fields, huh? Need a serpentrain for that ... I'd have to whistle five or six minutes to call one up. What's in it for me?"

"Uh ..." *The satisfaction of helping some nice strangers out?* I hesitated to ask what a dude buried in mud for eternity would possibly want that we had.

"For crying out loud," Julia said, wrenching her way over step-by-step. She came in on the other side of him and leaned her face into his field of vision. "We've got nothing to trade. If you want me to, I'll have sex with you. That's about the best we can do."

"Sex? That sounds like a lot of work. I'd have to get out of the mud, or support all your weight on my hips ..."

"Good god," Liv said. "No wonder they call them the Bogs of Indolence. People here are too lazy to open their own eyes or let someone fuck them?"

"Why don't you jack me off instead?" the face continued, oblivious to Liv's words and maybe to her presence entirely. "And if your friend screws you over my face while you do it, it'll save me the trouble of coming up with a fantasy."

Liv shook her head. "Wow."

"We'll do it," Julia said. "And that'll be enough for you to whistle up a ride for us?"

"Jeez, Julia, you might ask me before –"

"Yeah, that'll do," the face said.

"– you go offering me up for a sex show."

"It's not like we don't have to do it a bunch more times anyway."

I couldn't really argue with that, and ordinarily would have been deterred by the way she scowled her impatience at me. But ...

"Right – except these aren't exactly the conditions I'd pick for sex – a mud pit? It's ..."

"*Tell* me you're not going to say 'unsanitary.' After we did it inside a mermaid uterus?"

I shut up. Before I could think of a retort, the bog person said, "You might want to get to it. I'm really starting to feel like closing my eyes again."

"Come on," Julia said, walking into place with her legs wide on either side of the sunken head. "You won't be getting your junk in the mud or anything. Just slide in behind me and do your magic. I'm betting it's been forever since this dope worked up the energy to get himself off. It probably won't even take all that long."

When I glanced at Liv, I got a shrug and a permissive tilt of her head. "Really, what else are we going to do?"

"Ugh."

"Oh, thanks," Julia said as I shifted around behind her. "That makes me feel great."

In spite of several other things on my mind, the words hit my guilt spot, which made me even more aggravated. "That's not what I meant."

"Yeah, I know. I just want you to get your ass moving."

She bent at the waist, putting one hand down into the mud mound ahead of her, searching.

"What's up with the limp noodle?" asked the mud guy from between Julia's legs. His eyes went from my face to her crotch. "Are you not seeing what I'm seeing?"

"Give me a minute, would you?"

But he didn't respond to the request, because his attention stayed on the hovering vagina and pregnant belly above him instead of on my lips.

Well take a cue from him then, I told myself. *You're damn sure not going to get hard watching him lie there drooling in a pile of mud.*

"Aha. Found it."

"Ooh! You found it!"

"Yeah, I just said –right, he can't hear me. So what's the deal, Tim, is anything happening there or not?" Her head tilted my way, but she couldn't quite turn enough to make eye contact. She had her left hand down to support her weight, I guess on his thigh, and I could see her right shoulder roll a bit as she did something out of sight beneath the mud.

That's not much help either.

"Like I said, give me a minute." Shuffling forward through the mud, I tried to keep focused on her ass and twat, ignoring the face underneath and the wanking on the far side. In the position she'd taken, she gave me a really good view – her whole posterior basically thrust up above straight legs with her low-hanging pregnancy visible between them. Mud kissed and released the curve of her belly whenever she worked her shoulder, making a little sucking smooch sound each time. I got my pants down below crotch-level, then took hold of my penis and tried to tug it to life, but the mud and the staring eyes of the bog guy ...

"Tim, come on. He's really stiffening up in my hand, and it's making me horny as hell."

Grimacing, I stepped in close. *Goddamn, couldn't the angle at least be better?* To get anywhere, I had to set my feet far apart and go into a partial squat with bent knees. That put my crotch at about the right level. I leaned in and tried rubbing the head of my cock into Julia's slit. It made me chub up a little, but not nearly hard enough to go in.

She squirmed at the touch, though. "Yeah. There. Let's go."

Sparked to life by the eagerness in her voice, my dick thickened and pressed forward against Julia's crease. Her dry outer lips didn't exactly welcome me, but touching them throbbed me a notch harder.

"Fuck, yes, put it in her," said the buried man, close enough that I could feel his breath on my balls, which unnerved me. "Faster with the hand, please ... yes, a little faster ..."

With my right hand still muddy from wiping out his eyes, I only had my left to work on my erection and on Julia's still-not-wet labia. I'm not a big fan of going in before a woman is totally ready, but the mouth had started panting on my scrotum, and I knew I had maybe a second or two before things started going limp again. So I got some spit on my fingers, wet her vulva down, did the same to my tip, and leaned into her as quickly as I could.

"Nnnf!" Julia said.

"Dude, that's so hot! Plug her!"

"God, would you shut up?" I only said it because I knew he couldn't hear. It made me feel a little better. Julia made me feel a little better too – actually a lot better, pushing back against me with her plump bottom so that her cunt gobbled me deep as it could.

"Faster! Faster!"

Which one of us is he talking to?

If it was me, he was out of luck. Bumping Julia's ass and thighs any quicker would almost certainly push her off balance, and if she collapsed forward, odds were good I would go too.

"Yessss," she groaned, her spine rolling and her right hand working feverishly under the mud. My knees didn't much like the strain I had them under, but there was nothing I could do about it except pray I somehow managed to come before the shakes set in.

"Ooh, yeah, baby ..."

Mud sucking at my legs. A lazy muck-slug gasping and sex-talking into my ball sack. A woman who completely screwed up my wonderful girlfriend squeezing my dick in her vagina. My wonderful girlfriend standing nearby thinking who knows what ...

I wonder if this is the worst sex anyone has ever had?

But it wasn't, because no matter how crappy the atmosphere and circumstances, Julia's ghost snatch felt like heaven. (Probably because that's sort of where we were.) And it also wasn't, because just as I had that thought, I heard Liv choking back a laugh over to my right.

You'd think that would be the final straw, and I'd completely deflate. And I was ready for that to happen when I reflexively looked over at the sound she made. But when I saw her with one hand over her mouth, trying to keep quiet, my cock surged stiffer than ever inside Julia.

"What?" I asked, exasperated and yet exhilarated to see laughter in her eyes.

Her hand moved just long enough for her to say, "Honey, I've never seen anyone so miserable to be having sex in my *life*."

Then she clapped it back over her mouth and closed her eyes, shoulders shaking. Even with my cheeks burning, the sight of her happy, together with Julia's moaning thrusts, tickled me right to the edge of orgasm.

"Yes, yes, grab it there – squeeze it *there*."

"Tim – I think I'm –"

"Oh yes, this is it ..."

Holy fuck, I'm going to –

Without warning, a whale-spout of cum blasted up out of the mud, higher than my head.

I screamed and threw a hand up to keep the explosion of semen from raining down over my face. Julia screamed and contracted throbbingly around my cock, her vaginal walls a trembling vice. The bog guy screamed and blew another gout of brown-streaked jism skyward, and then another one. The stuff spattered down all over Julia's back and hair – thankfully, almost none of it reaching all the way back to me.

"*Uhhh!*" she cried out, banging back against me in a spasm. The impact tottered me off balance, and I grabbed at her waist to keep from falling backward. But I overcompensated, and she fell forward and I fell forward on top of her. "Shit – fuck me ..."

The mud surged up around her belly and in between her legs, lapping at my scrotum. A thick film of cum squeezed and spread between my stomach and her ass and back. I put a hand to her shoulder to try to push back and up, but it only slipped on a giant gobbet of spooge.

"Oh god," I said, gravity and inertia plunging me all the way up into Julia even though every nerve in my body was trying to recoil.

"*Hurry,*" she urged me, her face barely out of the semen-streaked mud over the bog man's hidden crotch. "Don't waste it, Tim, come *on*."

Mud and cum were everywhere, sticking my body to Julia's, clinging to her pregnant belly and down-hanging breasts, dappling her black-and-purple goth-locks. It made my skin crawl – and yet my dick felt so close to orgasm that I knew I still had a chance to get there. I just had to make up my mind and focus.

Fucking hit it, damn you. The shit's already all over you, just do it.

So I did. I gritted my teeth, grabbed Julia by the tits, and started humping. Cum and mud smeared slickly between us and made noisy sucking sounds with every stroke I pushed into her. Her body bucked and moaned beneath me as I moved. Swamp gunk lapped up into the hot, wet juncture between our groins, and the sweet, textured throat of her vagina swallowed and caressed my thrusting cock – tight, luscious, feminine, lustful, lovely –

I came.

The filth in which I lay, and the wet, loamy smell of the swamp around us, and the bleach-and-sweat cum-stink of sticky ejaculate coating my front, joining my shirt to Julia's back – all the nastiness of the moment zig-zagged through my body, through my brain, down to the tips of my toes and back up to a gas-burner in my nut-sack, pressure-cooking sperm and glandular fluids together into a great, hot, spouting orgasm that convulsed its way out of me and into the grasping clutch of cunt that held and surrounded my manhood. My spine arched and tossed my head back, throwing limitless blue sky across my vision as I groaned and emptied my prostate into the pregnant ghost-girl beneath me.

When it was done, I dropped forward onto Julia deliriously, feeling my forehead clunk into the back of her skull, not quite hard enough to hurt. I lay there huffing and panting, my chest and lungs expanding out of sync with hers. It didn't even occur to me that I had my entire weight on her – or that both of us lay atop the bog man.

"...fucking...crushing...me..." he gasped. After a moment or two, the source of the words registered, followed by their meaning. I rolled exhaustedly off of Julia, landing on my back in the sucking mud. She crawled to the other side and flopped down too.

"...so...tired..." said the bog man. "I could sleep...for a month now..."

Exhausted or not, that got me moving like a poke from a stick.

"Whoa, no," I said, jumping back up. Okay, not so much 'jumping' as clumsily extracting myself from the mud. But it was as quick as I could manage, for certain. "Nobody's going to sleep – you've got to call that serpentrain, right?"

He yawned and frowned. "I guess I did say so. But I wasn't expecting you two to lay all over me and wear me out."

"Dude, that's bull. Get whistling, or I'm going to dig you out and make you walk us to the train station."

"Oh, all right," he groused. Then he pursed his lips. A brief six-note tune bird-chirped out of them, then repeated, then repeated again, and kept going with only a pause for breath every few bars.

I shrugged out of my shirt – the back caked with mud and the front dripping semen. For a second I thought about trying to wring it out, but the thought only made me shudder, and I ended up throwing it aside without looking to see where it landed.

"You okay, sweetheart?" Liv asked as I hitched up my pants. Her eyes whispered sympathy, but I could see her mouth struggling to hold off a smile.

"I need a bath," I said. "A very long bath." *And then maybe some of that Wine of Forgetting.* Although the thought came naturally, I kept it in my head instead of saying it out loud. The reason we needed the wine in the first place was not exactly funny.

"We'll get you one as soon as we can," she said, patting my shoulder. I won't say that her hand on my skin felt better than the orgasm I'd just had. But it was close. Especially when she left it resting in place.

A few minutes later, the serpentrain showed up.

* * *

Obviously, being a role-playing gamer, I had my share of dog-eared paperback fantasy novels on my shelf as a teenager. Some of my favorites were the Conan books, despite Conan being not that nice a guy. And the copies of the books I had – yeah, they're actually still in a box somewhere in my garage, so I shouldn't be using the past tense – all featured mega-testosterone covers by Frank Frazetta, the most bad-ass fantasy artist of all time. And the bad-ass-est of those ten or twelve covers showed Conan in a prison of some kind, chained to the floor with this subway-train-sized snake about to try to eat him. The reason it's so bad-ass is that Frazetta made that snake something nobody in their right mind would want to be on the same planet with, much less in the same room with, much less manacled to the goddamn floor in front of – but when you look at the picture, despite all the tension and ominous lighting and unbreakably thick iron links of Conan's chains, you can't help but think, *That snake is toast.* You can't even see Conan's face in the picture, but that's how bad-ass Frazetta painted him. He's chained up with a ninety-foot monstrosity that wants to swallow him whole, and you know he's going to kick its ass.

If I had ever doubted it before, the serpentrain made me completely certain that I am no Conan the Barbarian.

For starters, when the thing snuck up on us, I screamed like a teenage girl getting carved into porterhouses in a 1980s slasher flick. It was *fast*.

Between me spotting it, drawing a breath, and actually getting out my girly shriek, the snake went from fifty or sixty feet away to curled in a circle completely around us and close enough to touch. Its back rose almost to my shoulder height, and while I stood knee deep in mud and it slithered along right at the surface, that still put it maybe four, four-and-a-half feet in diameter. A number of disturbingly larger bulges swelled its cylindrical body outward here and there. Its head, which it thankfully kept at ground level, had about the dimensions of my computer hutch if it had been laid on its side.

"There you go," said the bog man cheerily, putting an end to his whistling. "Be a pal and cover my eyes back up before you get in, okay?"

"Get *in*?!"

The guy still couldn't hear, so he didn't answer me. But the snake did.

"Don't worry," it hissed, black eyes the size of cantaloupes glittering at me. "It's just like being snug in your mud bath, except you'll have to hold your breath. And I do all the work, on the way in and the way out."

"Oh, *hell* no," Liv said. "I'm with Tim on this one. No way am I letting myself get swallowed and shitted out by a giant snake."

"New arrivals, huh? Trust me, you'll find it's a lot more work hanging onto my back than cozying up in my belly. And everybody says coming out is like a full body massage. Just lie down and close your eyes and we'll be to the baths in maybe twenty minutes."

"Twenty minutes? We can't hold our breath twenty minutes!"

"Of course you can, silly, you – oh, wait. *She'sss* obviously dead, but are you two badgies? Right, I see it on your rib cage now."

I grasped at my badge reflexively, suddenly needing to make sure it was still there even though the snake had just said so.

"Yes, it's right here," I said, pointing once I felt it in place. "We're alive. Do you need to see Liv's too?"

"No, no," the snake said. "Sorry to worry you. You can climb on right behind my head as soon as I swallow your friend. That's the easiest spot to get on and stay on."

"Look," Julia said, her arms crossed nervously over her front, "if it's okay, I'd rather ride up top with them, not ... inside."

"Sorry," it hissed apologetically. "Afterlifers travel roughage class. I turn my digestion off while I'm working, but I still get hungry without enough in my tummy. I promise, it's really not unpleasant at all."

"Yes, but –"

"Ding, ding! Serpentrain is departing!" With a ripping sound where it broke free of the mud, the vast snake reared its head twelve or fifteen feet up and back. Julia squeaked and cowered, throwing her arms in front of her face. Before I could so much as open my mouth, the creature struck, plunging snout-deep in the mud with its maw engulfing our ghost completely. I caught a half-second glimpse of her feet sliding away into its throat as the head came back up – then she was just a struggling bulge moving down the scaly neck. A long, black, forked tongue flicked out and back in, and the lipless jaws smacked. "Sorry about that. I'm not exactly on a schedule, but there are other folks inside who are expecting to get to the baths soon, and I hate to make them wait. Are you ready to depart?"

The head settled back to earth as it spoke.

"I, uh, I have to cover up this gentleman's eyes first," I said, moving as slowly as I could around toward the bog man's face.

"Sure. I'm peristalsing your friend down into my first stomach anyway, so you've got a second."

As Julia went all the way down, I scooped mud back over the guy's eyes – probably unnecessarily, since he'd already shut them and seemed to be snoring, and the surrounding glop had started flowing back into place. But it let me avoid watching the serpentrain finish swallowing.

"There we go," it said. "Hang on, and I'll make it easy for you to climb up."

With a few slithery back-and-forth motions, the creature wallowed its throat deeper into the bog, until the peak of its upper spine had dropped a good foot and a half – low enough to swing a leg over, which, reluctantly, Liv and I both did.

"All settled in? Good. First stop is the apple tree!"

A laugh skipped out of Liv's mouth. "You can't seriously think we're going to eat apples that a talking snake carries us to!"

"Haha, no, we're going straight to the baths. That's just a joke I use on new arrivals if they seem Judeo-Christian."

"Hilarious," I said. The mention of apples reminded me that I was hungry, and then the idea of having to pick them and eat them with my mud-covered hands made me cringe, and now I didn't know whether to be relieved or aggravated.

"Off we go!"

* * *

Despite the rippling back-and-forth of the serpentrain's body as it propelled us across the mud flats, the head and our portion of the neck stayed perfectly straight and level. With no real landmarks and an almost featureless brown-green surface, the bogs made it hard to guess how fast we were going – but there hadn't been any wind near the guy who'd whistled the snake up for us, and once we got to cruising speed, a pretty strong one blew my hair back from my face.

Liv had settled in behind me after I got on and now rode with her arms wrapped around me and her chin on my shoulder.

"You all right?" I asked her.

"Yeah." Her eyes were closed. "I was just thinking what it would be like to be one of these bog people."

"Really? Because I'm completely baffled. Why the hell would anyone want to spend eternity stuck in swamp goo?"

She peeked through her eyelids at me and laughed a little. The movement pressed her breasts against me in a way I found comforting and warm. "I guess I should have figured that, with your thing about germs. But I bet there aren't any germs here, and I actually thought the mud felt good around my feet. I can totally see it. You know, imagine that feeling when you're lying in bed on a Sunday morning, snuggled under the covers, cozy and relaxed and knowing you don't have to get up anytime soon. You can just rest there and enjoy being all cuddled in. Only here you're in a soothing mud bath instead of in bed. But it's the same thing, and you can just *be*, just let sleep fade in and out over you, tug you back down into dreams for a while, then float you back up."

"I didn't think you liked the dreams you had here last night."

A deep breath and a sigh. "No, I liked them. They were wonderful. Sort of *too* wonderful, because when I woke up, I didn't feel like I was ready for the things I'd been ready for, in the dreams."

I itched to ask her what that meant, but she'd been so evasive that morning, and I didn't want to pry if she wasn't comfortable talking about it yet.

But I'd already forgotten that someone else was there.

"Dreams!" said the serpentrain. "I *love* hearing about the dreams people have here. How did they go?"

"I don't think she wants to –"

A hand tightening on my stomach stopped me.

"No, I do ... mostly. It was a little too weird with Julia here earlier. But I guess she can't hear, right?"

"Not above my rumbly tummy and all the muscle-curling going on around her. Your secret's safe – let's hear it!"

"Well ..."

I lifted a hand from where I held onto the snake's scaly back and covered Liv's with it. "Only if you want to, honey."

"Sure. It's just a little ... racy. But I guess we've let plenty of strangers in on more intimate stuff the last couple of days."

"Ooh, racy and intimate!" hissed the snake. "Even better!"

Liv wiggled her nose and gave me a tighter squeeze, then started. "So, it was one of those dreams where you're back in school. High school. But instead of just being my high school, it was Julia's too, and she showed up in the nerd brigade I hung out with and tried being our friend. But she was kind of a bitch."

"Big surprise," I muttered.

"Right, but it was that high-school-outcast, insecure, bitter and lonely kind of bitchiness – the kind where you cut down people who are trying to like you because they're the only people who will listen to you long enough to be cut down, and because you've got to put yourself above *somebody*. It's ugly, but you know – high school. And honestly, most of the group had at least a little of that, although it didn't show up in anybody but Julia in this dream."

The snake asked, "Was it nice seeing your old friends again?"

"It *was*," Liv said. "I haven't seen those guys in a long time ... none of us went to college together. But mostly the dream was about trying to get Julia to fit in. She was smart and intense and she had a good sense of humor even if it was too sharp sometimes. But I worked at it, and by senior year she'd gotten a lot better, and the two of us were pretty close, even though she'd stolen a couple of my boyfriends. For some reason, the fact that they let themselves get stolen clued me in that they were dicks, and since they were dicks to her too, she ended up having to break up with them anyway and then we could compare notes on what big dicks they were. So we had a lot of the same problems and frustrations, and –"

"Wait, seriously? I know you hung with the uncool kids in high school, but it's hard for me to see you making the kind of trouble for yourself I'd see Julia doing."

She tousled my hair, breaking some of the crust on the muddy part. "It was a dream, Tim. We had to be at least kind of alike if we were going to be best friends in it. But I really *did* have some of those problems in high school too. I didn't want to be mean to people, but when the macho jock types asked me out because I was hot, a lot of the time it was by saying things like, 'What are you doing with these losers, babe? Why don't you ditch them and come to the game with me after school.' You can't help but sass somebody when they talk to you that way, especially if you want to make sure they don't ever talk to you that way again. And if you date a clingy nerd guy for a couple of months and then break up with him because it's just not good, you have to be pretty firm and even harsh if you're going to stay broken up. So I wasn't as much of an anti-Julia in high school as you would expect.

"And in this dream, we more or less turned into peas in a pod. I worked at her enough to sand off most of her sharpest edges, and she rubbed off on me enough to give me a few more than I started with. By prom time senior year we were both no-date virgins and peeved about it. So we had a sleepover by ourselves, and that's where things got *very* not-the-way-they-really-were-in-high-school."

Weirdly, even though it was a dream, and even though I'd now had actual sex with Julia six or seven times, I felt a little jealous at where this was about to go. Which of course brought out my guilt complex. *What kind of jerk gets jealous over a dream?*

"Anyway, I woke up from this wonderful physical thing that I'd done with this wonderful friend, and there was the real Julia –"

"Ho, hey! Stop right there!" the serpentrain said, tilting its head but not turning it as it kept us speeding smoothly across the bogs. "That's kind of a big jump-cut, don't you think? You're not seriously going to skip the juicy details, are you?"

"I, uh, didn't really think Tim would want to hear them. He's my boyfriend, you know."

"A boyfriend who doesn't want to hear about his girlfriend getting it on with another chick? Look, I've been around the block, and I'm pretty sure that's the number one fantasy of guys who are getting laid regularly."

"Well, Tim's not your typical guy," she said, leaning her cheek against my shoulder. "But I'll tell if he wants me to."

"Tim, come on. Give a snake a break. It's not like I'm charging you guys for this ride."

I actually didn't ever fantasize about Liv and another girl – but she was the first one of my girlfriends that was true about. Once Liv and I got together, I didn't really need to fantasize about much of anything – and I certainly didn't daydream situations in which she was getting something from somebody else that I couldn't give to her. Too many scenarios already ran around in my brain in which she got tired of me and decided to leave; adding the possibility of her turning into a lesbian seemed like a bad idea.

But the dream had meant something to Liv. I could hear it in her voice.

So I pushed back my jealousy and my general discomfort about the notion of Julia getting *more* intimately involved in our lives, and I said, "I want to hear whatever you feel like telling, honey. If you can stand to watch me fuck her for real, I don't know why I should get to shut out you fucking her in a dream."

"You're sure?"

"Not a hundred percent," I admitted. "But you know I'll always listen if you're talking. And if you want to talk, you should talk."

"All right," she said. "Well ... I do. I don't know why, but it was so different, so *real* seeming – it makes me want to share it."

"Share away, sister!"

Liv laughed. "Okay. It was at my house, because Julia's parents knew it was prom night and Uncle Nate was clueless about that sort of thing, so we wouldn't have to listen to anybody saying what a shame it was that no one had asked us to the dance. Or maybe it was at my house because my subconscious has no idea what Julia's house looked like. Who knows. The point is, we sat around in the living room playing video games and watching movies until Nate fell asleep, and then we went up to my room and closed the door and took off all our clothes. Fast. I was really hungry for it. I wanted to see what Julia's body looked like, and I wanted her to see mine. I wanted us to be touching. I wanted to find out what it was like kissing a girl, and if it was any better than kissing the couple of short-term geeky boyfriends I'd had."

"Was she all gothed out in your dream?"

"Yes and no. She had her hair dyed and used a lot of black eyeshadow and lipstick. But when she got her clothes off, she didn't have the tattoo."

"Wait," I said. "Did she have eyes? It's just a weird picture if she didn't have eyes."

"She had them, but I don't remember what they looked like. Also, at that point I wasn't really interested in eyes – I had her whole naked body to be looking at. Her breasts were really small, even smaller than when you and I first saw them. But they were cute – I mean, *adorable* – and I giggled at them and she went red like she was going to get mad. So I asked if I could kiss them and she kind of nervously said okay. It was *so* fun smooching on them and getting the nipples to harden up, and my hands went all over her, and she was *soft*. Pretty quickly she started breathing funny and pulled away and said we ought to get in bed and kiss for a while before we really got into touching each other's parts like that. She wanted to turn the lights off too, and I said yes, but first I lit this candle I'd gotten from the kitchen downstairs earlier in the day.

"It was magical, sliding under the sheets next to her in the flickering candlelight. She looked all nervous, with her lip between her teeth, and I felt the same way, but burning hot too, and we sort of ducked and dodged our faces near each other, trying to work our way into a kiss. I finally just put my arm around her back and pulled her in and did it. Her lips tasted like gum. I put my tongue in her mouth to see if she was actually chewing some, but all I found were her teeth."

With mud all around and wind in my face and everything whipping by at high speed, the circumstances didn't exactly lend themselves to conjuring images from Liv's descriptions. But on the other hand, her words and her breath were in my ear, and her arms around me and her breasts against my back – and I had a giant snake head pointing out from between my legs. So despite the weirdness of it all and my unease at thinking about Liv and Julia together, I found myself getting hard pretty quickly.

"We kissed for a *long* time, just holding each other. And she was a waaay better kisser than any of my boyfriends up till then. I don't know if it was technique, or the size of her mouth, or just the fact that I wasn't worried about whether I loved her enough to be doing this with her – which is how I always felt with my dates. We were just two friends playing around, and the only thing I had to think about was what we were doing and how it felt.

"The whole thing had me super turned on. I kept catching myself moving my hand down across my belly toward wank-off territory. After the third time, I said, 'I'm going to put my hand between your legs.' She made a little noise and kept kissing me, and it was definitely a 'yes' noise, so I went for it. *Pow*, hand in between another girl's thighs, finding her and fingering her and thinking how different it felt with my hand turned that direction instead of toward myself, feeling a mons and a clit and wet lips against my fingers but only feeling it one direction because there weren't any fingers on my own bits. I had her groaning into my mouth in no time, and it felt ... I felt like a stud. I felt so *powerful*. Maybe if I'd ever gotten past second base with a boy, it wouldn't have been such a surprise and such a rush to just touch somebody and have them squirm like that. But watching her face twist and tighten up with the candlelight dancing across it while I rubbed her and diddled her with my fingers – it blew me away. I had to have more.

"So I pulled away from her face and slid down along her cute little body toward her crotch, and she tensed up some and said, 'Wait, what are you –' But before she could tell me to stop, I went down on her."

Her arms circled even tighter around me, and she said, "Honey, I hope to god that when you're doing that for me, you like it as much as I liked doing it for her in that dream."

"It's pretty good," I agreed, in a tone that made it clear I was understating things by a lot.

"It was like ... eating an ice cream cone that never goes away and is the exact temperature of your tongue and your lips. Or maybe like kissing the world's best barbecue chicken. And pretty soon she was screaming and coming and if it had been real instead of a dream, Uncle Nate would have woken up for sure and come to see what kind of disaster was going on in my room. But it was a dream, so she just went on coming and coming, and I just kept licking and kissing, and eventually we turned around so that her mouth was on me while mine was on her, and we just kept rolling over and over in the bed until we were both so worn out from coming that we couldn't move. Then we just lay there next to each other with our sweat cooling and our hearts pounding and I got her hand and held it and I was *so* glad no one had asked me to prom."

I shifted a little, trying to get my erection more comfortable with the spinal ridge of a huge-ongous snake running right underneath it. That part I more or less managed. I had a tougher time getting my feelings comfortable – happy to hear Liv so obviously enjoying herself talking about something sexual, but also wishing I could be a more direct part of it. The fact that she'd gotten hot in a dream, and had been able to enjoy normal human sex, made a part of my brain think she must be getting better – that the memory of her multi-hour continuous gangbang orgasm had faded and let her want something physical that I could give her. But I couldn't ask. I'd sound like a shallow, horny guy who just wants to get laid. Probably not to Liv – she'd know I was just concerned about her. But I'd sound that way to myself, so I simply didn't go there.

"Wow," I said instead. And I did really mean it. "That sounds like a pretty awesome dream."

"Sounds like a shortly awesome dream to me," said the snake. "I mean, very spicy, but usually people's dreams here go on and on and on."

"Oh, it did," Liv said. "When we got our breaths back, we did all kinds of stuff – scissoring and hand-jobbing and jamming each other off with cucumbers I went down and snuck from the refrigerator. We were totally uninhibited. It was like having one night where you're allowed to do anything, and we had an insane amount of fun. By the end of it we were some kind of expert lesbians, at least as far as technique and range of experimenting goes. We fell asleep nestled together in my bed, skin touching skin and closer than I'd ever been to anybody in my life. And I expected to wake up and do even more in the morning. But –"

I tried to turn and look at her, but she put her cheek to mine and I couldn't see her expression.

"Yeah?"

"But then I woke up for real, and there Julia was for real. Naked and pregnant and this person who fucked up my sex drive by giving me something so good that nothing else would ever measure up. And I was *mad*. Not just mad that she'd done what she did, but mad because ... some of the feelings from my dream had stuck. They'd stuck in my head, and I felt close to her, and I wanted to go over and hold her – not sexually, just, as friends who'd shared something. I wanted to tell her I felt *better* about her. Maybe even that I was starting to forgive her. Is that crazy or what?"

"I don't know." I shrugged. "Maybe this place kind of pushes your forgiveness buttons."

"It does," the snake sibilantly remarked.

"Well it shouldn't. I mean, does she really deserve to get off that easy? After what she did, and just because I had a dream?"

I didn't have an answer for that, but the serpentrain did.

"Forgiveness doesn't free the person who receives it," said the great reptile. "It frees the person who gives it."

"Huh," said Liv, processing the idea.

In the distance ahead, the baths appeared.

CHAPTER TWELVE

"Now, you're going in on the bog side," said the serpentrain, "so you're going to have to follow the bog-side rules."

We had pulled up alongside a huge Greek temple of a building, all columns of white marble and classical statues in between. The statues depicted human nudes in every shape and sex and form, usually by twos or threes, with one sculpture relaxing while the other(s) tilted pitchers over them. None of the figures had carved mud on them and none of the pitchers had marble water flowing out, but the washing theme made itself pretty obvious. From the main, raised body of the building, ten feet of marble stairs descended to the edge of the bog. Our ride had parked itself next to these and proceeded to shit out its other passengers.

"Bog side is for the Indolent," the snake continued. "That means no washing yourselves. The attendants will do it all for you. Ngn. Jeez, this guy's a big one."

With a flatulent blurt, the serpent's bowels extruded a tubby man my height or bigger, with very broad shoulders and a head-to-toe coating of mud and some glistening substance I didn't care to speculate about. The man rolled a short distance toward the stairs and then lay on his back whistling a brief musical phrase.

"Also, no walking around yourselves. They're really picky about keeping the place clean, and they don't want you tracking crap all over the place – yours or mine."

From a door beyond the gleaming colonnade, six people now came briskly down the stairs, all of them perfectly formed with healthy complexions and Captain-Kirk wax jobs, the hair on their heads immaculate and every muscle in their bodies seemingly tuned and just in place. Naked as the statues, they carried an oversized stretcher and several crisp alabaster tarps.

"I'm not sure I like the sound of someone else carrying me around and washing my body for me," I said. "Could we maybe sneak around to the other side and come in from the Field way? Are the rules there any better?"

Smartly, the bath attendants threw their tarps down on the mud between themselves and the fat man, walked across the fabric to him, rolled him over it and onto the stretcher, and then carefully drew the sheets after them, folding as they went in such a way that they ended up with the muddy sides on the interior and no hint of drips or drops on the outside. They had him halfway up the stairs by the time the snake pushed out another passenger.

"Uwuh," it said. "They're not big on rules at the Fields, but most of the attendants on that side are locals who'll be looking to score, and if you don't put out, they have a habit of directing you to the vomitorium instead of the bathing pools. But it doesn't really matter, because you can't get through the hedges. They're impenetrable. Which is kind of funny, because just about everything on the other side is very 'penetrable,' if you know what I'm saying."

"Great." The hedges in question ran off to the horizon in either direction from the sides of the bath-temple. I didn't bother to ask about climbing over them – not if it might earn me a trip to a vomitorium as my reward.

The second passenger had barely started whistling when another set of six attendants dashed out to retrieve her.

Liv watched all the comings and goings with a curious frown. "So who becomes a bath attendant for all of eternity?"

"Sometimes people who've spent all their lives as servants and don't know anything else. Other times people fresh out of super-modest cultures, who want to get their hands and their eyes on as many naked bodies as they can. As far as I can tell from here, they cycle through pretty quick. I don't think it takes long to decide they're ready to reincarnate and get on with eternity somewhere else. Okay, here comes the next one ... grkk..."

"And what about you and the mermaids?" she asked. "How'd you get here?"

"Wouldn't you like to know! Ahh." Another muddy bog-person eased from the serpent's rear orifice. "There have to be some mysteries in the afterlife, don't there? Everybody needs something to wonder about if they're going to be happy, in the long run."

The second passenger had been spirited up the stairs by now, and the first team returned to head for this newest snake turd.

"Okay, here comes your friend," the serpent said. "Head on down next to her and you can all wait for the porters to carry you in."

Reluctantly, I did as the creature said – not at all in a hurry to be up close when Julia got disgorged by a scaly sphincter. Liv went with a bit more speed in her step, calling back over her shoulder on the way.

"Thank you!" she said. "You've been very helpful."

"Sure. Sex stories always put me in an amiable mood."

"Glughhh!" came Julia's voice from farther down the elongated body. I couldn't help glancing at the sound, and saw her head protruding first as the serpentrain excreted her. "That's got to be the worst economy class anybody ever traveled."

We reached her about the time her second foot popped loose. The snake hissed a farewell and serpentined away in a flash as the team of attendants bore the previous passenger through the door at the top of the stairs.

"Wow," Liv said as Julia got to her feet, drenched head to toe in some kind of gooey grey secretion. "We all need a bath, but you win the prize."

"Uh-huh," she scowled. Then she looked up at the bright marble temple above us. "I guess at least we're in the right place."

* * *

Despite Julia's snake-slime coating, Liv made me go first when the next set of attendants showed up.

"I can practically see your skin crawling from here," she said. "And I'm barely dirty at all above the knees, and Julia can wait her turn a lot better than you can, I'm sure."

Julia moved her arms out from her sides at that, snake mucus making a momentary web between the right one and her abdomen. When it soap-bubble broke, she looked up and said, "Whatever."

So I took the first ride, six polite but untalkative Venus and Adonis types bearing me on a very comfortable stretcher at a very comfortable angle despite the steepness of the stairs.

"Is there a self-service area?" I asked them. "I'd really rather –"

"No, but thank you for asking," said the woman at the stretcher pole over my left shoulder. I didn't try any further conversation.

The door behind the columns swung open for us, revealing an airy, spotless entryway ringed with white marble arches. Each arch wore a set of draperies – sheer and pale aqua and rippling as if with a breeze. The whole place murmured liquidly in a voice of water, running, lapping, splashing. My porters veered toward the middle left arch, and as the first two passed through, the drapes splashed across their heads and shoulders: curtains of tinted water, not cloth at all.

As soon as the water sluiced across me, I felt cleaner. Caked mud ran off and sank into the fabric of the stretcher. Along a brief hall, through another couple of cleansing paper-thin waterfalls, and down three gentle steps, we came to a bath, rectangular and tiled in sunny sky colors and about the size of two king beds end to end. My team of attendants walked straight down the graded tiles into the pool, letting the stretcher fall slowly away as I reached water level, where they transferred their hands to my shoulders, arms, and legs before I had any idea what they were doing.

We kept moving at exactly the same speed. The water felt rich and cool against my back and tickled along my sides as if it couldn't wait to get at the dirt on my front too. Halfway along the pool, without warning, the man at my right shoulder reached up to pinch my nose shut, while the girl by my left leaned and clamped her mouth over mine. I could feel her naked breast against my collarbone as we all dipped eight inches or so, fully submerging me. But before I could react to that or to the unexpected shock of her breathing into me, we rose again, and I surfaced, feeling another layer of sweat and soil and sludge wash away. She straightened and kept carrying me forward.

I ought to have been freaking out – a gang of naked strangers touching me, squeezing my nose between their fingers, *breathing* for me. But instead, all I could think was, *Holy shit, these people* really *know what they're doing.*

Maybe there was something in the water, a topical anesthetic or antianxiety drug. Or maybe it just felt really, really good – supernaturally clean. Whatever it was, the combination of the water, its perfect temperature, and the sure, strong hands of the attendants turned a switch in me, and I just relaxed, let them carry and float me through another half-dozen chambers of colored and clean-scented or lather-covered waters, sometimes cool, sometimes warm, sometimes half a degree short of too hot.

I may have fallen asleep at some point – I have no idea how much time passed before Liv's voice broke my sanitized haze.

"Hey there, squeaky clean."

I opened my eyes. We floated in a crystal green gel, viscous but not sticky, about three feet from each other.

"How long have you been there?" I asked, but even as the words came out, I recognized soft footsteps fading away across the tiles behind me.

"They just put me in. I have *never* been this clean."

"Yeah. It feels really good."

"Maybe the staff take turns bathing each other like this whenever they don't have customers. *That* would explain why they'd pick this place for their afterlife."

"Mm-hmm," I said, keeping my eyes on her dark, still form, hovering at ease in the gel.

She reached over and touched my nose, leaving a fingertip-sized wet spot on the end. "What's with the staring?"

"Oh, come on," I said. "You know. You're the most beautiful thing in the world – or in however many worlds this place is. I can't help it."

She smiled and flicked her eyes to where my body extended lower into the green fluid. Well, most of it was extending lower. "And I guess you can't help that either?"

"No, and I'm too relaxed to be embarrassed."

More footsteps behind us, this time coming nearer. Liv twisted her head. I just sighed. *And here comes Julia to tie off a perfect moment.*

Sure enough, a band of attendants appeared in my peripheral vision, stepping into our crystal-green pool and lowering Julia's shiningly clean body in beside me, opposite Liv. When they let her go, she floated there with only her face and the crest of her belly above the waterline.

"Oh my god, I am so clean," she said, keeping her green eyes closed.

I waited for the bath staffers to leave, but as the last of them moved back toward the steps – a sleekly muscled Asian guy – he noticed what Liv had been teasing me about.

"Do you want to have sex?" he asked.

"Gah – um, look, I'm flattered, but –"

"No, not with me. With one of them." He nodded at Julia and then at Liv.

My lips and eyebrows compressed, "Well if I do, I think that's my business, isn't it?"

The other attendants had paused just out of the pool.

"Not here it isn't," he said, waving them back toward us. "No one's allowed to exert themselves at the Baths of Indolence except for us. Which of them would you like to make love to first?"

"No. Really, no, that's not –"

"I can't," said Liv to the Asian dude. "But the two of them should. She's getting ready to rebirth – that's what everybody keeps saying, right?"

"Yes, that's what everybody keeps saying," I replied. "But –"

"Tim, when are you ever going to get the chance to have sex with someone without either of you having to move a muscle yourselves? I know when, the same time as I'm going to have a chance to see it – which is never, if you don't say yes now. And I notice Mister Happy-to-see-me down there isn't saying it's as bad an idea as you are."

I closed my eyes. *Give in, dude. This is bizarrely hot.* "Okay. Whatever."

Before I could figure out what I wanted to ask them to do, one of them rang a bell on a pull-cord and the others slid into the watery gel with us. My eyes opened reflexively, just in time to see the guy beside me make a series of gestures to his teammates, so that they hopped-to like everything that happened next had been choreographed and rehearsed for a Broadway show.

An Indian woman knelt between me and Liv, scooping her hands down under the water as though ready to support my ass with them, but not yet touching me. Four others surrounded Julia, taking a leg or arm apiece. The last guy held back while the quartet maneuvered our pregnant ghost out through the pool until they had her toe-to-toe with me, at which point they slowly eased her forward, legs spread, closer and closer – I thought – to my now-granite-hard cock.

But when her feet passed my knees and hovered at about mid-thigh, the attendant who'd stayed back dove smoothly under the water, all the way to the bottom. Once there he went belly up under my right leg, then grasped, lifted, and extended it until it pointed right into Julia's crotch. As he folded the little toes under, the others repositioned Julia fractionally, until the soft hood of her clitoris just brushed the tip of my big toe. The two statuesque men on leg duty each had one hand under a knee and one on a hip, and they now gently rotated Julia's pelvis to orbit her slippery vulva against my toe-tip.

"Oooh ... this is fucking crazy," she groaned.

"Shhhh," whispered one of her marionetters.

After a minute or two of clit-teasing, the guy beneath my leg flexed my ankle and sent the first knuckle of my toe up into a plush embrace. More groaning, and louder.

Slowly, Julia's attendants rocked her hips, riding her onto and off the knob of my toe.

"Fuck, I'm going to come ..."

As if that was a signal, they popped her loose from my foot and rolled her shoulders up out of the gel, folded her legs at the knee, raised her, carried her forward, and aimed her submerged vagina straight for my ramrod-stiff cock. Just as her lips touched my tip, I felt the Indian woman's hands cradle my ass and push up, helped by the guy who'd been fucking my toe into Julia a moment before.

They brought her down and me up at the perfect angle, slipping us together like a flesh key into an angel-soft ignition.

"Guhuhhhuuhhhh..." she said.

Now, I really like woman-on-top sex, and Liv really likes it too. So we do it that way a lot. But this was about as different from anything I'd ever experienced as you could get while still involving a vagina sliding up and down around a penis. For starters, the guys holding Julia scowled at me the second I moved my own hands, which reflexively wanted to reach up and touch her. So I went still and forced my arms to relax. They settled her all the way down until our groins touched flush and pressed together – and those were the *only* parts of us that touched. With her legs angled to barely avoid any contact with my hips or thighs or abdomen, I was buried to the hilt inside of her but could feel nothing except her cunt and the solidity of her pubic arch.

And I couldn't thrust up to meet her either. My legs floated in the gel with nothing to leverage against. Same with my spine and shoulders. If I tried to stroke my hips forward, it would only lower my head into the waterline. My ability to penetrate and withdraw depended entirely on the hands of the two attendants beneath my ass.

Meanwhile, Julia's bearers held her steady in the throes of her orgasm, which pulsed around my cock and brought more whimpers out of her for several seconds. Once she came down and her breathing steadied, the entire team gently, sensuously collaborated to ease us into a rhythmic intercourse – first of millimeters, then of inches.

The feel and temperature of the gel made it seem like my entire body was inside Julia's pussy – but better than the slide of sex I'd taken into Bubbles' womb by a lot. My partner rocked limp and blissful in their grasp above me, her eyes closed and whispered moans escaping her lips. Kneading fingers worked my buttocks as their attached palms raised my pelvis to meet Julia's. The absolutely effortless glide of vaginal flesh around my cock pushed me into a blinking, gasping daze.

Several more attendants arrived, summoned by the pull-rope bell that had been rung earlier. They glided into the water next to us and lifted my arms, positioned my hands, let me cradle Julia's breasts and caress her burgeoning stomach.

"This would be worth a fortune online if I had a camera," Liv said. I thought her breath caught a little as she spoke, but it might have just been the lapping, amniotic gel by my ears. I looked over at her to find her eyes wide as I've ever seen them. "Is that as good as it looks?"

The attendants swaddled my cock deeply into Julia with a long, strong thrust.

"Ooh – it's – mmn-hhh – it's pretty darned good."

"Hush," said the black guy at my right arm, who'd lifted it slowly up to trace the fingertip around Julia's lips and then insert it between them. I felt her humming with pleasure around it as she sucked it deeper and ran her tongue along it.

Slow, low waves rolled out through the pool at the same pace as our languid sex. The thickness of the gel petered them out quickly, but I saw them rising and reaching farther as the staff of the baths stepped up the pace.

"Olh glod," Julia mumbled around my finger, her brows knitting together. I could see her trying to work her hips, to drive herself more firmly against me – but the attendants loosened or tightened their holds just enough to foil her every time, keeping us on their schedule instead of letting us set our own. "Uuh, I need to come…"

"Soon," whispered a woman at her ear.

I could feel things starting to happen in my balls and in my groin. Julia's beautiful depths moved along the rigid, anxious beam of my cock like something magical. "Ooh … uhhh."

Faster by a hair, and faster by another, the attendants brought us apart and together, my hands puppeteered across Julia's face and shoulders, around and down her rocking, fleshy waist, into the gel to press against her wide-spread thighs as they undulated in the grasp of her manipulators. We both gasped and groaned with almost every stroke now, and no one bothered to shush us.

"Oh god, so close," she said.

"Ngh – yes – me too ... ah ... *ah* ..."

And then the strong hands that held us rotated the entire world in a second, and I found myself above her, plunging into her at a rapid-fire pace that would have exhausted me if I'd been making the effort myself. The swell of her tummy glanced against my navel with every full-length insertion of my cock into her cunt.

"*Oh shit!* Ah! Fuck! AHH!" Julia writhed in their grasp beneath me, the muscles of her neck standing out, her tremors threatening to dunk her head beneath the surface except that the flawless muscles of the attendants wouldn't allow it.

A fountain of luxuriant seed burst out of me inside her, as if my semen had transformed into one of the dozens of bath oils or lotions or gels that had been worked into my skin over the last several hours. The watery voice of the bathing temple called out in ripples to its silent brother fluid that gushed from my balls to Julia's uterus. I squirted and spasmed at the same frequency as the waves ringing their way across the surface of our pool.

"AH! *Sheez* –"

"So good ..."

"...fuck..."

"nghh"

The attendants' motions subsided with the lowering gasps of our breath. They wrapped my arms around Julia and brought my face in close to hers, aiming our lips together as surely as they'd done with our genitals.

"Wait, *wait*," I said. "We're not –"

Liv spoke at the same moment that the hands paused. "No, go ahead. That deserves to end with a kiss, Tim. If you don't it'll be like cutting off Bohemian Rhapsody before the gong note."

Julia's eyes opened, pools of emotionless monochromatic green. But her lips opened too, wantingly, and suddenly she was someone I felt very close to, who needed something. And it was weird because I had no desire to kiss anyone except Liv, and yet it felt right because of how the tension flowed out of her the second our mouths touched and made their soft, wet embrace.

It didn't need to last very long, and I didn't let it. But Julia looked very peaceful when I lifted my lips up from hers. Something about that turned over a warm sensation in my chest.

"Are we ready to get dried off and find the Dionysian Fields?" I asked.

"Yes," she said. Her fingers slid up and over her full belly. "I think I'm readier than I ever was for anything in my life."

Cripes, I keep forgetting she's dead. I've got my dick in a dead girl.

For some reason, it throbbed and swelled inside her at that thought, and she raised her eyebrows.

"Are you sure *you're* ready to get out and dry off?"

"Uh..."

Liv yawned on the far side of one of the attendants.

"Well I'm worn out just watching that," she said. "If you want to do it again, I'm going to have another of those warm-oil backrubs – assuming some of you kind folks would like to help me?"

A few of the staff moved instantly toward her.

The rest didn't even ask, but just maneuvered me and Julia apart and began repositioning us with expert care.

CHAPTER THIRTEEN

Whatever the hell they use for fabric softener at the Baths of Indolence, I would be a gazillionaire if I could patent the formula. When the attendants gave us back our clothes – after toweling us off and then doing a final air-dry with giant palm fronds – I'd have sworn they burned the real ones and made exact copies from some kind of cloth woven out of clouds. I half wanted to kill myself for throwing that shirt away back in the Bogs of Indolence just because it was covered in cum.

Liv repeatedly smoothed her t-shirt down over her breasts and stomach after pulling it on. "They don't make stuff this soft for *babies*."

"Or for ghosts either," Julia grumped.

"Here." Liv tossed her the hoodie that she had no use for in the perfect temperatures of the afterlife. "Just don't get ghost sweat all over it. I want to take it home when we're done and see how long it stays like that."

The jealous expression on the ghost's face changed to something else as she caught the jacket. Guilt? Gratitude? Both? I still found it hard to tell, with those eyes.

"Are you sure? I was just –"

"Wear it," Liv said, pulling on one leg of her jeans. "It'll save me from having to carry it around for a while. Ooh. Oh, that's good."

Julia ducked her head and put an arm into the hoodie. "Wow."

We finished getting our clothes on and looked toward the exit of the dressing room. I wasn't sure why the bath staff had left us here to change on our own, after doing absolutely everything else for us. Maybe it was to reduce the chance of us having second thoughts and asking for another series of massages or scrubbings. Or another round of hand-crafted sex.

The thought definitely tempted me. Through the other door, we'd supposedly find a passage to the Dionysian Baths if we went right and the Fields if we went left. Assuming M had assessed Julia's condition right, back in the bookstore, the three of us would need to hang out in the Fields long enough for me to screw our pregnant ghost another four or six times. Then she would "rebirth" – however long that took – and then we'd have to find the Wine of Forgetting for Liv.

And once we did, would it make her forget enough? Or was there a risk she'd forget too much?

If Liv's memory got blanked back to before she met me, what were the odds I'd be lucky enough to get her to fall in love with me a second time? Especially if she woke up in an afterlife paradise full of guys who looked like the ones in the Baths of Indolence?

But we couldn't hide in the bath temple forever, and even if we could, the idea of asking Liv to do that, with part of her broken the way it was ... well, it occurred to me, but I couldn't possibly give it serious thought.

Julia rubbed the sleeves of Liv's hoodie along her arms as we stood there. She'd left it unzipped – it wasn't exactly sized for maternity wear. For some reason, the way it fell aside around the curve of her pregnancy settled something in my head.

"Okay. I guess we should get going."

* * *

The door at the far end of the hall opened onto a classical Greek portico, semicircular, with marble tiles and columns in an opulent combination of blues and off-whites and lavenders. And it almost opened into a minotaur humping this fat chick doggie style.

"Oh geez, sorry," I said. But he was snorting and pounding her too hard to notice, and she squirmed and squealed so vigorously from the schlonging of his bull's pizzle that I decided I'd have to raise my voice to get her attention at all. Which I certainly wasn't going to do.

So we snuck along the wall in the opposite direction and hurried down some stairs, leaving behind his snorts and her grunting and the oscillating waves of her fat rolls and enormous, down-hanging breasts.

The stairs took us off the portico to a green grassy yard bordered in hedges and populated with a half-dozen picnics and orgies and picnic/orgy combinations.

"I guess this place is not where people with lots of inhibitions come to spend eternity," Liv said.

No kidding, I thought.

Spread before us on the park-like lawn was a pornographic array of humans and mythological creatures indulging in just about anything that could be indulged in. I saw satyrs having sex with leaf-haired nymphs, guy centaurs having horsey sex with girl centaurs, human guys having sex with girl centaurs, and even, scarily enough, human girls having sex with guy centaurs. And just when I thought all the centaur combinations had been taken, I saw a woman with an enormous strap-on moving lustily toward the up-tilted rump of a centaur mare. *Please don't let there be any cherubs having sex,* I thought. *That will just be way too creepy.*

Nearby lay a harpy with her wings spread flat against a checkered blanket, eating apple slices that a man dangled down to her mouth while another guy licked honey from her breasts and a third knelt between her bird legs, plowing away at whatever she used for genitals. I didn't look close enough to see if it was a cloaca. Paths of white steppingstones curved around and through the green swards where all this fucking took place, and also wound their way through gaps in the hedge ring. As we stood there taking it all in, a powerfully built dude in a toga came through the nearest divide, laid eyes on Liv, and immediately drew the front of his sheet-dress aside to reveal a burgeoning erection.

"Whoa-ho, hotness! You look new ... can I be the first to welcome you to the Fields?"

I stepped in front Liv and said, "Thanks, you just did, and we appreciate it."

The man, curly-bearded and curly-haired, leaned a little to try to make eye contact past me, saying, "Sure, no problem. Maybe later, after you've settled in?"

Liv raised her t-shirt enough to let him see the badge against her ribs. "Sorry, but we're not staying long."

The guy dropped his toga and raised both hands in front of him. "Oops, pardon. People who come to stay are usually happy to get propositioned right out of the gates. I wasn't trying to be rude. Is there someone you're looking for? Something I can point you toward?"

Yes, any source of information that isn't hot to put the moves on my girlfriend.

If he'd been a little less good-looking – or had been ogling Julia instead of Liv – his helpful blue-eyed expression might have made me feel bad for getting defensive. But as it was, I couldn't relax even with the change in his demeanor. It didn't help that his erection remained jauntily tent-poled against the front of his toga.

"We just need a quiet spot to help our, uh, friend do her rebirthing. And then we need to find some Wine of Forgetting."

"Gotcha." He turned and pointed across the yard – past a female cyclops being fisted by two guys at the same time. "That fourth path will take you through the Woods of Amorous Underbrush and eventually to the Letheside Vineyards. Plenty of shrubbery in the woods you can hide behind for privacy. Just watch for shaking bushes so you don't interrupt anyone else's trysting."

"We're also hungry," said Liv. "Is there anything to eat along the way?"

"Well, you'd be welcome to join any of the picnics here – but they'd probably expect you to *really* join in if you did. There are fruit trees all over the place, though, and you're welcome to help yourselves. There's also a pizza buffet about halfway through the woods."

"Pizza sounds good," Julia said.

It really did – if disorientingly anachronistic.

"Thanks," I said, forcing myself to offer a hand for him to shake, since I felt uncharitable and he'd turned out to be so helpful.

"Think nothing of it," he beamed – grabbing the hand and using it to pull me into a back-slapping embrace instead of just a handshake. His hard-on glanced off my thigh in the process, for less than a second but more than enough to make me beet red by the time he let go. Then he looked at Liv and said, "Look me up if you come back this way after you've, you know, kicked off."

"We'll see," she said. "But I'm hoping to be old and wrinkly by then."

"No one has to look old here unless they want to. But even if you do, I'm game!" Then he waved and headed up the stairs toward the portico, the minotaur, and the fat woman, shucking his toga as he went.

"At least people are nice here," Julia said. "I *guess* I can deal with living like this for some chunk of forever."

Thanks to the penis prod and that overly enthusiastic hug, I was already wanting to rush back into the baths and ask for some hand sanitizer. But instead, I headed in the direction the guy had pointed, saying, "I'm sure you'll do fine here."

As we passed the threesome with the cyclops woman – who had a single central breast to go with her single central eye – one of the men servicing her had literally gone muff diving, with his head and one arm all the way inside that mammoth vagina. Even though she was easily twice human height, it still looked like a heck of a stretch, but by the way she bellowed, she must have enjoyed what he was doing. "*Ohhh ... nobody's done this to me before, and I've been waiting so long for it ...*"

The other guy lay nearby at loose ends, licking his forearm and hand in a way that made me queasy. He looked up as we passed.

"*Wait,*" he called out to Liv. "Would you care for a quickie before it gets to be my turn?"

"Busy with an errand," I said. "Sorry!"

Liv put a hand on my shoulder as I attempted to hurry her along – not to fight against my pull, but to tell me something.

"Honey, you don't think I'm going to take any of these guys up on this stuff, do you? If you don't remember, the whole reason we're here is my sex drive being crushed by high expectations."

I stopped, steaming at myself and at the perverted mythological menagerie around us. The blue sky and the green hedges and the yard full of murmuring, moaning lovers all made me feel like some things were simply out of my reach.

"No, of course I don't," I told Liv. "But it's just like I know if I wash my hands with a little soap, there's no chance picking up some Ethiopian food with my fingers will make me any sicker than eating it with a fork. The only difference is, I can live without finger foods, but I can't live without you."

She took both my hands and looked at me, her eyes searching and disturbed. "Why would you ever think you'd have to?"

"Oh, come on, Liv. Look at me and look at you. Don't you think it's pretty natural for me to be worried that someday somebody's going to come along who's younger than I am and better looking than I am and less of a germ spaz? And then my goose would be cooked, and you'd end up with somebody who really deserved you, and all I'd be left with is trying to be happy for you."

"Holy shit, Tim," said Julia, taking her hands from the hoodie pockets. "What an *asshole* you're being right now."

Suddenly Liv was the one standing in front protectively. "That's not fair. Tim can't help –"

"Bullshit." She stormed up to the two of us fuming. We'd made it along the path just through the gap in the hedges, and the cyclopean ménage a trois looked over at the sound of our raised voices. Then someone had an orgasm and they turned their attentions back to each other. "You are so full of bullshit, Tim. You think I can't tell every time you've fucked me how you feel about Liv? The times I was inside her and the times since we got here? Do you have any idea what I would give –" She hiccupped a little and sprouted tears from her eyes. "– to have somebody look at me the way you look at her? To have somebody who would fuck a ghost for me, fuck a freaky-ass monster chick in a hole human beings don't even *have* for me? Literally be ready to go to hell for me? And then you have the nerve to tell her that somebody else out there might *deserve* her more? And she's not even mad at you for saying such an asshole thing to her. *Fuck* you. If you don't 'deserve' her, who the hell can *I* hope to deserve? Because I'm a lump of shit next to you, Tim. And now I'm dead anyway, and nobody *ever* felt about me the way you and Liv feel about each other. *Jesus.*"

Putting her hands over her face, she turned away and just stood there shaking.

My hands still held Liv's loosely, and I looked from the ghost to her unbelievable brown eyes.

I felt every bit as much a dick as Julia said.

"She's right, isn't she?"

Liv gave a little smile and a squeeze of my fingers. "What, that you deserve me? Or that you're kind of being an asshole about it?"

"Okay, I'm sorry," I said. Then I looked back to Julia. "I'm sorry to you too, Julia. And I like you, you know? Obviously not as much as I like Liv, but I do. You're not an unlikeable person. And in a place like this, if you just try to let your nice side out, you're going to have guys all over you. Or minotaurs, I guess, if that's your thing."

She took a deep breath and lowered her hands, but didn't turn back around. "All right. Thanks."

"You're welcome. I'm sorry I can be such an asshole. I just — well, I guess I'm just too used to thinking of myself as the low end of the food chain."

Going up on her tiptoes, Liv kissed my forehead.

"Lie down, on your back."

"What? What do you —"

She pushed firmly on my chest, almost firmly enough to move me backwards, and she stepped in closer as she pushed.

"Liv, you're not —" I gulped at the expression on her face. "You don't have to —"

"I know I don't have to. I want to."

"But I thought —"

"Not sexually. I'm not horny or aroused, even a little. Just lie down for me and let me do this."

"You don't have to prove anything to me."

"Yes I do. Lie down."

She gave another push, and I gave way and reluctantly went down to one knee and then stretched out on my back. Kneeling between my legs, she took hold of my penis, which was in the same ambivalent condition I was.

"Give me a second to get this going," she said, "and then I'm going to tell you why I want it."

"Okay," I said helplessly.

She smiled at me, dropped her head, and gently took the soft tip of my glans into her mouth. I felt her suction simultaneously drawing me in and engorging the meat of my cock. With just a few wet, slurping strokes, she worked me up to a raging boner.

Then she angled her neck and deep-throated me, driving my tip past the root of her tongue into the squeezing, deep embrace of her esophagus.

Just as quickly as that, she withdrew, drooling along the shaft as she let it out, then dropping a fat ball of saliva on the end to run down it as she crawled forward.

She got her face over mine and her eyes over mine and her groin over mine. I felt the lips of her pussy find my sopping wet crown and part around it. Then she plunged down and sheathed my cock inside of her.

"Oh my god, Liv."

"Sh." She settled into place and put her hands to the sides of my head, holding it as though to keep me from looking away – not that I could have in a million years. "Tim, right now, this feels O.K. Physically. But knowing what it does for you feels *wonderful*. Some stupid knee-jerk part of your brain thinks that because I look the way I look, you don't deserve me. But how I look is just sex. It's just millions of years of evolution and a bunch of boob-marketing pop culture telling you what you ought to want to fuck."

She started to move. I groaned, trying to keep the sound quiet, trying to keep my brain functional enough to process what she was saying. But it was hard, because she felt so good, and a part of me had been scared that she would never want to do this to me again.

"I don't need a sex-drive to have sex with you, Tim." She didn't roll her hips or grind the way she normally would at the start of her-on-top sex. Instead, she worked me like she'd already come and knew I was close enough to make switching positions a waste of time: with long, powerful lunges of her body that took me halfway out and all the way in, sweeping plushly around my rigid cock in a glide of ecstasy.

"Liv ..."

"No, listen," she said, breathing a little faster with exertion. "Your brain is programmed to look at my face and my body and want sex. But I know that if I looked like Julia, or even if I was outright ugly, you would still want to do this with me. And even if we weren't going to get my libido fixed, I would be happy to do this for you every day for the rest of our lives. No guy *deserves* to have a girlfriend who looks like me – biology just tells your dick that it wants a few meaningless characteristics that I happen to have, by a fluke. But you, my dear, neurotic boyfriend, deserve to have a woman who wants to bring you joy, and that's because of the person you are. Do you understand?"

"Yes," I said, or kind of squeaked. "Liv, I'm going to come ..."

She dropped her face down nose to nose with mine and used her throatiest voice to say, *"Do it."*

And then she sat down and milked the most powerful orgasm of my life out of me. Dionysian Fields, Baths of Indolence, hundred-foot mermaids, mile-high penises shooting spirits into the afterlife – in that moment, Liv did what none of the rest of it had and proved Heaven to me. The universe became her face and contained nothing but perfect beauty pouring into every one of my senses and echoing back out in waves of pleasure like ripples from an endlessly skipping stone upon the still and deep waters of infinity.

When I floated back down into my body, I was gasping, tears running down my cheeks. Liv caressed them away one side at a time with her thumbs, smiling down at me as she did.

"Do you get it now?"

"I think so."

"Good." She kissed me, then wiggled her hips. "Then you need to felch this cum out of me and spit it into Julia so it doesn't go to waste. And then I want some fucking pizza."

* * *

I had sex with Julia three more times at the pizza buffet. It was apparently kind of the thing to do – when we got there, after an hour of walking along our path through the woods, half the women and a couple of the male patrons were bent across the tables, one plate of pizza before them, another balanced on their backs so that their partners had simultaneous access to dinner and receptive orifices.

"Oh, you two are so totally going to do that," Liv said as soon as the trees opened up and we saw the clearing and the tables and the diners and the doubly engaged diners.

"What? No. I can't eat pizza off someone else's back. It's demeaning and –" *and how would I be able to use my knife and fork with the plate jiggling back and forth?*

"Dude," said Julia, "I took a cum-shower from a guy I jacked off in a mud pit while you doggie-styled me. How exactly is a little pizza going to demean me compared to that?"

I closed my mouth.

Encouraging me forward with a hand on my bicep, Liv said, "Come on, honey. It will be fun and funny, and I'll feed you pizza while you're doing it if you want."

I let her tug me into the clearing, but said, "Do I need to be worried about how much you seem to be getting into watching me and Julia do it?"

"I *always* enjoy watching you do it. It's just that right now all I can really enjoy is watching, as opposed to watching and participating."

Across the way, a satyr with a ridiculous Italian chef's hat covering his horns saw us and called out, "Hey! How's about-a you come and getta youselves some pizza?"

"Oh my god," whispered Julia. "That's terrible."

Thankfully, after the one line in that hideous mock accent, he went back to what he'd been doing before, which was playing European cafe music on a set of wooden pipes. We walked over to the serving table, an enormous thing that ran fifty feet long if it was an inch and held every kind of pizza imaginable along with a couple I might have preferred not to imagine.

"Is that a whole rat?" Liv asked.

The chef lowered his pipes just long enough to say, "The harpies, they-a enjoy it thataway."

We got ourselves plates and several slices from the more conventional looking pies, then found an end of a table that wasn't too close to anyone getting boffed or buggered. I had an awkward time starting things up, with Julia kneeling on a bench to get her bottom at the right height, and all those people around, and the noises of screwing and eating everywhere, accompanied by the capering and piping of the goat-legged chef. But once Liv began feeding me pizza by hand, everything got easier.

Weirdly, I didn't have any problem eating food that had been held in *her* fingers, and it surprised me that we'd never uncovered that particular quirk before. It was sexy. Especially when she would close her teeth and lips on the pizza slice to take her own bite before turning it and offering it to me. Add that to Julia rubbing her ass-crack against my naked dick, and I got hard pretty quick, then got well into fucking her before we'd finished our first piece.

"Holy cow ... that's good pizza ..." I mumbled around a bite, bumping up against Julia's round tush as I chewed and thrust. "It's not just ... ngm ... me, is it?"

Liv grinned. "You mean it's not just being fucked while you eat it, don't you? Either way, you're right. This is some amazing pizza."

"Yeah, but it would go better with some finger on my clit," Julia said.

I tried to hunch over to get a hand down and around the smooth globe of her belly, only to have Liv push my hand back up to her waist.

"I'll get it." Moving our plate to the center of Julia's back, she sat down on the bench and reached easily beneath the pregnant tummy where she could stroke both of our crotches, from my scrotum along my sliding shaft and then firmly onto the clitoral hood just beyond me.

"Ooh," said Julia. "Ooh, mmm, ooh ..."

We went through another slice of pizza that way, a bite for Liv, a bite for me, a finger-tickle for Julia, a finger-tickle for me.

"I'm close," she moaned as Liv tucked a last bit of crust between my lips.

"Oh no," Liv said, raising an eyebrow at me. "My hand is getting so tired."

Quicker than I got what she was doing, her hand left our crotches and she swung up from the bench, took a turn around me, sat down on the other side. There, she got her right hand back in where her left had been a second ago.

"Ah, much better," she said, flexing the fingers of her now-free left hand as if to uncramp it.

"Uhh, yes," said Julia. "Much better ... ooh, there ... there ..."

With noticeably glistening fingers, Liv picked up the next slice of pizza, bit off a huge chunk of its vertex, and lifted it up toward me while she smiled and chewed. It smelled like cheese and pepperoni and cunt.

"Fuck ... yes ..."

"Are you *trying* to make this more difficult?"

She swallowed. "Oh please. Your mouth's been there a couple of times now."

I opened up and let her put the pizza in. Of course, she was completely right. If anything, the smell of Julia lingering on Liv's fingers notched my urgency up and got me closer to coming all by itself. At that moment, Julia climaxed and groaned around her own mouthful of pizza, her spine arching so that our plate slid down it into the little valley she'd made at the small of her back.

"GhhHmmm!"

Her spasms and the toss of her head pushed me even closer.

"Put the pizza down," I gasped at Liv, hooking a hand around her wrist and urging it toward the plate as I stepped up my pace within the pulsating cunt that surrounded me. She dropped the slice – my fingers encircled her wrist and my thumb rode up into her palm and I raised her hand to my face.

"Oh, fuck, Tim –" Julia grunted, her hips gyrating arhythmically. I breathed the smell of her in deep from Liv's fingertips. Then I closed my eyes and sucked those sticky, dark fingers into my mouth, where I could swirl my tongue around through pussy lubricant and pizza grease.

"*Mmmm* ..." I moaned, digging my grip in at the left side of Julia's waist, plunging hard into and against her, feeling the heat and tightness build just under the root of my cock. "Nnn-hhnnn ... *AH!*"

My mouth and eyes flew open, releasing Liv's fingertips and showing me her smile as I clutched Julia two-handed now and held myself as far in as I could go, throbbing, jerking, jetting out more life-fluids to enlarge her ever-more-pregnant belly. It wasn't the transcendent thing Liv had given me earlier, but it held me and squeezed me in its gorgeous grasp a good long while before it let me go.

At last I groaned and dropped back and out of her, stumbling on shaking legs to find the bench and collapse against our table.

"Holy ..." I panted.

Liv laughed and moved the plate from Julia's back to the tablecloth beside me. "Eat up and get your strength back. If I'm counting right, we've got a couple more to go before we're done."

I waved at her and took my time recuperating, mind blanked by orgasm and the accompanying cardio workout. Eventually, though, I found myself ready to eat again and looked around for a fork. No luck. I closed my eyes for a second. Then, I guess out of sheer exhaustion, I just picked up a slice of pizza and took a bite.

Liv gave an audible intake of breath.

I closed my eyes and chewed for a second, then mumbled, "Yeah, yeah. Don't say anything or I'm going to think about what I'm doing and then I'll have to stop."

* * *

Two plates of pizza later, Julia sucked my cock back to life and rode me to another orgasm. It wasn't as good as the first and getting there took twice as long. By the point I finally gushed, I felt plenty ready to move on and give it a rest.

But when Julia stood up and took a step, something made her grab her now-gargantuan belly.

"It just kicked. The baby just kicked."

"Baby?"

"*I* don't know," she growled, still holding herself. "Whatever it is that's in here. Me, I guess."

"Are you okay?" asked Liv. "Can you walk?"

"It didn't hurt or anything. I can try." But the second she took another step, she doubled up again. "Holy shit. That was my leg. I'm feeling myself walk, inside. Oh man, there is no fucking way I can go anywhere like this."

"Great," I said. I'd been getting my pants on so that we could head out for the Letheside Vineyards. Now I just shucked them back off. "Well, you're going to have to give me a while to get ready again."

"Yeah, sure," she replied, easing herself back down to the grass where we'd fucked just a few minutes earlier. "Ooh. Hmf. This is so fucking weird."

It didn't take me all that long to get it back up. Something about Julia's pregnancy nearing completion dialed my excitement up – not in a fetish kind of way, but in a light-at-the-end-of-the-tunnel kind of way, a sense of relief that my life and my girlfriend might be at least sort of back to normal soon. She was close. All this crazy shit was about to be done.

I did her kneeling between her legs. The "kicking" sensations apparently distracted her too much for the sex to get her off – she kept *ooh*ing and giggling, but it was because I'd bump into her legs and her legs would bump the inside of her uterus. At one point, she had me touch her belly while she bicycle-pedaled her feet in the air to either side of me. It freaked me out and turned me on at the same time.

Okay, Tim. Let's go, buddy. This time tomorrow you could be back in bed with Liv instead of screwing ghosts in fairytale land. I decided to go with that, closing my eyes and imagining it was Liv in front of me and enfolding me. Groaning. Calling out my name. A white light of hope clicked on inside that image, made its way down from my brain through my spine, then hopped across to my gonads and went brighter and brighter until I came.

Better than the second time, not as good as the first time, I thought, opening my eyes with the assumption that I'd see Julia's abdomen plump out even farther.

Instead, hot fluid gushed through her cunt, all along and past my softening penis, flowing out into the grass below.

"Oh wow," she said. "I think my water just broke."

* * *

When it became obvious that Julia was rebirthing, the pizza buffet cleared out with a mad scramble from the tables to the path that led back into the woods.

"...never seen one? Trust me, you don't want to."

"What? Yeah, I could close my eyes, but I can't close my ears."

"...gross. Just ... ew, gross."

"Grab your plate and come on if you want to keep your appetite."

"...think they could have found a better spot ..."

I called an apology out after that last one. "Sorry! First timers ..."

"What do I do?" asked Julia, groaning. I guess the contractions had started – I'd pulled out when she doused me with that amniotic slosh.

"I don't know – deep breaths or something, right?"

Liv looked around and saw the proprietor, who'd taken his hat off and set down his pipes. "Do you have any towels or something? Can we use the tablecloths?"

He waved the idea away and lay down by the buffet table with a yawn.

"Don't worry about it," he said. "Pretty much nothing you can do except help pull her out once the head and arms come free – I mean, unless you want to get *really* gross and wishbone her when she starts to crown. Otherwise you might as well have some more pizza before it gets cold."

"Agh!" Julia's hands flew to the top of her head and her face screwed itself up in agony. "What the hell – my fucking *skull!*"

Her legs kicked, spread wide in front of her bulging belly. Then one hand grabbed for her groin and dug the fingers in just above the vulva. "Ow! Shit, OW!"

"Please," Liv pleaded toward the chef. "We don't –"

But he'd already started to snore. *I guess we should just be grateful he's not up blathering at us in that terrible accent.*

I put a hand on Julia's shoulder and one behind her neck, which strained up away from the ground as her body tried to bend itself double with every contraction.

"Oh god, please make it stop!"

Liv settled warily in front of her spread legs. "What can I do, Julia, tell me what – oh shit."

From between Julia's thighs came this sort of meaty tearing sound, and then a goddamn *fountain* of blood. Liv had to jerk back to keep from getting splashed.

"*AAAAHHH!!!*"

"Oh my god, Tim, she's, like, splitting open down here ..."

I wanted to do something, but the best I could manage was supporting her neck and shoulders and holding down my pizza. *I am definitely not going to grab an ankle and get Liv to help 'wishbone' her.*

"SHIT! FUCK! *GUAHghuhhh* ..."

"I think I see the top of her head!"

Awesome. Let's get this the fuck over with.

I figured keeping my eyes on Julia's face would hide most of the gore from me and maybe let me comfort her if she opened her eyes at any point. Instead, as a series of wet, popping, bursting sounds came from Liv's end, I realized that the head in my lap was *crimping in* at its crown, folding and disappearing into itself.

"Oh crap." Somehow, despite the lack of blood, that sight grossed me out more than anything else so far.

"The head's definitely coming out ... god, there's so much blood ..."

With a horrible *slurp*ing sound, Julia's entire skull collapsed into her neck.

"Fuck!" I couldn't help myself. I dropped her shoulders and fell back away from her.

"Tim, Tim, come on, here she is!"

Right along with Liv's voice, I heard a gasp from between Julia's blood-spattered thighs, and then, "*Oh my god this hurts so fucking much!*"

Against every instinct in my body, I got up into a stoop and saw what was going on on the other side of that taut round belly. Julia's vagina had torn open well past her pubic arch, which itself looked ruptured at a cartilaginous joint down the middle. Sticking out from the bloody mess was her head, dripping red and just as contorted with agony as it had been at the end of her neck a moment earlier.

"Can you get an arm out?" Liv asked. I just hung there staring.

"Aah ... uhh – I don't – ow, *gnuhh*, shit!" The last combination came as her right arm reached up to what should have been the base of her throat and got sucked right into the sort of fleshy sphincter there. A bare second later, the fingers poked out along her neck. "Ow, no – I can't do this ... I can't ..."

Shit.

I knelt down by her shoulders again, getting hold of her right elbow.

"I'm going to try to help push, Julia, okay?"

"No – yes – I don't know!"

With a deep breath, I thrust the forearm down into the hole where her body was inverting itself. The first few inches went pretty easy and came out through the ruin of her cunt, freeing her hand. Liv grabbed it and squeezed.

"You're doing great, Julia," she said. "Keep pushing, Tim. I'm going to pull."

The upper arm gave me a lot more trouble. But with Liv grunting and yanking and me steadily shoving against the elbow and both of us trying to ignore Julia's screaming, we managed to slowly bow the humerus into an unnatural curve, and then her whole shoulder popped through like it was nothing.

"Uhh – uhh, give me a second," she panted. We took a momentary breather. Then her left arm started feeling its way up after the right. "Okay," she said, tensing up. "Okay, let's go ..."

The second arm took even more work than the first. I could hear her vagina ripping wider as we worked to force it through. *Thank god Liv's on that end. I'd have fainted by now if I was down there.* Eventually, with enough sweating and wrestling and shrieking, we got the left arm through.

From there, things actually went pretty quickly. I took hold of Julia's waist while Liv held both her hands, and we tug-of-warred until the rib cage sunk in my side and emerged from hers. Once the flappy flesh of her emptying belly disappeared into the swallowing sphincter, it became a process sort of like rolling a giant meat sock to turn it inside out, with the bloody gaping vagina as the rolling part.

When I got it down past her toes, the last of her old body disappeared into their tips, and Julia lay there gasping with her eyes closed. I duckwalked up by her head and looked at Liv, who knelt on the other side.

Shrugging, she said, "It's a girl?"

Julia snorted out a laugh, then a moan, then blinked up at us.

She had green eyes.

But this time, they were a normal green, with irises and pupils where they ought to be.

"If it had really described that part in the book," she said, "I would have closed it right up and handed it back to that asshole warlock without reading another word."

"No you wouldn't have." Liv poked her shoulder to show she wasn't being mean. "You would've just asked if he had a book on ghost epidurals too."

Julia sighed and sat up. Most of the blood ran off her, and she shook her hands to hurry the process along. I saw that her tattoo was gone. "Yeah, you're probably right. What a bitch. I don't know why you keep helping me. I mean, I know why, I just don't know why you're being nice about it."

"Force of habit," I said. "If you work at it, pretty soon you won't be able to help it any more than we can."

"Don't be a dick, honey. Look, Tim's right that it's kind of just who we are, but it's more than that too."

She paused as if searching Julia's face for words.

149

"I mean, we've been through a crapload of stuff together, right?"

"Yeah – most of it my fault."

"That doesn't matter. We've gotten mermaid slimed and dragged through the mud and spooged on and –" She turned her bloody hands outward. "–bled all over. And now bits of us are stuck to each other. I could work on pulling away and scrubbing you off of me. But then I'd just feel icky whenever I thought of you. I'd rather go ahead and let you stick, so at least I'll have the good parts of you to think about whenever I remember all this."

"Well, you don't have to remember, or you won't have to once we find this wine. You can just flush me away completely and not have to worry about your brain being cluttered up with all my shit alongside whatever couple of good parts I guess there are."

I made a face at that. "Cut that crap out, would you? That's the whole reason we're here, you know – you moping over everything you didn't like about yourself until you got so down on your own life and everybody around you that it made you start doing crazy shit. There's nothing wrong with you that you couldn't fix by admitting that there's nothing wrong with you."

"Whoa," said Liv. "Do I hear the pot calling the kettle insecure?"

Julia laughed – a nice enough sound to keep me from feeling too called-out by Liv's point.

She put a hand back on Julia's shoulder. "And anyway, I don't want to forget you. I want to forget the way I felt about you when you tricked me into putting on the necklace, and when you took me to that frat house. But ... I mean, look where we are, Julia." She gestured up and around, sweeping her hands over the blue of the sky and the green of the trees and grass. From somewhere down the path we heard laughing – the other buffet guests returning, probably, now that the screams from Julia's rebirth were done. "I know things I couldn't have known without you. I met my *mom*. Just for that, you're one of the most important people in my life. Why would I want to give you up?"

Tears tracked down through the sticky pink on Julia's face. She sniffled. "I'd hug you if it wouldn't ruin your shirt."

Liv didn't take half a second to lean over and pull her in tight.

* * *

Every table at the pizza buffet had several bottomless decanters of both wine and water. We moved to an edge of the clearing and used one of the second sort to rinse off Julia's rebirth blood. Since none of us felt the need for more food, we headed on along the path to the Letheside Vineyards.

Julia's hair was brown now, to match her pubic thatch. She also had armpit and leg hair, though not enough to be gross.

"I hope I'm not gonna have to shave for eternity," she said when she noticed the downy brunette haze on her legs. "It sucked enough doing it when I was alive. There better be some kind of treatment or something so I don't start looking like one of those goat guys below the waist."

For most of the walk to the vineyards, she nattered on like that. Now that rebirth was behind her, the reality of endless afterlife must have sunk in, because she discovered dozens of questions they hadn't covered in her orientation. Obviously, Liv and I had no idea where she was supposed to get a toga if she wanted one, or how she would apply for reincarnation when she got tired of eating and drinking and screwing here at the Dionysian Fields. "And why's it called the Dionysian Fields anyway? We've been walking through woods for hours now." I admitted that I had no clue, unless it was just because "Dionysian Fields" was easier to say than "Dionysian Fields and Woods and Vineyards and Pizza Buffets."

Mostly, though, Liv and I stayed quiet and just let our friend speculate.

And the farther we walked – and the softer the afternoon light fell through the forest canopy above us, and the more relaxed and natural Liv's hand felt in mine – the more that's how I thought of Julia: as a friend. She had passed beyond any ability to cause us more suffering or grief, and with the tattoo gone and her hair rumpled and brown, she gave off some aura of renewed innocence: childish curiosity, a sense of being in a world full of wonderful unknowns – everything that her cynical goth persona had denied. I really couldn't hear the change in her voice without feeling happy for her, and it's hard to be happy for someone without liking them.

So Liv and I followed her along the quiet path, listening to birdsongs as much as to the endless string of questions and guessed-at answers. I looked over at Liv a lot, and sometimes she looked back and smiled, or other times her gaze stayed out in the trees or up in the blue sky snippets that danced between branches overhead. The whole thing seemed unreal, including how beautiful she was, how perfect and flawless in spite of the bloody imprint of Julia's breasts across her front where they'd hugged. I halfway didn't want to go, and I wondered what they'd do if Liv and I just decided to stay here after she drank the Wine of Forgetting.

Duh. They'll keep propositioning us for sex, since that's the national pastime around here. And eventually we'll probably both start saying yes. It didn't take more than a second of imagining Liv getting it on with a minotaur – or me up to my elbows in a sheclops – to remind me that I really, really did want to go home. Peaceful and beautiful and dreamlike walk through the woods aside, when the path opened up an hour or so after the pizza buffet, my heart took an enthusiastic jump.

* * *

The satyr in the Italian chef's hat, with his half-dozen banquet tables and fifty-foot spread of pizza, had nothing on the Letheside Vineyards.

We came out of the woods to a wash of late-afternoon sunshine, streaming golden down a shallow hillside before us to a series of gentle slopes and a river that glinted police-light blue behind them. How far the vine-trellised hills extended, I couldn't tell you, but I'm betting it was miles. Hilltop chateaus and pillared monuments had been scattered about willy-nilly, along with wooden-staved vats ranging from hot-tub size to the equivalent of an aboveground pool. People were everywhere, picking grapes, stomping them in the vats, taking breaks to fuck in the stomped grapes, carrying great urns of purple juice uphill to the winery buildings or hauling bottles and tuns of wine back down. And drinking, of course.

Minotaurs and dryads and nymphs and fauns seemed about as common as human beings, followed closely by centaurs and a dozen other varieties of part-A-of-human-stuck-to-part-B-of-animal creatures that even my years of memorizing role-playing bestiaries didn't let me recognize. Not everyone wore togas – I spotted plenty of medieval costumes here and there and even one guy in a musketeer uniform. But overall people stuck with the Ancient Greece theme, plucking golden lyres and playing pan flutes amongst the colonnades when they weren't actively involved in winemaking or orgies.

"Uh, yeah," said Julia as we stood there taking it in. "I think I can deal with this for a while. But I hope there's a library or something someplace for variety."

I shook my head at the panorama of debauchery before us. "Sure, there's a library. As long as you don't mind the pages of all the books being stuck together."

Liv laughed. "Come on. Let's go."

People waved at us as we came down the path – some in friendly greeting, others more beckoningly and with provocative expressions. We waved back and headed toward the nearest large building we could see, hoping to find some kind of organization where we might ask about magical wine without interrupting – or being asked to join – anyone's carnal entanglements.

The way took us down between two hills and up a third, where a sun-glazed villa of tangerine stone made a semicircle around this cozy, blue-ceramic-tile plaza. A little fountain chuckled off-center of the plaza, its spout a golden wine-bottle in the clutches of a cherubic statue.

As we finished the stairs up to the plaza, Julia glanced around and then pointed. "Look – a guy with a ledger. Let's ask him."

I'm not sure I've ever heard anybody as enthusiastic about spotting some guy with a ledger. But I pretty much felt the same way, and followed her toward the man's position, near the entryway of the largest building. He seemed to be checking baskets and wheelbarrows of grapes as people brought them in, making notes, and then redirecting the carriers to other parts of the villa or the hillsides.

Up close, he wore a button-up shirt and knee-pants, with a pair of half-rim spectacles low on his nose. Unlike most everyone else, he looked to be middle-aged – older than me – hair thinning and a slight paunch at his middle.

"Excuse us," Julia said at a break in the incoming grape porters. The man looked up from marking his books and pushed his glasses to the bridge of his nose with a pinkie. "I'm a new, ah, citizen here, and I need some Wine of Forgetting for my friend. Someone told me on the other side that I could find it here."

He compressed his lips. "Not *here*." His stylus jabbed over his shoulder toward a stairway down the other side of the hill. "They make that swill down by the riverside. I didn't spend eighty years of my life and hundreds of years here cultivating the perfect grape just so that people could blank their brains."

"Sorry," she said. "I didn't meant to ..."

The winemaker sighed and let his expression soften. "No, no. I'm the one who's sorry. You're new, and everyone's here for their own reasons. I shouldn't get cranky because we all have a different idea of heaven. Down the path, take a left, there's a reed shack by a water-wheel where they'll be happy to help you."

"Thank you so –"

His eyes had already returned to his ledger, but bobbed back up. "Oh, and don't decide to take a stop and swim in the river or dangle your feet. Not unless you *really* want to do some forgetting."

* * *

A bright meadow sat just inland of the bank where the shack and its water-wheel played neighbors with the river. Pairs and triads and quartets of lovers lounged or lunged across the meadow's grass, in each case with a wine cask and glasses close at hand. For once no one offered to screw us as we approached – the people here held each other's attentions more firmly than elsewhere in the Dionysian Fields, apparently. As the path carried us by the amorous sward, a middle-eastern-looking couple well ahead of us made their way inside the reedy hut. They came out with their own cask and glasses a moment before we reached the door.

"Oop – excuse us," the man said, swerving to one side so that he didn't bump into Julia with the cask. "You might be quiet – the winemaker's asleep in there."

"Oh."

The idea stopped Julia where she stood, and while her hesitation might have turned out to be momentary, I stepped in to make sure the two didn't wander off and leave us forced to rouse whoever made the wine.

"Sorry – I hate to interrupt you, but we've just gotten here and we need Wine of Forgetting."

"Right in through there," the woman said, gesturing with the glass in her hand. Both of them made as if to continue on.

"But," I said, "we don't know how it works. Would you mind ... so we don't have to wake anyone up ... ?"

"Yes, of course." The man hitched up the little keg beneath his arm. "It's easy as anything. You just think of what you want to forget, hold that in your mind, and take a drink."

The woman put an educational smile on her tea-with-cream face. "For instance, we're going to forget what it's like to have sex with one another. Then we're going to find out again."

They gave each other a grin.

Stepping forward, Liv said, "How specific can I be? Do I have to forget a whole chunk of time, or –"

"No, no. Pick whatever you want. Remember the perfect dinner you cooked but forget that you spilled the plate on your wife's lap as you tried to set it before her. Erase the guilt that you felt for breaking your mother's favorite vase but keep the happiness it gave you to see her cry with joy when you replaced it with one twice as expensive."

"And it's as easy as that?" I asked. "You just –"

The woman cleared her throat. "Remember how it pleased you to help the strangers, but forget how annoyingly they continued to distract you from your lovemaking."

I stepped back out of their way with my face burning and mumbled an apology, but they both laughed and waved as they walked on, and then the business at hand seemed much too important to worry about making an ass of myself.

"I guess I'll go in and get it," Julia said. "No sense all three of us clunking around and maybe waking the guy up."

"Sure."

She ducked inside, leaving me and Liv alone. Liv took up my hand again, her fingers a little fluttery as they found mine.

"You okay?"

"Uh-huh," she said. "Whoosh. Can you even believe it's been, what, less than a week?"

"I know. Everything's upside down."

She squeezed my hand. "Not everything."

"You know, we could take some of this wine with us, go back home and forget any of it ever happened."

"Would you?"

"No," I said, meeting her eyes as she fixed them on mine. "That lunch with your mom was great. I couldn't get rid of that. And I'd be an idiot to get rid of the things you and Julia told me when I said that dumb crap about not deserving you."

"But you could forget that part too."

"What, saying I didn't deserve you?"

"No, whatever it was that made you think it in the first place."

I shook my head. "I'd have to forget a whole lifetime of being me if I wanted get rid of what made me think it in the first place. Anyway, I don't need to forget that as long as I remember you making it go away."

"So..." she lifted her eyebrows. "It's gone? Completely?"

"It'll never be gone completely. I have to hang on to some of it to make sure I don't turn into a total narcissist and start taking you for granted."

She swiveled and bumped a hip up against me. "I wouldn't let you do that."

Julia came back out before I could reply. She held a wineglass in her hand, its bell half-full of rosy liquid.

"This is it, then," she said, holding it out to Liv, who took it. "What all are you going to forget?"

With her eyes on the glass, Liv raised it up against the slanting sunlight. "All the necklace orgasms, for starters. That's got to go. Everything else is kind of optional."

I watched her bring the glass back down. "Really? You're not going to get rid of the ... you know, from the frat house?"

"Well, I could, I guess. But except for the nonstop orgasm, it was all really dreamy and, uh, sort of an ego boost. No way in hell would I ever do that myself, but jeez, you know ... taking care of *that* many guys ... I think without the orgasm part, it'll be a really hot thing to remember. Do you want me to get rid of it?"

Yes. Actually, hell yes.

"Sort of, but if you want to keep it –"

"Don't bullshit me, Tim. If it's really going to bother you, I'll flush it."

I opened my mouth, only to have Julia chime in before I could speak.

"Hey, I worked my ass off fucking all those guys. Or I guess I worked Liv's ass off. Anyway, it was sick, but ... in an awesome, look-what-I-can-do way. Tell me if I'm wrong, Liv, but having that many people that fucking amazed at how incredible I was being – I sure as hell wouldn't want to forget it."

"I didn't say –"

"Yeah, but I could see the look on your face. And I get it, and I get why Liv would let you make the decision instead of just doing what she wanted.

But maybe instead you should get your own glass of wine and forget it yourself. Then she can remember it all she wants, and you won't have to know anything about it."

Yuck. But you have to admit it's a lot more fair than making her give something up. Only ...

"Would you want to remember and keep that a secret from me?" I asked her. She shrugged, and I knew exactly what the shrug meant: *It would suck having something I thought was cool that I could never tell you about.* But what would be cool about remembering dozens of guys having their way with you? The question kind of answered itself when I pictured a room full of naked college chicks all waiting their turn to have sex with me. *Shit.*

"Okay. If you want to remember, I want you to remember. But you're going to have to come up with, like, a really sexy way to tell me about the whole thing. When I'm ready. When I don't think I'll put my fingers in my ears and go *la-la-la-la.*"

She laughed that laugh. That perfect sound. I imagined her using her sultriest voice to describe the room, the bed, the frat-boys and the things Julia made her body do for them, to them. *No, I guess that won't be so bad.*

"So what else, then?" Julia asked. "Is it just the magical orgasms and that's it?"

Liv turned to her. "I'm going to forget hating you too."

"You don't have to do that. I deserved it."

"Sure you did. But Tim said I would forgive you, and I have. How often do you get the chance to *really* forgive and forget?"

With her lip quivering just enough for me to spot it, Julia gave a flinch of her shoulders.

"Here goes then."

The glass went up. Liv tilted it, and her neck too, drinking down the whole glass with closed eyes. When she was done, her hand and the glass lowered a couple of seconds before her neck straightened and she looked at us.

"Wow. That was some good wine."

"Did it work?" Julia asked.

Liv answered her first with a huge hug. Only after a moment did she say anything: "Yes. And I'm going to miss you so much."

Julia hugged her in return, tearing up. "Thank you. I don't want it to be a long time until I see you again, but I hope it is."

Then they let each other go, and it was my turn. Despite having had sex with her a dozen times, I felt awkward hugging this naked little woman. I tried to think of something to say, but couldn't. So I just held her and waited for her to stop holding me.

"You're great, Tim," she said at last. "Keep Liv happy and try not to be too much of a pain in her ass."

The hug suddenly became much more real for me.

"Sure."

"Is that it, then?" she asked, sniffling a little as she stepped back. "Time for you to rip up your badges and go?"

"Yeah," Liv said, looking at me. "Tim and I have things to do." Then she smiled back at Julia. "But we've got forever to bump into each other again. And one of these days, we need to schedule a reincarnation where we go to high school together. A private school with those cute uniforms, right?"

"Ooh, don't tease me like that!"

"I'm not teasing you." She squeezed my arm and gave me a peck on the cheek. "I'm teasing Tim. We'll make him be reincarnated as the Peeping Tom next door. Peeping Tom, Peeping Tim, whatever."

I pulled the badge loose from my ribs, trying not to swallow at how hot that scenario sounded.

"I think we should go before I get too jealous or too horny from all these plans."

Liv took her own badge from under her shirt and hooked her arm through mine. "Too jealous would be bad. There's no such thing as too horny. I'll prove that to you when we get home."

Julia waved both hands at us.

"Have good lives, okay?"

"We will," I said.

"And you have a good afterlife," Liv added.

Julia nodded, and then we tore our badges in half.

EPILOGUE

"Wow, that is a *lot* of lube. You really think we need that much?"

"Uh..." I looked from my hand, more or less holding the full contents of the tube of lubricant I'd just squeezed over it, to Liv, lying on her side in the center of the bed, head propped up with one hand. "The stuff I read on the internet made it sound like you really can't use too much, especially the first time."

"Yeah, but if there's so much that it just runs off, I don't think my ass is going to be helped out by the extra."

Two weeks had passed since we'd torn our afterlife badges and reappeared in Gio R. Gioenne's basement workshop, with the scaly woman nowhere in sight. We thought about calling down the dark stairway that I assumed led to her living quarters, but a mush of indecipherable and disconcerting sounds from the stairwell made us decide to just go up to the ground floor and let ourselves out, where we found it was 9:00 Monday morning.

I called in sick, and we spent the whole day having sex and talking about the future. That night, we went to the Ethiopian restaurant.

"Well, it's not going back in the tube," I said. "So it's going to have to go on one of us."

"You first."

Things had quickly and easily gotten back to normal, although it was never going to be the same normal it had been before – a much better normal instead. We kept our lips stubbornly zipped when we saw Bill at the game. But every time the adventuring party came to a decision juncture, we deliberately asked if he had any ideas, just so the rest of the group would say, "Never listen to Bill's ideas!" He took it like a good sport. And when

Liv's necromancer character started getting it on with a ghoul, I was the one who scooted my chair closer to hers.

Work still sucked. Only it didn't matter that it sucked – I had, what, maybe twenty, thirty years of it to go, and then the entire rest of Time after that I wouldn't have to lift a finger if I didn't want to.

"Brr!" Liv said, flinching at the touch of the cold gel at her ass-crack. "That's definitely too much, and it's freezing."

"Sorry ... I got as much of it on myself as I could ..." Which was true – I'd more or less encased my cock in a thick transparent coating of the stuff.

"Uh-huh. Next time, we're warming that shit up in a hot-water bath or something first."

"Sure. I mean, assuming we both like it enough that there *is* a next time."

"If we don't, we're probably doing something wrong and we'll definitely have to try again."

"Okay." I snuggled in alongside her, spooning up against her perfect mahogany bottom. My dick bumped against it, then slid along the crevice where her buttocks and thighs met each other. "Are you ready, for sure?"

She laughed. "Readier than you are, it sounds like."

Then she twisted her upper body to angle her face toward mine for a kiss, and we held that and shared it for a good long while.

"Right," she said, breaking away and smiling with her mouth and her eyes alike. "So let's do this thing."

I kissed her shoulder, then shifted where I could see at least a little of what I was doing. Liv had tucked her knees up to her chest now and wiggled her behind beckoningly.

Getting hold of my cock and positioning it, I took things the same way I'd taken them on our three trips to the Ethiopian restaurant over the past two weeks: very, very slowly. The first time, I'd just eaten with a fork. The second, I let Liv feed me a few bites by hand toward the end of the meal. And the third, we moved from her tearing off the spongy *injerna*, to me guiding her hand to my mouth each time, to me transferring a bread-wrapped morsel from her fingers across the last inch or so to my lips, and finally to me just picking up the food and eating it myself. It was weird and unsettling to do that. But the way she smiled made it okay, and then better than okay, and then outright enjoyable.

Of course, we weren't going to draw the anal sex out across three different evenings over two weeks before finally making it work, so it wasn't *exactly* the same.

At first, I just touched myself to the tight little crimp of flesh there in the crease of her ass. (Hygiene note: we made sure to time things so that she'd emptied the whole region out and gotten it as spic-and-span as that particular area gets. Even so, a part of me wanted to use a condom, and if I hadn't previously forced myself to fuck M in her cloaca, I probably would have chickened out and worn one.) Liv made an *mmm* sound at the contact, although the truth is, we both had so much lube on us that I was surprised she could even feel that initial touch.

Her hum encouraged me, though, and I started rubbing my tip gently back and forth across her dark-fleshed asterisk. She shivered.

"I'm liking that," she said. "For sure. How are you doing?"

"So far so good."

"Good. Are you going to start pushing?"

"In a minute."

I circled the sphincter a few more times, then shifted a little. Strangely, only a few images of swarming bacteria flashed through my brain – mostly I hesitated because I wanted to make sure I didn't hurt her.

She wants you to, I thought, pressing forward ever so slightly. Liv took in a sharp breath. *She wants it, and the gut bacteria can go fuck themselves, all right? Just be careful and slow.*

Millimeter by millimeter, I eased my hips toward her. Hell, maybe even micrometer by micrometer. I could feel the flesh around her ass-button bowing inward, and at the same time her breathing sped up.

"Is that okay?"

"Yeah, but you're *killing* me with the suspense."

"Well, I don't want to force anything. If you're relaxed enough, I think it's supposed to go in pretty easy."

"It's kind of hard to relax with something poking you in the ass. Maybe if I was already a yoga master instead of just five classes in – anyway, it feels pretty good, and I'm trying to loosen up. Just give it a little more oomph."

By now, she almost completely surrounded my tip. If I hadn't done all that reading, I'd have assumed I was already in.

I tried a little more oomph.

"Ng," she said. I felt a spasm right at the spot where my urethra opened. The dimpled flesh around me closed in and tried to push me back out, then quivered and relaxed and quivered and relaxed. I had to use my hand to stay in place.

"You sure you're all right?"

"Uh ... huh," she said raggedly. "It's good. Just push. Push."

I did. Harder and harder. Little by little.

And then suddenly the ring of muscle *popped* open to let me in, squeezing tight as it rode out around the ridge of my glans and swallowed the first centimeter or two of shaft past that.

The penetration forced a primal grunt from deep in Liv's throat – a sound of pure animal biology with only faint overtones of human pleasure.

The strength of her anal grip on me made me gasp too, and I couldn't help but thrust forward, another inch and then two, my rod gloriously constricted by Liv's butthole. She panted and moaned, and I was just about ready to plunge deeper, and then: "Ow! Ow, ow, *ow!* Take it out!"

I pulled out in a panic, feeling her anus clutch and twitch at me as I went. But then she was laughing and rolling onto her back, her legs clamped tight together, her face scrunched up in something halfway between a grin and a grimace of pain.

"Ow, ow – *haha* – *ass cramp* ..."

"Are you okay?"

"Ohoo, ha – uhuhuh ..." Her eyes opened and then rolled and then focused on me as she crossed her legs and squirmed. "Oh my god, for a second it felt *so* good, and then all of a sudden it was like the hardest, biggest, most constipated shit I've ever taken."

"That doesn't sound so great."

"No, but it felt amazing going in, and it was a *hellacious* relief going out." She blinked a few times and unkinked her legs, one at a time. "How about you?"

"Aside from thinking I'd killed you, it was kind of awesome."

"Not too disgusting and feces-germy?"

I shook my head. "Pretty sure I would have gotten all the way to coming without remembering to be grossed out. Wow. You were, like, super-tight right at the, uh, sphincter, and then all different and soft inside that."

"So you'd like to do it again?"

"Not if it's going to hurt you that way, no."

"I think I just need practice relaxing and getting ready."

I ran my hand along her thigh and up her hip, and she intercepted it with her own, weaving her fingers together with mine.

"I guess it's pretty dumb that we went through everything we went through with Julia just because I was freaked out about doing that."

With a gentle movement of her wrist, she rocked our hands back and forth where they lay on her hip. For a second, we both watched the light glinting off the diamond in the ring I'd given her at dinner earlier in the evening.

Then her eyes turned back to mine. "You were freaked out because you're you. And I love who you are, *so* much. I wouldn't undo a second of it now."

"Uh, I could probably think of several seconds I'd undo. But there's a lot more I wouldn't."

"Good."

"Do you want to wash up and do it the old-fashioned way now? We can try again some other night ..."

Her lovely, brilliant head shook. "No. I taught you to eat with your fingers tonight. The least you can do is teach me to take a cock up the ass in return."

"Okay," I said. "But try to be a quicker learner than I was."
She laughed and smiled and got me to do what she wanted.
From then on.

END

ABOUT THE AUTHOR

Ian Saul Whitcomb is a good-hearted but perverse soul who lives with his wife and a number of other mammals in an undisclosed but sizeable city somewhere between the Eastern and Mountain Time Zones. In between novels, he can be found blogging or, sporadically, on Twitter.

bigheartednarcissist.blogspot.com

@coolgasmic